The Gathering of Clan McFee

Karen Baugh
MENUHIN

ISBN: 979-8-2901163-7-2

To Lianne & Gerry Leddy
for all your kindness!

CHAPTER 1

**The Scottish Highlands
April 3rd 1924**

'Where?' I asked, having just come indoors and sat down for the first time since breakfast.

'Castle McFee,' Swift replied, trying to keep the excitement from his voice. 'It's up towards Loch Torridon, among the mountains.'

'Laird McFee died on Hogmanay,' Florence said, frowning at her knitting. It was a tiny baby coat in cream wool, the little arms sticking out; she was working on the neck. 'He was quite reclusive. He and his wife never left the glen.' She spoke in a soft Scottish accent, strands of pale blonde hair falling forward around her pretty face.

Swift carried on with his explanation. 'There's a group of prospective heirs gathered at Castle McFee and one of them has died after falling down the stairs the night before last. He wasn't found until yesterday morning. The late Laird's lawyer thought it could be suspicious and decided to call Scotland Yard. DCI Billings wants us to go up there, Lennox.'

We were seated in Swift and Florence's cosy parlour above the ancient keep of Braeburn Castle. Spring was slower to emerge in the highlands, and a crisp chill nipped the air despite the sunshine streaming through the windows. Orange flames blazed from blackened logs in the stone hearth. A tray of mid-morning coffee and sliced clootie dumpling waited for us on a low table in front of the chintz sofas we were occupying.

The fug of warmth had just begun to thaw my face and hands after a walk around the island with my dog, Mr Fogg. He'd gone to flop in front of the fire, long golden spaniel ears drooping as he closed his eyes to sleep. Mr Tubbs, our fat little black cat had already cuddled up alongside Nicky – Swift and Florence's Jack Russell terrier. Together they formed a pile of furry bodies dozing contentedly on the hearthrug.

'They must have plenty of detectives in Scotland, Swift,' I remarked dryly.

'Yes, but the Laird's heirs are toffs,' Swift replied.

Florence put her knitting down to hand out cups of creamy coffee and plates of clootie, still lightly steaming from the oven.

'And Billings says you're his detectives to the toffs,' Persi teased, her eyes alight with mischief. She was right: whenever blue blood was spilled DCI Billings called us. He, or rather Scotland Yard, had recently made us official consulting detectives for a nominal monthly pittance. They were keen to extract their pennies' worth – much to the delight of Swift. He'd given up his career as a detective to marry Lady Florence Braeburn and move to live with her and the Braeburn clan up in the highlands. Now he had the best of both worlds.

'These would be the type of toffs who live in castles similar to this one?' I remarked dryly, then took a forkful of clootie.

He ignored that. 'There are foreigners among the gathering.'

'What sort of foreigners?' Persi asked, wrapping her knitting up with a sigh. Persi was my wife of a year or so. The pale green jacket she was attempting was as tiny as the one Florence had been working on, but Persi's was rather knotted, with one arm distinctly longer than the other. Both garments were intended for the baby we were expecting later in the year, an event which filled me with alarm whenever I thought about it.

'Canadians, Americans, some English, and a Dane,' Swift said as he sipped his coffee.

'Castle McFee is poorly neglected,' Florence said, brushing crumbs from the lap of her blue woollen dress. 'Daddy was telling us about it when he saw Laird McFee's obituary in *The Oban Times*. The Laird and his wife, Lady Peggie, didn't have any children, and the coffers ran dry over a century ago. The land's thin in the mountains and there's nothing to be made in sheep now.'

Given punitive death duties and the perilous state of farming, penury was increasingly common in ancient family estates. 'Which one of the potential heirs died?' I asked, reaching for my coffee cup.

Swift picked his notebook up from the low table. He was wearing a fairisle sweater and charcoal grey trousers, rather than the kilt he'd adopted on moving to Scotland. He was looking quite relaxed for a man who didn't actually know how to relax. 'William Sullivan, aged 53. English. He was from Newcastle. According to the late Laird's lawyer, he had one of the best claims to the title through the bloodline,' he read out.

'Then why were other contenders invited?' I asked.

'I said *one of* the best,' Swift repeated. 'There's no definitive heir, and those identified as potential claimants are apparently all descended from the female line, which puts them in contravention of the tailzie.'

'The what?'

Florence smiled. 'It's called an "entail" in England. It's a legally binding settlement on an estate to preserve it intact within the male line. We've a tailzie on Braeburn. It means Angus will inherit everything one day, regardless of any other bairns we may have.'

We were all aware that Swift's and Florence's little boy, Angus, would inherit the sprawling Braeburn estate, including the castle, loch, distillery and land. Swift, being English and only related by marriage, would never own the home he lived in.

'It's the same law as primogeniture in England,' Persi said, then asked. 'Is it only men gathered at Castle McFee? Because it is ridiculous in this day and age to exclude women.'

'I asked the same question,' Swift said, who not only had socialist tendencies, but also had modern ideas on women's emancipation. 'It's a mixed group. The lawyer, Sir Richard Fitzroy, has persuaded the Laird's widow to have the tailzie amended.'

'They're able to overturn an entail...I mean, a Tailzie?' I asked, surprised to hear it.

'Yes, the Entailment Amendment Act was begun last century,' Swift replied. 'In certain circumstances it allows estates to be split up, or passed down the female line. It's safeguarded spousal rights, too.'

A sudden silence descended as Florence, and Persi, and I, realised he must have researched this at some time.

The door opened to break the quiet. Greggs, my butler, entered. '*Ahem*, sir. I have packed your carpet bag, and the Inspector's. The boat is ready. Mr McDonald is fretting to be off. He says the wind might turn.'

'What?' I sat up.

Greggs adopted an air of innocence as his eyes slid in the direction of Swift.

Swift's lean cheeks showed a faint flush of guilt. 'I thought we should get moving. It will take a few hours to drive there.'

'Swift–' I began, then realised my wife was smiling.

'You can hardly refuse, my love,' Persi said. 'And you'll enjoy it. You always do.'

'No I don't.'

She raised her brows in feigned disbelief.

'Are you and Florence coming?' I asked, unable to resist her teasing. She looked particularly beautiful in the early stages of pregnancy. She wore a blue dress the colour of her eyes, her blonde hair pinned back from her lovely face, a flush to her cheeks and a smile never far from her lips.

'No,' she replied lightly. 'There's a cairn on the mainland I've been dying to investigate, and Florence and the Laird have promised to take me there tomorrow if the weather holds.'

'So you've already planned—' I tried objecting.

Swift cut in with an explanation. 'Billings telephoned while you were out walking, Lennox. We thought it best to pack…and, erm…prepare.'

I swore under my breath. We'd only arrived yesterday, supposedly to enjoy a couple of weeks of peace at the castle with Swift and Florence and the Braeburn clan. I'd been trying to persuade Persi to stop digging things up and take some rest. She was an archeologist and it hadn't taken her long to discover our home in the Cotswolds was surrounded by history going back to the iron age and beyond. She'd recently heard rumours of a Roman Villa under an old plague pit in our village of Ashton Steeple and wanted to investigate. I'd immediately called Swift and invited ourselves up here. I'd been rather looking forward to fishing in the loch, and touring the whisky distillery that Swift and the clan had rebuilt over in Braeburn village.

I finished my coffee in irritated silence, then put the cup down. 'Greggs. You're coming,' I told him.

'What? I mean, pardon, sir, but I thought—' he tried quibbling.

'If the place is running into dereliction, the least you can do is come and make things comfortable,' I said.

'I didn't say it was derelict,' Swift countered. 'Florence mentioned it was neglected.'

'Well if Castle McFee was neglected, and the funds ran out a century ago, it amounts to the same thing,' I replied tersely. 'Greggs, you'd better get a move on if McDonald is waiting.'

'Sir…but…but–' he spluttered.

'Now,' I ordered.

'You can help find the killer,' Persi told him.

He stopped spluttering. 'Can I, milady?' His face brightened at the thought.

'Assuming there is one,' I replied.

His face dropped again.

'A group of heirs gathered together, vying to inherit a castle, and one just died after falling down the stairs,' Persi said. 'I'd be surprised if it truly was an accident.'

'Indeed, milady.' Greggs cheered up again.

'The skiff is waiting, Greggs,' Swift warned him. 'McDonald gets tetchy if he's held up.'

'I will not be a moment, sir,' he assured us and tottered off, a grin of excitement on his old phiz.

A good thirty minutes passed before we were seated in the rowing boat ready to be waved off by the small crowd gathered on the island shore. Fogg was with us, sitting shivering on my lap; Swift had donned a suit and tie and was buttoned up in his new trench coat, scarf, gloves and whatnots. Greggs had reverted to a balaclava under his bowler, which was tied down with a black scarf. He'd enveloped himself in a voluminous green cloak and looked like a mobile tent.

I was in a dark greatcoat over my usual winter tweeds, cream sweater and a dark red scarf that Persi had given me for Christmas. We held carpet bags on our knees because there was water swilling around our boots in the bottom of the shallow boat.

'Ye'd best hang on. The wind's got up and it'll be pitchin',' Donald McDonald, the Laird's gruff Ghillie Mor told us. 'If ye'd come when I'd told ye, we wudn'ta be tossed aboot like this.' He set the oars into the white-tipped waves and pulled away. Icy salt spray hit us in the face, the wind buffeting cold about our ears.

We waved to Persi and Florence, both now wrapped in thick paisley shawls over their winter woollen frocks. Angus was with them; he jumped up and down, arms in the air, a happy little three-year-old with Swift's dark hair and dogged determination. Nicky raced up and down the shore yapping madly, in the usual manner of excitable Jack Russells. The Laird had strolled down to join the group – a dignified man, with leonine white hair, beard, and togged in full Scots garb of kilt, black jacket, sporran, cream socks, dirk and a flowing cape. His piper came with him, as was usual, and piped us off to a mournful tune.

Greggs pushed a gloved hand from the folds of his cloak and fluttered a white handkerchief.

You'd think we were going to war.

The clamber to get out of the boat almost ended in disaster. Greggs wobbled on the slippery dock and would have ended in the water if McDonald hadn't caught him. Foggy spotted a duck on the sandy shore and raced off and I realised I'd forgotten the half bottle of Braeburn I'd intended to bring.

I went off muttering to myself to find my Bentley in the Braeburn boat house and cranked her up. She started on the first turn, which was a relief and it lifted my mood somewhat. Greggs tottered over and took up position in the rear, unable to hear a word under the scarf and balaclava. Swift had picked Foggy up and hauled him over to place next to Greggs, then he climbed into the passenger seat to navigate.

It took hours.

Winding lanes, wrong turns, sheep on the road, a fallen tree. We stopped to ask locals when we got lost. They advised that it was just over yon hill, or mountain, or the other side of a distant loch. The colours of spring lit the land in a patchwork of glorious hues of heather, russet, copper beech and budding green, though I have to admit my mind was on the future, and the baby. Words like 'responsibility' and 'commitment' rebounded around my head. How was I going to provide funds for nannies, and schools, and all the usual? And what if there were more babies? It was perfectly likely, given…well, given the usual marital…actually, I decided not to think about that.

Pink-tinged dusk was sweeping across the sky as we drove between steeply rising foothills on a single-track road and turned a corner to see a glen spread out before us.

Magnificent trees just coming into leaf circled the tranquil clearing. A crystal clear river broadened out into a wide arc, bordered by swathes of spring-green grass spread between the sparkling water and the tall castle standing solid, grey and rather intimidating on the other side of an arched stone bridge.

It seems we'd arrived at Castle McFee.

CHAPTER 2

'A wee doggie. Ah, that's better than all them ootlanders.' An elderly chap in butler's garb had opened the massive front door. He held an umbrella over his head, despite the lack of rain and him being indoors. Foggy ran a circuit around the echoing hall, then headed for a broad stone staircase. The butler watched him go, then turned back to us. 'I'll thank ye kindly for that,' he said and closed the door in our faces.

I'd driven through a vaulted archway into a cobbled inner courtyard and parked the car some distance from the grey, stone-framed entrance. We'd unloaded our bags and carried them to the raised front doorstep. Foggy had, as usual, run straight into the house when the doddery butler opened up.

We stared at the studded oak door for a moment then I lifted the heavy iron knocker and rapped loudly once again. Nothing happened. Swift stepped forward and tried the same.

The door swung back open.

'What?' A short stocky chap stood in the lofty door-frame, he wore ill-fitting Scots garb that looked ridiculous on the man. A black jacket too tight across his chest and plump stomach, his grey shirt creased, the tartan kilt reaching halfway down his calves, cream socks gathered round his ankles, and he'd hitched the sporran up around his paunch. 'Are you guys from the village?' he said, then spotted the Bentley. 'Oh, you're swells.' He was American by accent. 'Well, if you're thinking about claiming anything, don't bother. The place is falling down.'

'Police,' Swift predictably announced. 'Scotland Yard.' He stepped forward.

'Police?' The American tried to stand his ground. 'You got a badge?'

'Don't be ridiculous,' I said and walked past him, into the expansive hall.

Greying white walls hung with stags' heads, sooty portraits of grim-looking men in tartan bonnets, a few dark paintings of bleak landscapes and an impressive collection of antique battle axes, swords, staves, spears, battered shields and all the usual warmongery you'd hope to find in a Scots castle. There was the inevitable massive stone fireplace blazing with logs on the opposite wall, the mantel adorned with a carved and painted crest and the words 'Clan McFee' below it. Despite the width of the hearth and leaping orange flames, the fire barely lifted the temperature above the evening chill outside. Numerous candlesticks with flickering candles had been set about the place, but they didn't add much to the dimming light, and a few had already been blown out by the draught from the open door.

'We'd like to talk to Sir Richard Fitzroy.' Swift had put

his carpet bag on the stone flagged floor and was pulling off his gloves. His eyes were on the stone staircase, or rather the faded Persian rug at the foot of it.

'I'm not a servant, y'know,' the American complained, then focused on Greggs, still swathed in his ridiculous outfit. 'You brought your own mortician?'

'That is my butler,' I said. 'Who are you?'

'You got a butler?' He sounded surprised. 'Gee, our cops only get doughnuts.'

I eyed him. I guessed him to be in his late fifties, with thin greying hair combed over a bald patch and unkempt brows above beady brown eyes.

'Major Lennox asked who you are,' Swift cut in.

'I'm Malone. Mick Malone. And I ain't got no reason to be running round at your say-so. If you want the lawyer, you tell your butler to go find him.'

'Mr Malone?' A female voice from above shut him up. 'Craggie mentioned some men had arrived.'

We craned up to see a lady standing with her hands on the balustrade running the width of the next floor up. A heavy black chandelier hung above from a chain, the light from the candles illuminating her white hair like a halo.

'Hi there, Lady Peggie,' Malone replied in a friendlier tone. 'They wanna see Fitzroy.'

'Greetings,' I called up.

'We are police,' Swift added. 'Inspector Swift and Major Lennox. We've been sent by Scotland Yard.'

'Oh, you're the detectives. I was informed you were attending,' she called back, her accent distinctly English.

'Would you mind coming up? And Mr Malone, please don't leave the front door open, the air is really quite frigid.' She gazed down at us for a moment more, then stepped back and disappeared.

Greggs had been staring about, his eyes framed by the round sockets of the black balaclava. When he spotted the lady, he'd whipped off the scarf tied around the bowler, removed his head gear and smoothed down his hair. 'I am ready to assist, sir,' he announced.

'You can take our bags to our rooms,' I told him. 'Assuming you can find the butler.'

'He's called Craggie.' Malone had closed the heavy front door with a bang and was now marginally more friendly. 'He's as rickety as everything else in this place. Come on, we can go see her ladyship. She'll have gone back to the drawing room, it's too cold to hang about in the hall.'

'Fine,' I agreed.

'Sir, milady said I could assist in the detecting,' Greggs reminded me.

'And you can, when we have some detecting to do,' I replied.

That didn't seem to help and he remained on his spot, the bags at his feet and a distinct sulk on his hangdog face.

Swift had already moved to the bottom of the stairs and was staring up them, presumably looking for blood stains. There weren't any.

'Did you see the body?' he asked Malone.

'Yeah, me and everyone else,' he replied. 'Mrs Craggie found the guy yesterday morning. She's the housekeeper, married to the old butler. She hollered the place down and woke us all up. It was still dark; she was in her nightdress and carrying a lantern, it was real spooky. There's no electric nor nothing here. They've got a telephone in a room in the hall, but that's as modern as it gets. I had to use a flashlight to find out what was goin' on.'

We were walking up the stairs, the stone treads worn smooth and dipped in the middle.

'When was the victim last seen alive?' Swift asked, already shifting into police mode.

'What do you call him a victim for?' Malone bristled. 'He fell down the stairs 'cus he drank too much. Jeez, you guys are all the same. Suspicious of everyone an' always looking for trouble.'

We arrived at a wide landing jutting out over the hallway below. Tall narrow windows in the opposite wall were filling with pink and orange light as the sun dropped into the sliver of pale sky between layers of grey clouds and the jagged peaks of distant mountains.

'You didn't answer the question,' Swift persisted.

'I don't know when he was last seen alive, do I,' Malone complained. 'We were all talkin' and havin' a drink, then we went to bed. He was still drinkin' when I left.'

'Oh, Mr Malone, there y'are.' An American lady of mature years arrived from a passageway at the end of the landing. 'I believe they're about to serve drinks in the drawing room.' She looked up at us. 'Are y'all more heirs?'

'No, I'm Inspector Swift and this is Major Lennox,' Swift announced. 'From Scotland Yard,' he added. Now that he was back working for Scotland Yard he found every opportunity to mention it. And to wear the new trench coat he was still sporting over his suit.

'I'm Miss Susannah Bellamy.' She held her hand out. We made the usual formalities.

'They're detectives,' Malone told her. 'They think Sullivan was pushed or somethin'.'

'We're simply here to determine the facts,' Swift said.

'No-one said anything about detectives coming,' Miss Susannah Bellamy said. 'But I'm thinking there's not going to be much for y'all to do. Poor Mr Sullivan had too much to drink and fell down the stairs. Although I do believe it's a fine thing to have two handsome young men about the place.'

Greggs must have heard us because he'd rushed to the top of the stairs. He came and gave a simpering bow.

'This is Greggs, my butler,' I introduced him.

'Oh a real butler!' She laughed, her face lighting up. She was quite short, slim with a high-collared lace blouse under a cashmere sweater and matching skirt in lavender blue. 'Now I wish I had someone like you back home, Mr Greggs. We'd have such a time of it.' She put a thin hand to her chest. 'And I insist y'all call me Susannah.' Brown eyes crinkling in her delicately lined face, her tinted blonde hair was carefully swept back behind her ears. She wore elegant diamond earrings and a bracelet to match. She probably had a necklace in the same style too because the cut and quality of her clothes spoke of understated wealth.

'I would be delighted to be of any assistance I can render, madam,' Greggs said, bowing even more deeply.

'Greggs,' I warned, because he wouldn't be able to straighten up if he carried on.

'Can we getta move on,' Malone cut in. 'The drawing room's over there. I'm goin' in, it's freezin' out here.' He stomped off towards an imposing doorway with a white painted surround and dark oak double doors. He swung one open and marched in, leaving it ajar.

'May I take up your kindly offer of assistance?' Susannah looked up at Greggs.

He grinned, making his chins wobble. 'I would be delighted, madam.' He offered an elbow.

'I already told you, it's Susannah.' She smiled, a look of delighted mischief in her eyes as she slipped her hand through his arm.

He escorted her through the open door with chest puffed out and paunch held in. We followed.

'Detectives?' a young man's plum voice was saying. 'Why on earth are there detectives here?'

'Shh,' a young woman answered with a hiss. 'They'll hear you.'

'There are detektifs come? For what?' a man's voice with a nordic accent asked. A group of people were ranged on a collection of mismatched sofas about a black-framed fireplace the height of a man. A stack of huge logs roared in the brick-lined hearth. The room was high ceilinged with dark beams and planks in the traditional manner. The only illumination, other than the fire, was from an iron chandelier fitted with stubby wax candles. Tartan curtains were drawn across the windows, the colours the same as

Malone's kilt and in the crest above the hall fireplace. Dark red, blue, and black – I assumed it was the McFee tartan. There were more stags' heads and dour portraits of long-dead Lairds on the ox-blood walls. The place was dark and shadowy and felt as though little had changed since its mediaeval past.

'Inspector Swift, Major Lennox, I presume?' A distinguished man with silver hair, a square chin and grey suit advanced on us, his hand out held. 'Richard Fitzroy.'

We all shook, and exchanged polite greetings.

'I hope your journey wasn't too arduous?' He raised trimmed brows; his manners were gentlemanly, his voice mature and reassuring with a subtle Scot's burr.

'Perfectly acceptable, thank you.' I glanced over at the fireplace where Greggs had seated Susannah Bellamy and was now offering to arrange drinks. It seemed Craggie still hadn't turned up. My dog wasn't anywhere to be seen either.

'I informed Lady Peggie that you were coming.' Fitzroy indicated the white-haired lady we'd seen out on the landing.

She came forward, tall and slim, her outstretched hand thin and knotted by arthritis. We all introduced ourselves formally. We were some distance from the miscellany of sofas and people seated around the hearth, but I could see them straining to listen.

'I really do not believe there is anything for you to investigate, gentlemen.' Lady Peggie spoke quite loudly, as though for the others to hear. Dressed in a high-necked, buttoned-up cardigan in dark blue over a woollen dress in the same colour, she looked strained. There were lines deep-set around her grey eyes; she had high cheek bones and hollowed cheeks. She would have once been pretty, but time and perhaps a hard life had taken a toll. 'But it will lay our minds to rest that it was a mere accident and not something worse.' Her gaze flicked to Fitzroy for a moment, and the lawyer gave a light nod of agreement in response.

Malone's loud voice broke over from the muted group around the fire. 'I want some of that whisky I had last night,' he was telling Greggs. 'Why do they only serve wine or sherry before dinner? What kinda drink is sherry anyway?'

Lady Peggie grimaced but didn't look round. 'How would you prefer to proceed?' she asked us more quietly.

'We'll join the crowd,' I replied before Swift had a chance. 'And ask a few questions over drinks.'

Swift frowned at that, of course. He probably had a whole list of investigative procedures drawn up, but I needed to sit down and drink something comforting after the long drive.

'I think that is an excellent course of action,' Fitzroy agreed. 'Lady Peggie?' He turned to her.

'Yes, please come and meet the…' She hesitated, as though unsure how to describe them. 'The gathering of the clan McFee.'

CHAPTER 3

'Now, we shall not stand on ceremony,' Susannah Bellamy said as we moved to join the small throng. 'Y'all sit down, there's plenty of room.' Susannah smiled up at us from the corner of a worn sofa nearest the fire. She was open and friendly in contrast to Lady Peggie's more rigid formality, although given the situation it was hardly a surprise the widow of the late Laird was on edge.

'Here.' A young lady with long auburn hair shifted across on a dark green sofa to make room. 'I'd love to hear more about your work, I think detecting crime must be fascinating.'

'Swift's the expert,' I said.

'Oh, that's dandy.' Her face lit up as she fixed bright eyes on him.

'I think I ought to–' Swift began.

She reached up and tugged at his arm. 'You English are real uptight, aren't you? I'm Molly Patterson, all the way from Calgary, Canada.' She laughed as Swift unbalanced and plonked down next to her.

'Oh, you shouldn't admit to coming from Calgary,' another young lady drawled. Her face made up, bright blonde hair shingled and fixed with brilliantine. She wore a sequinned green dress and jangled with gold jewellery. 'It's totally Hicksville.' She raised eyes narrowed with speculation in my direction. 'You're the man who brought his own butler. I think that's so copasetic. I'm Belinda Guthrie, by the way. My family started in Toronto. We made our fortune there, but we're in California now. The weather in Canada was just too grim. Why don't you come sit down and tell me about yourself, Major Lennox.' She patted the seat next to her, a coy smile playing on her pouting lips. She looked about the same age as the fresh-faced Molly, but her attempted archness added years to her, and not in an attractive way either.

'Thank you, but I have business to discuss.' I went to sit near Fitzroy, who had settled on a sofa alongside Lady Peggie.

'Huh. Whatever, but you're wasting your time. Sullivan just fell down the stairs.' Belinda Guthrie's mouth twisted in irritation as she lifted her wine glass to sip from it.

'Do you use your instinct to tell you who's guilty, or is it a forensic process, or both?' Molly Patterson began interrogating Swift. She wore beige slacks and a rollneck sweater in a rich reddish brown – a modern outfit, practical and comfortable. It suited her.

'I've always thought detectives are natural-born hunters who use their skills to track down assassins in the dark.' Susannah Bellamy turned to address me.

'Possibly,' I said, trying to catch Greggs' eye. Everyone around the fire was already clutching glasses of white wine or sherry, and he was now beetling about serving those sitting further back. He had paused to hold out the drinks tray to a chap with half-moon spectacles perched on the end of his nose. The man had thin grey hair; lean and rather sinewy, he looked intense even from where I was. Sitting bolt upright, a notebook in his lap, he was observing everyone very closely. He reached to take a sherry, drank half of it in one swift motion, then carried on watching.

'I'd like to establish William Sullivan's movements before he was found yesterday morning.' Swift had managed to quieten Molly and was reaching for his own notebook.

Molly watched him with fascination. 'I could help,' she said.

'No thank you,' Swift replied as he held his pen poised over a clean page.

'I believe I was the last to see him,' Fitzroy offered. He was a handsome man; obviously intelligent, and with a sense of solid reliability about him. 'He and I were drinking in here after everyone had gone to bed. He had asked to talk to me privately, and I stayed behind to hear him out.'

'What did he want to talk about?' Swift asked as he wrote the date, April 3rd, at the top of the page.

'He insisted he was the heir,' Fitzroy replied, a hint of wryness in his Scots brogue. 'He demanded I have the other contending heirs removed from the castle and hand him the deeds. He was rather the worse for wear.'

'Sullivan was a low life,' Belinda Guthrie cut in loudly. 'I expected everyone to have money. He obviously didn't. I'm surprised he was even asked.'

'He had every right to be here,' Fitzroy replied. 'And he was actually very wealthy.'

'Huh,' Belinda carried on. 'There's no way he would have stayed and looked after the castle. He'd have sold it soon as he got his hands on it.'

'The tailzie does not allow the castle to be sold,' Fitzroy stated, suddenly stern. 'I thought I had made that clear to everyone.'

'Well, most all of us understood it when you said it,' Susannah Bellamy replied. 'But I guess not everyone was listening.'

Belinda Guthrie's thinly plucked brows snapped together. She retorted, 'I didn't say he *could* sell it. I simply said he'd have wanted to.'

Greggs was pottering slowly in our direction. I gave him a meaningful stare.

'I'll take a sherry, please.' A young man, slim, long faced and long limbed waved a hand at him. His was the plum English voice I'd heard earlier. He was sitting some distance from the others.

'Certainly, sir.' Greggs lowered the tray for the chap to help himself.

Swift ignored the tart discourse around the fire. 'Did Sullivan leave the room before you?' he asked Fitzroy.

'No, he was…' he searched for his words, 'crass, and argumentative. I found his manners wanting. I explained the situation to him and then left.'

'And he'd had a lot to drink?' Swift continued as he made a note.

'Yeah, that's what we said already, and he was slurring his words.' Malone had gone to wander around, but now came over from a tall display cabinet full of fussy gilded ornaments and the like. 'He was a lug.'

'Much as I dislike to talk ill of the dead,' Susannah said, 'I have to agree.'

'Me too,' Molly Patterson echoed.

Lady Peggie didn't say anything, but her expression indicated she was of the same mind.

'What is this *lug*?' The pale blond-haired chap asked. He was obviously the Dane by his accent and Scandinavian good looks.

Both Molly and Belinda turned eagerly in his direction.

'A nasty guy,' Molly explained.

'A real louse,' Belinda added.

'A bad man,' Malone said.

'Ja, he was.' The Dane agreed in heavily accented English. 'A fellow not to be trusted.'

'And you are?' Swift asked him.

The Dane frowned. 'Lars Olafsen. You are these detektifs.'

'Yes,' I replied.

'I think you have nothing to detect,' Lars declared and leaned back to cross long legs clad in stone-coloured trousers, his heavy cable knit jersey in the same colour.

The upright chap with the half-moon glasses came over.

'May I join you?' he said, with a stiff bow.

'Professor Coltrane!' Lady Peggie broke into a smile. 'Please do. I was surprised you had not done so already.'

'I apologise,' the professor said. Another American, he wore a dark red dickie bow with a plaid shirt below a brown jacket complete with elbow patches, and dark corduroy trousers. It was an interesting ensemble. 'I was having a contemplative moment. I prefer to remain solitary. When I am required to talk to people before I am ready, it quite disrupts my equilibrium.'

'But it's sometimes good to be disrupted,' Susannah said to him. 'I live on my own and I can tell you too much solitude is bad news. I end up talking to my cats, and once they start talking back, I just know I have got to go out and get some company.'

'I'm used to being alone.' The young, plummy chap had followed the older one. 'Though I'm not terribly keen on it.' He was too tall for his sparse frame, although well-dressed in a tailored waistcoat and trousers with tie and formal shirt. 'I'm Daniel Addison, by the way,' he said.

'Sit down will ye,' Malone called to him. 'You're blocking the heat from the fire.'

'Sorry, sorry,' Addison stuttered and sidestepped away to perch on the edge of a flaking leather armchair.

'Sir, may I offer a choice of white wine or sherry?' Greggs had finally deigned to bring me a drink. He leaned in closer to whisper, 'I suggest you avoid the sherry, sir. It has lingered too long in the bottle.'

'Wine,' I said, 'and you'd best give Swift the same.'

'Inspector Swift has declined to drink while he is on duty, sir,' he said and held out the tray.

'So you've left me 'til last,' I remarked as I took the glass.

He looked about as though counting the assembled. '*Ahem*, it is possible, sir,' he replied, then headed for the safety of the ancient sideboard on the other side of the room.

The wine was thick and slightly sweet. I sipped it slowly, watching the back and forth between the claimant heirs. Despite Swift's determined questioning, he was being sidetracked by a burgeoning argument.

I interrupted the quibbling. 'Sir Richard, you say you were the last to see Sullivan the night of his death. What time did you leave him?'

'I left this room at around eleven and went directly to my bedchamber,' Fitzroy replied. 'I did not see Sullivan again until yesterday morning when he was found dead at the foot of the stairs. I have already stated this,' he reminded us, his Scots accent deepening as he spoke more firmly.

'What about the butler, Craggie?' Swift said. 'Would he wait until all the guests had gone to their rooms before retiring?'

'Craggie keeps very early hours,' Lady Peggie answered in her precise English accent. 'He retires after serving dinner. Mrs Craggie washes up, and then she too retires.'

'So who locks up, then?' Belinda demanded, reflected firelight catching the waves of her bright blonde hair.

Everyone looked at her.

'Why would anyone lock up?' Molly asked.

'Why wouldn't they?' A flush reddened Belinda's rouged cheeks. 'Our maid always does every night. We have six outside doors, and a triple garage, plus the pool house,' she replied, then added sharply, 'we don't all live in the middle of nowhere.'

'Are you living among thieves?' Lars asked in his deep voice.

'No, of course not!' Belinda was indignant, her cheeks now almost scarlet. 'We're just careful, that's all. We live in a city and you never know who is around.'

'Then why do you live there?' Lars continued pedantically.

I heard a few sniggers from behind me.

'Because there are stores, and restaurants, and street lights, and cars, and…and people!' she replied, then added vehemently, 'And we like living there.'

'Whaddya wanna live here for then?' Malone asked the obvious question.

Everyone waited as she glared around, then sat up with her chin held high. 'I am here to represent my family. We think it might make a fine property for hunting vacations. And now that I've seen it, I think we should have it because we can afford to pay to have it properly maintained.'

'Well, there's a modest reply,' Molly said. 'I'm not surprised you left Canada with an attitude like that.'

'I think Canadians are nice people,' Lars said.

Molly flashed a big friendly smile at him. He smiled back, a glint in his pale blue eyes.

'What time did you all go to your rooms last night?' Swift interrupted loudly.

'I went at nine thirty,' Susannah Bellamy said.

'Just before ten o'clock,' the young man, Daniel Addison, replied. 'I went at the same time as Molly.' He looked at the Canadian; he'd been intently watching the interchange between her and Lars Olafsen.

'He did,' Molly confirmed, then she smiled at him too. He blushed, and managed a shy smile back.

'Not until almost half past ten,' Lady Peggie said. I heard the note of weariness in her voice. 'Mrs Craggie and I stayed up late to clean the dishes in the kitchen. We aren't accustomed to catering for so many people. We ascended the stairs together and we went to our respective living quarters.'

'I am ashamed to admit it, but I left for my bed before our generous hostess,' Professor Coltrane said. 'I turned in before ten. I was very tired. I'd had a long journey to get here.'

'I always go to my bed at ten,' Lars said. 'It is my custom.'

'I was so cold,' Belinda said. 'I went earlier to try to get warm.'

'You should try wearing more clothes then,' Malone said.

'Like that ridiculous get-up you're wearing?' she retorted.

'Enough,' Lars said, which silenced them.

Swift continued writing. 'So nobody saw Sullivan leave this room, or go to the stairs,' he stated, then asked, 'Who doused the candles?' He indicated the chandelier with the end of his pen. 'And the ones in the hall?'

They all looked up at the chandelier and then at Lady Peggie.

'They were already burning low when I went to bed, as were the hall candles,' she replied. 'I asked Craggie the same question myself the next morning. He said they were almost ready to be replaced and the guests would need to see their way, so he had left them to gutter out overnight.'

Swift nodded and turned to a fresh page.

Belinda, Molly, and Daniel stared up again at the iron candelabra. They'd probably grown up with electricity and hadn't ever given the trimming, dousing and replenishing of candles a second thought.

'I left chamber candles on a trolley by the door.' Lady Peggie indicated the double doors behind us. 'I had advised everyone to take one with them. Everyone should have been able to see their way.'

Swift was sticking to his list of questions. 'Why would Sullivan fall down the main stairs if he was heading upstairs to bed?'

'He wasn't supposed to be goin' up or down stairs,' Malone said. 'The bedrooms are on this floor, and like we said already, he was drunk.'

Professor Coltrane spoke up, his voice a little high and taut. 'I have given it some thought. I believe he left here, headed for the passage and took a wrong turn, or simply staggered toward the staircase and fell down it.'

'Yeah, it ain't that difficult to figure out,' Malone agreed.

Fitzroy let out a barely suppressed sigh. 'Thank you Mr Malone. I will explain with more precision,' he said. 'If one exits this room onto the landing, then turns left and through the archway ahead, one finds oneself in the section dedicated to the chambers for unaccompanied gentlemen. However, as one approaches the archway I have just described, the staircase down to the hall lies on one's right. If Sullivan wasn't paying attention, or was fuddled, it's feasible he could have turned towards the stairs in the dark and fallen.'

'Lady Peggie said the candles were still burning in the hall,' I reminded him.

'They were failing when I went onto the landing,' Fitzroy replied tersely. 'And I've no idea what time he left this room.'

'Did Sullivan take a chamber candle with him?' Swift asked Lady Peggie.

'I don't know,' Lady Peggie replied. 'I ensured there were more than required. And matches had been left with the candles.'

'Was a chamber candle found with his body?' Swift turned to Fitzroy, who hesitated and looked at Lady Peggie.

She too hesitated. 'No, it was not. May I show the trolley to you?'

Swift got to his feet. 'Please do.'

Lady Peggie rose stiffly from the sofa. 'Very well.'

I stood too, along with a few others. 'Stay seated please,' I told them. 'Sir Richard, please come too.'

We walked to the double doors and stopped at a rickety old serving trolley. Its stained wooden top held five unused candles in typical enamel holders – shallow white dishes with blue rims, finger loops, and creamy beeswax candles gripped by metal stems.

'Where are the others?' Swift asked.

'Left in people's bedrooms, or bathrooms I imagine.' Lady Peggie glanced back at her guests and replied quietly.

'It's Craggie's job to keep the candles filled, but none of the heirs think about that. They have very little idea how a residence such as this is run.'

'Do you often have guests, Lady Peggie?' I asked.

'Not at all,' she replied, keeping her voice low. 'The Laird never wanted anyone here. He would have been furious at this...this invasion!' She suddenly glared at Fitzroy, anger creasing the lines of her face. 'I cannot thank you for this, Richard. It was not what I wanted.'

Fitzroy lost a little of his gravitas as she took him to task. 'I apologise, Your Ladyship, but as there is no true-born heir there's really no choice.'

'Is that my fault?' she hissed.

'No, of course not. Please do not take offence, dear lady, I mean none,' he replied.

That raised my brows but neither Swift nor I questioned it.

The conversation behind us had dropped to a hushed tone. Those gathered around the fire were all peering in our direction, including Professor Coltrane, who was sitting up rather in the way of a scrawny chicken listening out for a fox. Greggs had wandered closer to us, and paused to polish some glasses on another long sideboard.

'That was a great misfortune for which it seems I am still paying.' Lady Peggie spoke harshly. I could see hurt in her eyes, and hear the bitterness in her voice.

'And I am sorry for it too,' Fitzroy answered sincerely. 'But we have been through this, and you did agree to the course of action.'

'Did you consult the Laird on what he hoped to happen to the estate on his death?' Swift asked, also keeping his voice low.

'Yes, some years ago,' Fitzroy answered patiently. 'He was aware that there was no clear answer. I advised him that the tailzie could be amended to expand the possible group of heirs. I asked him if he would like me to do this, but he refused because he did not want the expense.'

Anger still burned in Lady Peggie's eyes. 'And the cost will now be borne by the estate, which will further impoverish us.'

'How did the tailzie affect the inheritance?' I cut in because things were getting a little heated.

'In its original form it was the same as the English primogeniture,' Fitzroy replied. 'Only a son, or the nearest first born male could inherit. But this can now be amended to include the female line and women. As you can see from the gathering, there are ladies present. If they had been omitted from the list, any one of them could have contended the inheritance on the basis of the tailzie amendment act.'

'You didn't have to invite them here,' Lady Peggie hissed.

'I thought I had just made clear why I was obliged to,' Fitzroy hissed back. 'It is a matter of the law and their legal rights.'

'Surely you must know who has the most right to the estate,' Swift said.

'We do not,' Fitzroy answered tersely.

Lady Peggie added, 'There is a family tree in the library, but it does not include the outlying branches. And there are many, many offshoots. These people are descended from them.'

'I narrowed it down to these few,' Fitzroy continued. 'And I have asked them to bring legally recognised documents, letters, old wills or even photographs they may have, to support their claim. One of them might possess something that could definitively secure their right to the estate and the title.'

'Fine,' I said. 'But it sounds like Sullivan just fell downstairs. Why did you contact the police?'

Swift quickly added, 'We are prepared to investigate further if you have any evidence of foul play.'

Fitzroy closed his eyes for a brief moment. 'Please come with me.'

Lady Peggie's creased lips pursed. 'This was a profanity on the Clan McFee,' she muttered. Which made both Swift and I exchange looks.

Greggs made to follow.

'No,' I said. 'And don't let any of the others out either.'

'It was my intention to guard the door, sir,' he lied smoothly.

Fitzroy led us from the room and onto the landing. He paused and made a point of firmly closing the doors behind him, then crossed to the balustrade to lean on it. 'Sullivan didn't fall down the stairs. He was murdered on the spot where I am now standing.'

CHAPTER 4

'Why did you tell us he fell?' Swift demanded.

Fitzroy straightened, he wasn't about to be intimidated. 'I informed the police there may be grounds for suspicion, but I judged it unwise to say more over the telephone. I felt it prudent to let the heirs believe it was a simple accident and avoid alarming the culprit into rash acts.'

We both nodded in understanding. He was probably right.

'What actually happened?' I asked him. I could see Lady Peggie from the corner of my eye. She was holding back tears, and had taken a handkerchief from her sleeve. She may have had an angry exchange with Fitzroy, but she was obviously quite distraught.

'Lady Peggie?' Fitzroy stood back to let her talk.

'As I said, Mrs Craggie found him,' she said, then briefly raised the handkerchief to dab her eyes. 'I'm sorry…this is an abomination on top of everything else that has happened since my husband died.' She wiped her eyes again. 'Mrs Craggie cried out very loudly. I heard her. The house is quiet, and loud noises carry around the hall and along the passages. I was still in my nightwear, but came immediately. Sullivan was lying at the foot of the stairs on the persian rug. There was blood on it, and on the stairs, and naturally I assumed that he had tumbled down and hit his head on the stone treads. He had…damage to the back of the… the skull.' She stopped and held her hand over her mouth, closing her eyes. Despite her life in the Scottish highlands, her English reserve was still very much evident. She took another deep breath and continued, her voice under control but strained. 'Richard had heard the commotion too and arrived shortly after I did. We could see the man was dead. We were so shocked. Richard called the doctor, he lives in the next glen. His name is Doctor Kildare.' She cast tearful eyes at Fitzroy.

He took the story back up. 'Mrs Craggie was dreadfully upset, crying "milady, milady." Craggie was with her but he had become dizzy at the sight of the blood and went to sit by the fire. After calling the doctor I returned to the body. Mrs Craggie told me there was candle wax in the man's hair and something was not right. I examined him. The wound was deep and I thought perhaps he may have been hit with a heavy candlestick, but the ones in the hall were untouched.'

'We checked each of them,' Lady Peggie added. 'They were all undisturbed.'

'Was this before the heirs had seen him?' I interrupted with the question. 'Malone said everyone had seen the body.'

'It was done after they saw him,' Lady Peggie replied. 'They were slower to respond to Mrs Craggie's cry of horror.

Malone came onto the landing. He looked down and shouted out, asking what had happened. Then the other men came to see. I simply said he'd fallen. It wasn't long before everyone had gathered and were staring down at the body.'

'There was still blood on the stairs and the body lying at the bottom,' Fitzroy added. 'I ordered them to return to their rooms.'

'I don't think any of them realised it could have been murder,' Lady Peggie said. 'The hall was dark, we only had lanterns. It was difficult to see anything clearly.'

'When they'd gone,' Fitzroy continued, 'Mrs Craggie decided the hall chandelier should be lit before the doctor came. She went to fetch the candles from the cupboard under the stairs and trod on the rug below us. There was blood on it.'

We all duly looked down. There was an ancient circular rug in the McFee colours of dark red, blue, and black.

'We have cleaned it now,' Lady Peggie said. 'But at that moment we thought Sullivan must have been pushed over the bannister. Though it made no sense…' Her voice cracked as she tried to hold her tears back.

'Let me understand this.' Swift put a halt to the confused explanation. 'The candle wax didn't come from a candle-stick, therefore it must have come from the chandelier?' He pointed up at it, suspended over our heads.

'Yes, that is what I was about to say,' Fitzroy replied as we gazed up.

The chain holding the black iron chandelier was hooked to a rope which looped around a pulley attached to a beam, high up in the ceiling. The rope ran to a hoist fixed to the wall at the other end of the bannisters, furthest from the stairs.

'So the chandelier was dropped on his head when it was released, and it killed him,' I said and strode over to the hoist. I'd no idea why they didn't just say so to start with. I reached to turn the iron handle and lowered the chandelier. The mechanism was of standard design, very old, of course, because this method had been in use since they did away with flaming torches. It worked smoothly and silently; the rope connecting the chain was relatively new, or less than a hundred years, anyway. I stopped when it was at head height.

'Blood.' Swift had taken hold of the wheel-like rim of the chandelier and tipped it for a better look. 'It's on the under edge of this dish.' There were a dozen black metal 'dishes', each fitted with a spike holding a thick candle. The flames fluttered as Swift manoeuvred the heavy structure around, the black chain creaking as he did so.

'Oh, I thought Mrs Craggie had wiped it all off,' Lady Peggie said. 'She tried her best.'

'Where was most of the blood?' Swift asked, bending to peer at the underside of the chandelier.

'On the rim nearest you,' Fitzroy replied, then lowered his voice. 'I believe two of the heirs worked together. One must have been down in the hall and called up to Sullivan to position him under the chandelier, and the other waiting in the dark, poised to release the hoist. Sullivan would have collapsed over the bannister rail, causing the blood to drip onto the circular rug below. Then the person down in the hall went up to help the other drag Sullivan to the top of the stairs and roll him down them.'

'How heavy was Sullivan?' I asked.

'Almost as heavy as me,' Fitzroy said. The lawyer was a tall and solid man for his age.

Swift had allowed the chandelier to sway until it hung freely on its chain, then he went to wind the handle to raise it back up into its usual position. 'When was the hoist last oiled?' he asked.

'Just before the Laird's funeral,' Lady Peggie answered. 'Craggie has always looked after the candles and lamps. He had been asking to overhaul the chandelier for years, but the Laird refused. I gave him permission to do so after my husband died.' She was clasping her knotted fingers together.

'Craggie,' I said in question. 'Why is he walking round with a brolly?'

'He is not an eccentric,' Lady Peggie explained. 'The umbrella was a form of protest. My husband had refused to mend a leak in the roof of the old sector and the umbrella was Craggie's response. We did have the leak mended, in the end.'

That made me smile. It was the sort of thing Greggs would do.

'He was carrying it when he answered the door to us,' Swift said.

'Yes, I know.' Lady Peggie sighed. 'I'm afraid he is now protesting against the guests in the house. He is not accustomed to providing for visitors.'

'Could you send him to us, please?' Swift asked. 'He can show us to Sullivan's room.'

'I…' Lady Peggie glanced at Fitzroy. 'I will do so.'

'Thank you,' Swift said.

They hesitated for a moment then parted. Fitzroy to the drawing room, Lady Peggie to head through the opposing archway to that near the stairs.

'He was hit on the head by the chandelier,' Swift said when we were alone. 'He collapsed with his head and arms hanging over the rail, and the wound bled onto the circular rug below. Then the killer carried or dragged Sullivan's body along here,' he indicated the landing, 'to the top of the stairs and let him roll down. The killer must have had enough strength to do so, or there really were two of them.'

'If it was planned then it was a damn poor plan. Letting him bleed onto the rug below the bannister gave the game away immediately,' I remarked. 'It would have been easier just to push him down the stairs.'

'Falling down stairs is not necessarily fatal, Lennox, particularly if he's drunk. He'd probably just collapse and roll down to land none the worse, apart from a few bruises.'

We walked across to trot down the steps to reach the faded persian rug at the bottom and knelt down to examine it. The pile had been scoured flat in places; the housekeeper must have used a heavy scrubbing brush. There was no sign of any blood left on it. 'I'm surprised they didn't just throw it away.'

'It's an antique,' Swift said. 'One of the predecessors must have brought it back from somewhere abroad.'

'Presumably when they had some money to spend.' I walked over to the circular rug below the chandelier. That too had been cleaned…with vinegar by the smell. The cloth was threadbare in places with ragged edges and wasn't worth saving either, to my mind.

I shoved my hands in my pockets and gazed up and about. Everywhere was brushed free of cobwebs and dust but damp patches were clearly visible below the narrow leaded windows and in dark corners. The furniture was made up of heavy oak antiques, rather battered and chipped but all highly polished, as were the myriad pewter candlesticks.

Despite the dusting and polishing and the roaring fire in the hearth behind us, there was an air of mouldering decay about the place. What was needed was a great deal of money and someone with the enthusiasm to spend it. I wondered how many of the heirs were really prepared to do that.

'I was told ye were seeking me,' the voice of Craggie called out from above.

I looked up. Only the umbrella was visible on the upper landing.

'We'll come up,' Swift called out.

There was some muttering, then, 'Toss some wood on the fire afore ye do.'

Swift frowned then turned back to throw a huge log on top of the others. It caused a shower of sparks to fly up into the sooty chimney, and he waited to watch them fall before coming to join me.

We walked up to the old butler on the landing.

'Why the umbrella?' I said, even though I knew the reason.

'Things fallin' doon in the castle,' he answered. 'Includin' the dead now.'

I eyed him. Bent back, sparse white hair, wiry hands, a thin hooked nose in a face wrinkled with deep creases around brown eyes, which carried a hint of humour.

'What time did you see William Sullivan last alive?' Swift asked, predictably.

'Just afore I went up to m' bed.' His forehead furrowed even more deeply, pulling his thicket of brows together. 'That were at eight, as it always is. The Laird and the Lady was always the same. But now there's ootlanders here and they stay up to burn the candles doon. The Lady kept with them, eatin' and drinkin', and m' wife with her. She din't come 'til after late. Chided her I did. Then she was up at the skreich o' day, an' found one of 'em dead.' He let the umbrella tip back so he could peer up at me. 'Murderin' each other now, like in the old days. Maybe there's some Scots' blood in 'em after all.'

That made me smile, though I suppressed it when Swift frowned at me. 'What time is skreich o' day?'

'Six o' the clock,' he replied.

'How did you know what time it was?' Swift demanded

'By the chiming o' the clock on the mantel,' Craggie replied, unrepentant. 'We have our own rooms, and I keep the time right by the kirk bells.' He lowered the umbrella and turned around. 'Now ye want to come and find that sassenach's room.' He marched off towards the archway, and the area Fitzroy had described as the men's chambers.

We continued along the unlit corridor. 'Where's my dog?' I asked, swivelling to look about, and almost walked into the wall. I realised they'd turned a corner. I swore under my breath, then hastened to catch up.

'With your man. M'wife gave him some scraps. He's been well cared for. We like dogs. Always had them here. Last one died a year afore the Laird. The Lady wanted another, but he said she was to wait till he'd gone to his grave. Then she could find one suited to her new abode.'

I'd no idea how he could see anything, and the umbrella hardly helped. I took my torch from my pocket and lit it.

Craggie stopped, turned about and said, 'It's ingenys you're minded for, is it?'

I didn't reply because I had no idea what he'd said.

'Where will Lady Peggie move to?' Swift asked.

'There's a cottage in the village waiting on her, and another for us,' Craggie replied. 'It'll be an easier life for all. I'm ready for it, an' so's Mrs Craggie.'

The thin carpet beneath our feet was also in the McFee colours. I could only see it by the light of my torch. I ran the beam along the wall. It was hung with dark paintings of men in full highland kit, and stern-looking ladies with buttoned-up blouses, pursed lips and hair pinned in tight buns. I think this section overlooked the east side of the castle.

'Lady Peggie is English,' I remarked.

'Aye, the Laird found her in the south and brought her back nigh on fifty years since. A good lady and never stinted from work, and there's always plenty o' that here,' Craggie replied, then stopped in front of a door. 'This was Sullivan's.' He took a large key from his black waistcoat pocket and gave it to Swift. 'I'll be away,' he said and turned to leave. His black trousers and black brolly caused him to vanish almost immediately into the darkness.

Swift unlocked the door and we stepped into a pitch black room.

'It's freezing,' I said as the cold hit my face.

'The fire will have been out since Sullivan died,' Swift said.

I swung my torch about and spotted an oil lamp on the mantel shelf. There were matches and tapers next to it. I kindled a flame to the wick.

'It's like stepping back in time,' Swift said as he looked around.

'How far back?'

He grinned. 'The dark ages.'

I laughed.

'I don't think Mrs Craggie provides room service.' He glanced at the unmade bed, then began to pull open the drawers in the dressing table. 'All empty,' he said, banging them open and closed.

I hated searching through people's private whatnots so I mooched about shining my torch at this and that. A book lay on his bedside table. *The Little Minister* by J. M. Barrie. Florence had read it. I knew this because she'd been telling Persi about it over breakfast. It was a 'romance set against a vividly portrayed Scottish backdrop.' I don't remember anything else because I'd stopped listening the minute she'd mentioned 'romance'. There was something slipped within its pages. I pulled it out.

'Swift,' I called him.

He came to look over my shoulder. It was a black and white photo of a man wearing full Scots regalia including a kilt, sporran and tam-'-shanter. The chap was grinning broadly, his chin held up. He had the look of a navvy, or someone who'd spent a lot of time in hard labour. A flattened nose, battered ears sticking out like pudgy wing nuts, small eyes deep-set under a low brow shadowed by the over large cap.

'Doesn't look like he's had a privileged life,' Swift said.

I turned the photograph over. There was an inscription on the back. *William Sullivan, soon to become Laird Sullivan-McFee of Clan McFee of the Glen.* I turned it back over.

'The kilt…'

'What about it?' Swift replied.

'Look at the sporran, and the pattern of the kilt. It's the same one Mick Malone is wearing.'

CHAPTER 5

He didn't take my word for it, of course. He went through Sullivan's cupboard, and then his wardrobe, to find those too were empty. Then he dragged the suitcase out from under the bed and opened that up to find it stuffed with clothes. After he'd searched through it, including the pockets and linings, he stood up.

'Nothing?' I enquired.

'As you can see,' he said tetchily. 'And you could help.'

'Hum,' I replied.

'We'll go and talk to Malone,' he declared.

'Fine,' I agreed. 'Over dinner.'

'No, Lennox—'

'Nobody's going anywhere, Swift. Just let things take their course.' I headed for the door. I was cold, it had been a long day and I was in need of food, and my dog.

Craggie must have taken up his duties as lamp lighter because the passageway was now illuminated by oil lamps in a series of niches in the walls. We made our way back to the drawing room to find it vacant apart from Foggy and

Greggs. The little dog raced up to us, barking and jumping about in greeting. I bent to ruffle his ears.

'Ah, sir.' Greggs straightened up, trying to hide a glass of wine behind his back. 'I believe dinner is about to be served in the grand dining room. You are expected.'

I went to the fire to thaw the extremities. 'You were enjoying something to warm the blood?' I raised a brow at him.

'*Ahem*, yes sir.' He slid the glass round then finished the contents in one.

'Come on, Lennox,' Swift said. 'We can't keep them waiting.

He was right. 'Has anyone dressed for dinner?' I asked Greggs as he showed us from the room.

'I believe a number have donned heavier sweaters, sir,' he replied. 'And the young lady from California has asked for her fur coat.'

'I thought Canadians were weatherproof,' Swift said.

'Only those who have remained in Canada, sir,' Greggs said.

Foggy led the way downstairs, tail at a jaunty angle, trotting ahead of us. A dog of very little brain, but very attuned to the whereabouts of food. We crossed the hall; I could hear the clattering of crockery from a distant passage, presumably the kitchen was somewhere along there.

We approached an imposing portal of overlarge proportions.

'I have offered to help Mr Craggie, sir.' Greggs opened the heavy oak door. 'On the provision he returns the umbrella to its stand.'

'Did he agree?' I asked. The noise of chatter along with

the delicious scent of fresh bread and hearty soup greeted us as we entered.

'As you can see, sir.'

Craggie had indeed ditched the brolly. He now held a white napkin draped over his left arm and was hugging it close to his body, thus leaving him, yet again, with only one arm functioning.

'Ah, the detectives!' Susannah Bellamy called out from her seat at the long table. 'Have you solved the mystery?'

'What mystery?' Belinda Guthrie demanded.

'The strange and tragic death of William Sullivan,' Molly Patterson said in mock horror.

'Will ya just si'down and let us eat,' Malone shouted out. He was still clad in the tartan get-up. I was inclined to ask why he was wearing the dead man's clothes but decided to wait.

'Ye can put ye'self doon here.' Craggie was trying to seat me next to Belinda Guthrie despite my shaking my head at him behind her back. She wasn't wearing a fur coat but had wrapped a cream mohair shawl around her shoulders. I've no idea why because, unlike the rest of the castle, it was actually warm in the room. Swift had gone to sit next to Professor Coltrane, who I'd have found more interesting than the petulant blonde.

'We are waiting to say grace, Major Lennox,' Lady Peggie said.

I sat down, and bowed my head. The young man, whose name I'd already forgotten, was on the other side of me. He'd clasped his hands on his lap and closed his eyes.

'Oh, a dog!' Molly called out. 'Isn't he cute!'

Everyone instantly snapped out of prayer pose and looked around. Foggy came out from under a Jacobean refectory table set against the end wall, where he'd no doubt gone hunting for lost morsels.

Most of the assembled called encouraging words and held their hands out, which naturally caused Foggy to trot from one to the other in the hope of titbits. He finally realised they hadn't any and came to lie under my chair.

'He belongs to the detectives,' Sir Richard Fitzroy said. 'And if we could please be silent for grace.' He looked at Lady Peggie.

'Thank you,' she said and then spoke in a clear voice, her earlier anger seemingly overcome. *'O Lord, who provides for all. Bless this table and those who gather at it. Grant us grateful hearts and generous hands, that we may share Thy bounty with those in need. May our speech be honourable, our actions fair and just, and our hearts ever mindful of Thy grace. In Thy name, we give thanks. Amen.'*

*Amen*s echoed around the table and we all reached for our spoons. The soup was oxtail with chunks of meat and carrots and a thin layer of dripping floating on its surface. It was delicious, as were the warm bread rolls spread with salted butter. Mrs Craggie must be an excellent cook.

I ate in silence as the chatter rose around me. The room was tall, narrow and imposing, but somehow convivial. It hadn't seemed to have changed since its early days of inter-clan hospitality. A massive stone fireplace with a mantel decorated with clan insignias and Gaelic mottos above a crackling fire loaded with a bed of peat and more huge logs.

The high ceiling was vaulted, the stone walls lined with hangings made of applied fabrics embroidered onto heavy canvas. There were depictions of men in plaid out hunting on small, sturdy horses with huge hounds running at their sides. Others were feasting at tables laden with roasted meats and goblets of liquor, the dogs lying below, gnawing on bones. It was the sort of life I'd have enjoyed, although probably not for very long given the propensity for warring, fighting, and getting killed in battle.

We were seated either side of the dark oak table lit with a line of heavily embossed silver candlesticks. Celtic symbols were cut into the high chair backs; the Laird's chair at the head was the most elaborate of all. It stood empty, a symbolic reminder of why everyone was gathered here.

'You are English, Major Lennox,' the young chap next to me said.

'Yes.' I dunked another chunk of buttered bread roll into my soup.

'Were you a pilot in the war?' he continued.

'Yes.'

'I read about you in *The Times*. You solved the Birdcage Murders.'

'Along with Swift,' I replied, because I couldn't reply 'yes' to that.

'My name is Daniel Addison, by the way.' He had finished his soup and put his spoon down. 'I did introduce myself but people hardly ever remember me.'

'Hm.' I finished my roll.

'I think Sullivan was murdered.'

I eyed him. An unprepossessing sort, with light brown hair and eyes, pale face too long, his narrow chin and thin lips were downcast and nervous. 'Really?'

His Adam's apple bobbed in his throat as he cleared it. 'Mrs Craggie scrubbed the circular rug from the centre of the hall. There wouldn't have been any need to clean it if he'd fallen down the stairs.'

'Was the body still there?'

'Not when she was cleaning it, no. The doctor and ambulance had recently left.'

'Weren't you on the landing with Malone and the rest before the doctor arrived?'

'Yes, but this was later, as I said it was after the body had been removed.'

I nodded. 'How closely did you see Sullivan?'

'Only from the landing. He was sprawled on his back at the bottom of the stairs. We could see his head was a mess, there was blood everywhere, including some on the stone steps.'

'Any blood on the top step?' I finished my soup and put the spoon down.

'No, but there was on the second one down, and most of the others. I thought that strange too, surely he'd have fallen his body length before hitting his head and making it bleed?'

'Not necessarily.' I was non committal.

Greggs had been pouring white wine into glasses etched with the McFee coat of arms. He leaned over to fill mine.

'I discovered a very nice Sauternes in the wine store, sir, with a claret, which will follow with dinner.'

'Which claret?'

'Latour, sir.'

I frowned. 'Is it drinkable?'

'I tried a soupçon, sir, while opening it to breathe. It is entirely drinkable,' he burbled happily and went off to serve the professor and Swift.

'I have a case of Chateau Margaux in my room,' Daniel whatever-he-was-called said.

'Really?' That surprised me; it was hideously expensive and utterly sublime.

'I wasn't sure if they would keep a decent cellar,' he replied in all seriousness. 'So I brought my own.'

'Where did you acquire it?'

'My father laid it down years ago. He was rather a connoisseur.'

I noted his use of the past tense. 'He's dead?' I said, then realised that he must be or he'd be the putative heir rather than his son.

Daniel nodded. 'Sir George Addison, he was Consular General in Hyderabad.'

'Ah,' I muttered, recalling the name, and the scandal. Sir George Addison had been murdered in the embassy at Hyderabad just as the war had ended. The motive had been publicly stated to be political, but there had been rumblings of misuse of diplomatic privileges, which usually meant smuggling large sums of money through diplomatic bags. Apart from the mystery surrounding his death there had also been a great debate in the newspapers about the trust fund he'd successfully set up to shield his estate from death duties. This was said to be letting the side down – mostly by those who hadn't thought of it first. 'You inherited, I assume?'

'Yes,' Daniel said. 'It's been tremendously complicated, but it has allowed me to better understand the finer points of inheritance law.'

I regarded him more closely. Looks could be deceiving and he might not be the nonentity I'd initially taken him for.

'Given the funds you've already inherited, why would you want a remote highland castle that will probably be a bottomless money pit?'

'I'd like the challenge of running this place, if I was chosen,' he replied. He picked up his glass of wine; his hand shook very slightly as he did so.

'It's not a question of being chosen.' Belinda leaned around me to speak to him. She must have been eavesdropping. 'It totally depends on which of us has the best lineage.'

'I'm not so sure,' Daniel replied, his eyes flicking across to Fitzroy, who was in close conversation with Lars and Susannah. 'Why should the lawyer decide on someone without any funds? We must have nearly identical claims to the castle; if we hadn't, the heir would have already been fixed on.'

'Well, my family has more than enough money, so it's not a worry for me.' She was dismissive. 'Though if it weren't for the title, my father wouldn't be particularly interested.'

'You're here representing your father?' Daniel asked her.

'I already said so, weren't you listening?' she replied.

I carried on drinking my wine as they quibbled across me, he more polite than she was, or deserved, to my mind.

'I offered to come and fight for our rights,' she continued. 'We Guthries won't let anyone get one over on us. What's ours is ours.'

'Your claim is on the maternal side?' Professor Coltrane said from the other side of the table, his thin neck stretching so he could view them more easily. 'Both of you, I believe?'

'Yes,' Daniel said. 'My mother's great, great grandmother was a McFee.'

'My father's great, great, whatever grandmother was a McFee, which means we're ahead of you,' Belinda retorted.

Malone laughed loudly. 'You're both way out. I'm second in line after Sullivan, and now he's out of the picture, I'm the heir.' He looked at Fitzroy. 'And there's nothing anyone can do about it.'

'Mr Malone,' Fitzroy replied calmly but coldly. 'You are not only incorrect, you are also disrespectful. I will not have Lady Peggie's meals continually marred by squabbling.'

Malone shovelled a piece of bread roll into his mouth.

'I apologise,' Daniel said. 'It was not intentional.'

Belinda pulled her mohair shawl more closely around her shoulders, a truculent moue on her lips. It was clear that she wasn't in the habit of apologising. Neither was Malone.

The loud rattling of crockery, cutlery, and squeaky wheels presaged the arrival of a trolley, pushed one-handed by Craggie. Greggs had heard the approach and opened the door in readiness.

'Tiz venison stew,' Craggie announced. 'With tatties and neeps.'

The scent was heavenly. I watched as the doddering butler moved at a snail's pace to the top of the table. Greggs put the wine carafe on the ancient refectory table and went to join him.

'We had venison stew last night, and the night before that,' Lars said in his heavy accent.

'So ye'll know what ye're getting then,' Craggie replied and slid open the top of the silver domed lid.

'Is this what you eat always?' Lars asked.

'No. Sometimes it's venison broth. And we have haggis on the Lord's day.' Craggie picked up a silver ladle and dipped it to stir the stew. Steam and more delicious smells rose from the tureen, which almost covered the entire top of the trolley.

'I've never had haggis,' Molly said. 'What is it made from?'

'Sheep innards,' Professor Coltrane answered. 'Mostly offal, but quite nutritious. The ingredients must not put you off.'

Molly laughed. 'Oh, it wouldn't put me off. I've had far worse.'

Greggs had lifted china dishes from the second shelf of the trolley to place on the table. He held the first one up.

Craggie's thick brows lowered. 'Bide ye time, man, there's nae haste.'

'I'm sure the guests would not want their stew to be cold,' Greggs replied. 'Nor would your esteemed wife wish for her excellent cooking to be delivered in a less than perfect manner.'

His effort at diplomacy was met with a fierce glare under brows now decidedly bristling. 'And what would ye know of me wife's wants and wishes, then?'

'*Ahem*, I, um… I know nothing, Mr Craggie, I was merely, erm…' Greggs took a step back, stammering nervously.

Craggie raised the ladle. 'I'll not have a soother moother lordin' over me.'

'Craggie, that's enough,' Lady Peggie called out sharply. 'Please accept Mr Greggs' help and hasten the meal.'

Craggie slammed the ladle into the stew, causing droplets to fly up. 'So that's the way it is, is it? Then yon man can do it his'sen,' he declared, eyes still fixed on Greggs. 'I'm goin' to get me brolly.' He threw the napkin on the floor and stomped off.

I raised brows at Greggs, his eyes wide in shock. 'Sir, I…I…'

'I'm so sorry, Mr Greggs. Poor Craggie has found all the changes most disturbing,' Lady Peggie said. 'Could I call upon you to stand in, please?'

That was all he needed to propel him to action. 'Of course, milady, it will be a pleasure.' He bowed, then picked up the napkin, and then the ladle, and began serving. He left me till last – again.

'Lady Peggie,' Molly said as we all ate the excellent stew. 'The road here was really narrow. Do you get snowed in come winter?'

'Oh, yes,' she replied. 'Every year. We're used to it.'

Belinda frowned as she looked from one to the other. Greggs had served the claret all round; it was quite superb.

'This is normal,' Lars said. 'I use skis, but I keep also horses and a sled. Do you have the horses here, your lady?'

'Not now, but there are a pair in the village,' Lady Peggie replied. 'We prepare for winter well in advance and are stocked up before the first snows cut us off.'

'We do the same,' Swift said. 'Although our problems are mostly caused by crossing the Loch to the mainland.'

'You also live in Scotland, Inspector?' Susannah Bellamy turned to him.

'Yes, Braeburn Castle. It's further south,' he replied, spearing a piece of tender venison with his fork.

'You got your own castle?' Malone seemed astounded.

'It is not mine, it is the seat of my wife's clan,' Swift replied.

'And the home of Braeburn malt,' Professor Coltrane said.

'Braeburn malt?' Addison asked, his eyes suddenly bright with interest.

This turned the conversation to discussions of whisky production and life in a castle. I quietly enjoyed my stew, sharing a few choice morsels with Foggy at my feet.

'Have the McFee's ever had the opportunity to produce their own whisky, Lady Peggie?' Professor Coltrane asked her, his American accent curiously clipped and precise. He was rather uptight, I concluded.

'Our land is not suited to such an enterprise, Professor,' she replied. 'I wish it were.'

'Then how did you pay for everything here?' Belinda asked.

'We had our own gold mine. It is the reason the Glen was so hard-fought over,' Lady Peggie replied as she picked at her stew.

Everyone's ears pricked up at the thought of a gold mine.

'Gold?' Malone sat up. 'You mean real gold? Out of the ground?'

'Yes,' she replied. 'The McFee's eventually secured the area and became rich and powerful, but the mine was exhausted over a century ago, and clan fortunes declined as a result.'

'It must have been a substantial seam,' Swift remarked. 'We had a lead mine but it was depleted within a few decades.'

'Yeah, but this gold mine,' Malone continued. 'You must have some of the gold left. A little pile of nuggets hidden away somewhere.'

Lady Peggie gave a tight smile. 'Every nugget was spent, right down to the last grain. Believe me, Mr Malone, the last few generations have scoured the mine, the castle, the ground, the river, and under every pebble and stone in search of any remaining gold.'

'I believe there are a number of gold mines in Scotland,' Professor Coltrane said. 'The Cononish mine in Tyndrum is the largest.'

'It is,' Lady Peggie agreed. 'We were minor in comparison, but the proceeds built and extended this castle and estate, and enabled the old Lairds to raise militia for the king when needed. The McFee's were once a great power in the land,' she added with some pride.

Talk turned to history, and wars against the English, as Greggs cleared plates and topped up the claret. The pudding was served in a dish of ice. It was cranachan, which I hadn't had before. A mix of toasted oats, honey, raspberries, a spoonful of whisky, and topped with whipped cream. I assumed the castle had an ice house or ice box somewhere.

'Mr Malone,' Susannah Bellamy finished her cranachan and placed her silver spoon neatly on her dish. 'Why are you wearing the tartan?'

'Because I'm the next Laird.' He grinned at her, eyes glinting. 'I believe in coming prepared.'

'This skirt does not fit. You could not have it made for you?' Lars asked.

'Sure I did,' Malone said with such confidence it was almost believable. 'The guy wasn't used to making Scots stuff.'

'It wasn't you who had the outfit tailored,' I said.

'How would you know?' Malone challenged.

'Sullivan had it made, and you stole it,' I said in an even tone and scooped up the remains of my dessert.

That caused a few gasps, and a spluttering cough from the professor.

'You killed him!' Belinda shrieked, and pointed an accusing finger at Malone.

'You said he fell down the stairs,' Molly reminded her.

'He stole Sullivan's clothes?' Susannah said, horror in her voice.

'He wasn't wearing them when he died,' Malone retorted, not in the least contrite about his lie being exposed. 'And it ain't none of your business. None of you.' He waved a defiant hand in the air.

'How did you get them?' Professor Coltrane had stopped coughing enough to ask.

'From his room. Where else?' Malone said. 'We came on the same train. He told me I was wasting my time, he was going to be the Laird and had a tartan suit all made.'

'So you killed him and took his clothes.' Belinda wasn't backing down.

'I did not kill him, no-one did. I took them outta his room.' Malone sat back in his chair and started picking his teeth. 'He was dead, he didn't need 'em.'

'Were any papers with his clothes?' Swift instantly asked.

'No, and I wouldn't have seen them anyway,' Malone said. 'I just picked these out of his wardrobe. It was the only thing he bothered to unpack. His room was a mess, clothes all over the place, even left on the floor.'

I looked at Swift. They'd been bundled into the suitcase when we searched it earlier, someone must have been in there. Other than Malone, obviously.

'That's despicable,' Daniel was saying. 'And as I've just pointed out to Major Lennox, there is no one here with a greater claim than the other, or Sir Richard would not have invited all of us.' He turned to Fitzroy, and so did everyone else.

'Can you confirm that this is true?' Professor Coltrane asked.

Fitzroy had the grace to look embarrassed. 'In theory, yes. But one of you may produce a document from your own family archives that proves a definitive heir.'

'Do you know if Sullivan had any such document?' Swift asked him.

'He said he had, but I have not seen any,' Fitzroy replied.

'Maybe the thief took his papers with his clothes,' Lars said, his blue eyes narrowed and fixed on Malone.

'I already said I didn't, and I ain't no thief,' Malone replied evenly. He may have been brash but he kept his wits about him and didn't overreact. 'And I don't give a damn what you say, I'm gonna be the next Laird 'cos I'm next in line.'

'You can't know that,' Professor Coltrane countered.

'Did you kill William Sullivan?' Molly demanded. She was cool-headed too. Maybe it was a McFee trait.

'Nope,' Malone said. 'An' anyway, he wasn't killed, he just tripped and fell down the stairs.'

'Do y'all think Mr Sullivan was murdered,' Susannah asked. 'Inspector Swift, Major Lennox?'

'Yes,' I replied.

CHAPTER 6

Swift was unamused by that particular revelation.

It inevitably caused a degree of chaos.

'Are you saying, Major Lennox,' Professor Coltrane leaned stiffly forward to address me, 'that William Sullivan was murdered in this house two nights ago?'

'Yes,' I replied again. I noticed Fitzroy close his eyes as I confirmed it.

Professor Coltrane turned to Swift next to him. 'You implied that Sullivan's death was an accident.'

'I…' Swift began, then corrected himself. '*We* have barely begun making enquiries yet. I was reluctant to cause any unnecessary alarm,' Swift extemporised then glared at me.

I emptied my glass of claret, which had grown more exceptional the more I drank of it.

'You mean someone in this room actually murdered Mr Sullivan!' Susannah Bellamy was looking about her in astonishment.

'This is evident,' Lars said, apparently unconcerned. He too finished his claret; it brought warm colour to his sharply defined cheeks.

'Seriously?' Belinda was finding the news hard to digest. 'I mean…seriously? One of you murdered Sullivan?'

'This is too much. Sir Richard, I am going to retire,' Lady Peggie said to him and banged her napkin on the table.

'Do you have a chamber candle?' Fitzroy replied. 'Craggie will have doused the lamps and candles.'

'I got a flashlight,' Malone declared. 'I'll go with you.' He stood up, reached into his sporran, pulled out a torch and held it aloft.

'No, thank you, Mr Malone,' Lady Peggie replied coldly.

'Whatever,' he replied. 'And I don't need no stupid candle.' He marched off towards the door.

'You look foolish in the skirt you stole,' Lars called after him.

'It's called a kilt, and I didn't steal it!' Malone called as he went out, slamming the door behind him.

'Goodnight to you all.' Lady Peggie rose from her chair.

'May I escort you, Lady Peggie?' Professor Coltrane instantly asked.

'Thank you, that would be most kind.' She turned to him and attempted a smile.

Susannah Bellamy looked up, watching them.

Fitzroy must have noticed, as he turned to her. 'And may I escort you, Miss Susannah?'

She jumped up, forcing a bright smile. 'How delightful, of course you may, Sir Richard.'

Greggs went to open the door and stood bowing as everyone filed out. Swift and I made up the rear, along with Foggy.

'I shall come along now, sir,' Greggs called out, and then started to blow the candles out along the table. 'If you would wait.'

'Who's going to clear up?' Swift asked him.

'I shall help Mrs Craggie in the morning, sir,' Greggs replied rather breathlessly. He caught us up and closed the door behind him. 'And you will need my assistance to find your room, sirs.'

'You don't want to wander about alone in the dark?' I remarked.

'I do not, sir. There is an atmosphere in this castle which I find rather disconcerting.'

'Nonsense, Greggs. You're letting your imagination run away with you,' I told him as we crossed the hall with echoing footsteps. The chandelier had indeed been extinguished, the lofty space lit only by flickering shadows cast by the fire dying in the huge hearth.

'It's often like this in Braeburn,' Swift said. 'The electricity fails and everyone is back to carrying oil lamps. There's always talk of ghosts and I'm forever telling them it's nonsense–argh!' He suddenly shouted out and leapt sideways.

'What the–?' I cried out. Something small had skittered across the floor ahead of us, then ran around and made a grab for Swift's feet. Foggy started barking.

I dug out my torch from my pocket and swung it about, trying to make out what it was, briefly catching sight of a pair of small eyes before whatever it was darted off.

'*Ahem*, sir,' Greggs said. 'I believe it may be Mr Tubbs.'

'What?' I said.

'I have not had time to inform you, sir, that Mr Tubbs came with us. He travelled under my cape.'

'Greggs, why did you bring him?' I demanded.

'It's the cat?' Swift could hardly believe it, but at least he'd stopped dancing around.

'Indeed, sir. Lady Persi said he would miss Major Lennox, and that the major would miss the cat. As would Mr Fogg. And also Mr Tubbs is not terribly keen on Nicky, except when he is asleep.'

He was right about that: the Jack Russell regarded the cat as a perfect playmate. Tubbs was usually up for most games but Nicky was still in his rough and tumble stage and Tubbs had quickly tired of being bowled over by the pup.

I caught the little reprobate in my torchlight. He'd sat down to lick a paw. Foggy went to sit next to him, watching proceedings with his tongue hanging out.

'Come on,' I said and leaned down to scoop the cat up. 'Bed time.'

We went warily upstairs then entered the same 'gentleman's' corridor in which we'd found Sullivan's room earlier.

'Mr Craggie informed me that this is the warmer end of the east wing, sir,' Greggs said as he threw open a door.

An oil lamp hanging from the ceiling was lit, showing two single beds, one each side of the dull green room. A large moth-eaten rug lay on the floor, a circular table placed on it with two hardback chairs, a low bookcase, and chest of drawers doubling as a washstand. It offered little comfort, except for the beds, which were covered with thick blankets and green, feather-filled eiderdowns.

'Why is it "warmer"?' I asked as a chill blast hit us.

'It is sheltered from the prevailing winds, sir,' Greggs said. 'I lit the fire when I brought up the bags.' He gazed at the embers beneath some charred logs piled in the stone hearth. ' I believe it may need some encouragement…'

'I'll do it,' I said and went to the nearest bed to deposit Tubbs on the quilt.

Foggy jumped up to join him then curled up to gaze at me with brown spaniel eyes almost hidden by his long golden ears.

'Aren't there any other spare rooms?' Swift asked as he regarded the other bed set under the window.

'Only the late Mr Sullivan's, sir,' Greggs said. 'I have a small antechamber next door, we could exchange if you–'

'No, I'm not going to be kept awake half the night by your snoring, Greggs.'

'As you say, sir,' he intoned then aimed for the door. 'Good night, sirs,' he said and was gone. It's amazing how quickly he could move when he wanted to.

I banged the ashes with a poker and watched as flames began licking around the wood. Swift put a half bottle of Braeburn malt on the table, then added the water glasses that had been left on the chest of drawers. I reached for a pair of worn leather bellows propped on the stone hearth, then changed my mind and picked up the unlit lamp on the mantel shelf. I unscrewed the base and poured some of the kerosene from its reservoir onto the fitful fire.

'Lennox,' Swift objected as it flared up then burst into yellow flames, the escaping gas hissing as it blazed.

'It was that or the whisky, Swift,' I told him. 'And that's all we've got because I forgot mine.'

He frowned and poured us each a glass of golden liquid while I quickly got ready for bed and dived under the covers. He placed a shot glass of amber liquid on the bedside table next to me, then retired to his own bed.

'Perfect, thank you.' I drank it in one and lay back to feel the warmth of high-grade alcohol spread through me. It was bliss.

'Malone is an idiot.' Swift had made a rapid change into pyjamas as well and reached up to turn the lamp wick down. It created an instant gloom in the room, with only the fire to ward off inky blackness

'He is if he killed Sullivan,' I replied.

'Any thoughts on who might have done?'

'No.'

'Neither have I,' he said then sighed. 'I didn't ring Florence.'

'No…' I hadn't rung Persi either. The thought had crossed my mind, but somehow the time had slipped away. 'Go to sleep, Swift.'

'Right.' I heard the tap as he placed his glass onto his bedside table. Then I didn't hear a thing until the door banged open at dawn next morning.

***

'Murder!' Craggie shouted from the threshold.

'What?' My eyes flew open.

'Murder. Murder!' Craggie repeated. 'Come quick. Quick now!'

That got me moving. I leapt out of bed. 'Who's dead?'

'Murder?' Swift had burrowed down in the covers, but now pushed them from over his head.

'There's a body.' Craggie waved his arms, panic setting in.

'Whose body?' I struggled into my trousers. Foggy sat up on the bed and yawned, not in the least concerned by the sudden commotion.

'Another ootlander. In the water.' Craggie was almost breathless. 'Floatin' away. Ye've got t'come afore he's gone.'

I pulled my thick Arran sweater over my head and shoved bare feet into my boots. 'Show me,' I ordered.

'Lennox, wait,' Swift called. He'd pulled his trench coat over his pyjamas and was now trying to tie his shoelaces.

'No time, Swift.'

Craggie shuffled ahead, but I overtook him. Foggy decided to come and bounded ahead of me. That caused me to break into a run and I raced down the stairs, across the hall and out through the open front door with Foggy lolloping at my side.

The early morning sun threw long shadows across the ground; a layer of light frost was turning to dew on the grass and ground. Lady Peggie was on the shore of the river, a thick woollen dressing gown held tightly around her. Fitzroy was with her, he too in nightclothes. They were staring in horror at the body of a man floating in the broad stretch of water some way beyond the bridge. He was already beginning to gather pace as he reached the arc at the end of the broad water and entered the narrowing river where it flowed downstream.

I couldn't see a face. His head was hanging down between outstretched arms; he was entirely bald, which confused me. Who was he? Not one of the heirs. The cause of death was easier to spot: there was a large knife stuck into his back, a circle of black-looking blood spread around it, staining his drenched overcoat.

Swift raced out of the door and paused momentarily at my side.

'I'll get him.' I pulled at an arm of my sweater to take it off.

'No, you must not,' Lady Peggie called to us. 'The river's in full spate from the mountain snows. He's too close to the narrows now. It's far too dangerous.'

'Don't go in, Major.' Fitzroy was striding towards us. 'Go to the cascade, you might catch him there.' He pointed east, where the water flowed downriver.

The body was moving much faster now, caught by the water funnelled between narrowing rocky banks.

'Come on, Lennox,' Swift shouted.

I yanked my jumper back in place and we sprinted off along an earthen path running parallel to the river toward a tree-covered promontory. Foggy raced alongside us, barking as though it were a game. The body was still visible ahead, the speed of the water propelling him faster and faster. We reached the bluff where large rocks divided the river into numerous roiling runnels, and Swift sprang off the bank and onto the nearest boulder only a couple of feet from the shore. His feet instantly slid from under him, a thin layer of ice making it almost impossible to find a grip. He scrabbled with fingers clawing to save himself from falling into the torrent.

'Hold on.' I almost threw myself onto the rock to lay flat over it, steadied myself and grabbed his wrist. I was nearly yanked off as he lost a toe-hold. 'Damn it,' I swore as I was almost pulled down with him. Foggy was now frantic and barking behind me from the bank.

'Lennox…' Swift was flailing, his shoes scraping against the ice-slicked stone inches from the churning water. 'Lennox,' he shouted. He swung his free hand and managed to grasp my upper arm.

I pulled, almost slipping backwards. He clambered, legs kicking out, then he was up beside me to lie alongside on top of the damn rock. We stayed still, panting to catch our breath, as the body swept through the water-filled gap between us and the next huge boulder.

Foggy was still barking. I called out to him, trying to give him some reassurance. I sat up carefully and watched as the body swirled, tumbling in the white water, before being carried around another rocky bend to disappear from sight.

Swift stopped panting and put his hand to shade his eyes. 'He was bald. Who was he?'

'I've no idea. Come on. Let's go and find out what the hell is going on.'

We were careful as we vaulted from the boulder to the shore, then we limped back to the path. Swift had gashed his knee which was bleeding through his pyjama bottoms, his trench coat grubby and streaked. My thigh muscles were aching, the exertion having fired off an old injury from the war. Fogg walked alongside, glancing up at us, his ears down, all exuberance gone.

Lady Peggie and Fitzroy had followed as far as they could and we met them on the earthen track weaving between the tall pine trees.

'Are you alright?' Lady Peggie held her hands clasped tightly together over her dressing gown.

'Fine,' I lied. 'Who was he?'

'I don't believe it was anyone local.' She looked to Fitzroy.

'It might be another claimant heir. A man called Douglas Brodie,' he replied slowly. 'He wrote to me a number of times and said he would arrive on April the second. I was surprised he didn't, but assumed he'd been held up. I had intended writing to him this morning.'

'Someone here must have killed him,' Lady Peggie said, then raised a hand to her mouth.

Fitzroy turned to me and Swift. 'How could he be killed when we didn't even know he was here?'

'We need to find the body,' Swift said. 'I'm sorry but I need some answers, Lady Peggie. Does the river go through the village?'

She let her hand drop and straightened her thin shoulders. 'Yes, it does, but the body will not be held back there, the water is moving too quickly,' she explained with a quavering voice. 'The river continues through the mountains and then into the loch.'

'Is it a land-bound loch?' I asked.

'No,' she replied. 'It is open to the sea.'

'I'll go and call Scotland Yard,' Swift said. 'They will alert the coast guard and the local police stations along the route.'

He limped off.

Craggie had been standing some way off, his back hunched, misery on his face. He still held the lantern in his hand. Swift passed him by, which seemed to rouse him from his shocked stupor, and he turned to trudge behind him back to the castle.

'Two men are dead, Major Lennox,' Fitzroy said. 'This is becoming dangerous. You must permit the heirs to leave.'

'No.'

'But–'

'No.' I cut him off. 'One of them is responsible for two murders. We'll talk later.'

There were any number of questions I wanted to ask, but there was something far more pressing first. I made for the castle, crossed the cobbled courtyard. The front door was still open. I ran through it and up the stairs, the pain in my thigh already subsiding. I aimed for the men's bedchambers and opened the first door I came to, stalked in and tossed the bed covers aside.

CHAPTER 7

'What the–?' Daniel Addison blinked his eyes open, then squinted to frown at me. 'Major Lennox?' His pyjamas were creased, his hair dishevelled. There wasn't any indication he'd been up before now. I reached for his boots left on the hearth to warm by the fire. They were dry, the soles relatively clean. 'What are you doing?' Addison sat up.

I didn't reply, merely walked out and stalked into the room next door. Lars Olafson was washing his face in a bowl of water on a washstand. He was bare chested, wearing only a pair of white sleeping shorts. He straightened up and turned around, then reached for a rough towel hanging from the rail of the stand. 'Hvad?'

'What?'

'I mean to ask what you want?' He was puzzled. 'Is there some alarm?'

I didn't answer. His boots were also standing by the hearth, which was blazing with a freshly lit fire. Made of thick brown leather, they were knee high and laced all the way up. I strode past him to pick them up. They too were bone dry, as were the soil and stones caught in the thick treads of the soles.

Lars came to stand next to me, looking quizzically at his boots in my hands. I gave them to him and stalked out. Addison had come out in the passage; he'd pulled a grey sweater over his striped pyjamas.

'What's going on?' he asked me as I passed him.

Soft snoring greeted me in the next room. Professor Coltrane was deeply asleep, his head on the pillow, mouth slightly open, hair astray, grey stubble on his chin. His clothes were neatly laid over a plain oak chair near the fire, which had burned down in the night. His shoes were on a folded newspaper – *The London Times*. I could see they weren't stained by damp but reached to check them anyway. I turned them over, felt inside, then put them back. I hesitated to pull the covers off the professor, he was the pernickety type, and I couldn't quite bring myself to be so disrespectful.

Addison was now in the open doorway; Lars had joined him, the tall Dane seeming twice the size of the gangly Englishman despite them both being the same height. The Dane had pulled a thick jumper on and some loose fitting trews.

'Something is wrong?' Lars said, his voice a deep boom.

That penetrated the consciousness of the slumbering professor. He opened his eyes, then looked at me in surprise, before realising there were two other men behind me. He sat up, reaching for his spectacles. 'What is it?'

'A death,' I said.

'Who?' Addison asked and stepped forward.

'I can't say,' I replied.

'Malone?' the professor guessed.

'No.'

'It is not Malone?' Lars repeated. 'But who then? A man or woman?'

'Man,' I replied.

'Was it murder?' Addison came closer.

'Professor, could you please step out of bed?' I asked him.

'I could,' he said, then fidgeted with the covers. 'My pyjama pants fall down if I do not move with care,' he confessed. He fidgeted some more, then moved the covers aside to swing his legs onto the floor, bare feet first.

'Now, Major Lennox, you must explain yourself.' The professor stood up. He was a good ten inches shorter than I, but fixed me with a stern eye – authoritative even in his blue striped pyjamas.

I took a breath. 'I will, but you must wait here,' I said, then made for the door because I still had one more suspect to confront.

'Whadda you want?' Malone was sitting up in bed wearing a thick grey vest, reading a book, which surprised me.

I made for his thick-soled shoes which had been kicked under his dressing table. I could see they were dry before I bent and pulled them out, but examined them anyway. Then I turned back to him. 'Get up.'

'No.'

I reached for the water jug on the dresser top. 'Get up now.'

'You'd better have a good reason for this, Lennox,' Malone griped and climbed out of bed. 'Ow!' he shouted as his feet hit the freezing floor.

There was nothing to see, apart from his appalling hairy legs below a pair of shapeless grey shorts.

Foggy had come in behind me; he whimpered.

'If you didn't have such a nice dog, I'd be tempted to sock you one right now,' Malone said.

I looked down at him, and raised a brow.

'Once I've found a box to stand on,' he said, then grinned.

The rest of the men had crowded in, ignoring my order to stay put.

'You must tell us what is happening Major,' Professor Coltrane said. 'I insist.'

'There's a body in the river. A man,' I replied. 'Someone in this house must have killed him and pushed him in there early this morning.'

They looked at me then each other. 'But who is the dead man?' Addison asked.

'He hasn't been formally identified.' Actually I'd forgotten who Fitzroy said he might be.

I stalked into the next bedroom. It was empty, but I could see it must be Fitzroy's. I backed out into the passage and closed the door. They'd all followed me, I almost bumped into them.

'Now what?' Malone looked up expectantly.

'I have to go and wake the ladies,' I replied.

'You're gonna go and drag the dames outta bed?' he said. 'Boy, I wanna see this.'

'Um…' I realised I might have to rethink that plan. 'Swift will do it.'

'Do what?' Swift walked up behind us. He'd changed into his suit and even brushed down his trench coat.

'He woke us all up.' Addison pointed at me. 'He said there's a body in the river. A man was killed.'

'I was checking shoes,' I told Swift. 'To see if any of them had been outside this morning.'

'Good, well done. Had they?' he replied.

'I didn't find any evidence, but any of them might have hidden a spare pair, or thrown them in the river.' I narrowed my eyes as I glanced at the men crowded round us. They looked back, puzzled but unabashed.

'Right, we need to check the ladies,' he replied. 'Come on.'

He strode out. I was perfectly happy to let him take the lead. The others followed behind us. Fogg had brightened and now trotted jauntily along.

We walked onto the landing to find the women gathered down in the hall, which caused me a sigh of relief as I hadn't wanted to barge in on them.

'God darn it,' Malone said. 'I really wanted to see you guys wake them. You'da had a black eye from one of 'em at the very least.'

'Mrs Craggie came and woke us,' Susannah Bellamy called up as we trotted down the stairs. 'What's happening? Where is Lady Peggie?'

'Where are your shoes?' Swift demanded.

'On my feet.' Susannah pointed to them, which she was wearing without socks or stockings, below a pink nightdress and dressing gown.

'Listen to me.' Swift stepped back and raised his voice. 'Return to your rooms, pick up all of your footwear and bring it here.'

'But the major has seen mine already,' Professor Coltrane said.

'Do you have slippers?' I asked.

'Yes, but–'

Swift cut him off. 'I am requesting your cooperation. This is a formal murder investigation and I do not want to have to caution anybody.' He was very serious, and totally in his element.

There was some muttering and shifting of feet.

'I'm not going anywhere until you tell us who was murdered,' Belinda piped up. 'I'm an American citizen.'

'You're Canadian,' Molly reminded her.

'Well I live in America.' Belinda rounded on her.

'As do I,' Susannah said. 'But I don't need to make a big deal of it.'

'Or be an embarrassment like you are.' Molly turned on Belinda.

'You do what these police say you do,' Lars said sternly to Belinda, his voice booming in the high-ceilinged hall. He turned to Malone. 'And you go put your skirt on.'

'It's not a skirt, it's a kilt!' Malone put his hands on the hips of his grey shorts and squared up to the big Dane.

'It's not yours,' Addison joined in. 'It was Sullivan's.'

'That's enough. Go and fetch your shoes.' Swift suddenly shouted very loudly, then added, 'Please.' Which finally caused them to shut up and move off towards the stairs.

We waited until they were out of earshot.

'Who was he, Swift?' I said, meaning the body.

'Didn't you hear Fitzroy, he said he could have been Douglas Brodie.' The furrow between his dark brows had deepened, his features hawkish.

'It doesn't make any sense,' I said.

'No…' Swift let out a sigh of exasperation. 'I called Billings at Scotland Yard. He's ordering an all-points watch for the body downriver.'

'Good. I'm going to take another look,' I said. 'The body may have caught on something.'

'Fine,' he replied. 'Lennox, this is deadly serious now. We can't let any of them leave. Billings was very clear, everyone must stay until we find the killer…' He glanced at me. 'I don't think the culprit has finished.'

I nodded agreement, understanding the implications. 'You're assuming the motive is Castle McFee and the estate,' I said.

'What else?'

'I don't know. Daniel Addison's father was murdered…'

'Addison…' He looked surprised. 'Wasn't he the diplomat?'

'Yes.'

He frowned. 'I can't see a connection.'

'No,' I replied.

'Did you bring a gun?'

'Yes.'

'Good.'

'Right,' I decided. 'I'll try to find the body.'

He didn't move, just watched me go out of the front door, Foggy at my side.

The early morning chill had begun to lift, although it was still only a few degrees above freezing. I retraced our steps along the path towards the promontory, pausing for a moment on the broad swathe of grass to gaze out across the water.

The river widened out in front of the castle, slowing on the further bank but faster in the middle where it had been confined by the arches of the stone bridge. The banks either side of it had been built up with stones to stop erosion, the rest of the river's edge was left to nature – a jumble of rocks interspersed with thick, springy turf. Trout were already rising to snap at insects flitting across the surface. I watched them as the rising sun threw rays of light bouncing off the ripples. There was a wildness about it, and yet it was utterly peaceful. Even though I'd witnessed the body, it still somehow seemed unreal and hard to imagine in such a tranquil spot.

I turned to look up at the massive stone edifice of the castle itself. It was less grim in the sunshine, although the dark granite could never be described as homely. The oldest section of the castle was at the rear; it was huge, severe, and possessed very few windows. A conical roofed turret did nothing to alleviate the impression of a grim bastion. A newer building had been added to the west, another had been tacked on to the east. The wall containing the archway linked them both to form the inner courtyard sheltering the front door.

Foggy began barking. He'd run along the path winding between the tall trees. I strode towards him, the scent of damp earth and crushed pine beneath my feet, the pure, cold air filling my lungs. I crested the rocky promontory to see the dog leaping around the base of a tree, from where a red squirrel was chittering at him in irritation.

The river raced by in spumes of bubbling froth, but beyond the boulders and white water I could see a section of soft ground and a sandy stretch of bank. There was no sign of the corpse, but I walked down to peer into the crystal clear water. It was full of tiny fry, which darted away as I approached. The sand extended into the shallows, then gave way to green-streaked stones in the swirling eddies. Beyond that the water raced towards the steeply rising hills and mountains beyond.

I whistled for Fogg who came bounding over and we carried on along the track paralleling the river. The exposed rocks on the bank grew larger as the course of water grew narrower. We trailed between tall firs and pine some distance then turned about yet again when I saw him. A man lying on a flat stone, reaching into the water to grasp something caught amid yet more jagged rocks.

'Greetings,' I called out. 'Did you find something?'

'Aye,' he called back. A lean man, a red moustache and beard, with dark red hair above a weather-beaten face. He wore a faded kilt in the McFee tartan with a thick jersey under a sheepskin jerkin. 'Summat caught in the crag. Yours is it?'

'It could be,' I replied.

Foggy raced toward him as he clambered back to the shore, obviously familiar with the river and terrain.

'Nice wee doggie ye've got there,' he said in a broad accent. He leaned down to ruffle the golden fur on Fogg's head. 'Ye stayin' at the castle?'

'I am,' I agreed.

'Well, ye've saved me a trek then. I was goin' to have to tek this by there, but ye can do it for me.' He held out something that looked like a dead leaf curled in on itself, limp and soaking wet. 'It's been caught between them two rocks these last couple o' days an' I've been walking by it, thinkin' it was just a bit o' cloth. But I know there's a bunch of ootlanders stayin' up at the castle, an' there's been a death. So I decided I'd catch it up and tek it to the Lady.'

I took the cloth from him. It felt slimy and rather repulsive. 'You haven't seen anything else in the river today have you?'

'No.' He shook his head. 'What was ye thinkin' of?'

I looked at him. He was shorter and older than I'd first thought, streaks of grey in his red beard. 'Are you from the village?'

'Aye, Hamish Gordon, and ye didnae say what ye was seekin' in the river.'

'A body.'

Lines furrowed below his red brows. 'A dead body, ye mean?'

'Yes.'

He stared at me. 'Are you the polis?'

'Yes.' I could have said more but thought it might complicate matters.

'Is the lady safe?'

'You mean Lady Peggie?'

'Course I do. What other lady would I mean?'

'Right, well I'm sure she's perfectly safe,' I replied although I had no way of actually knowing that. 'Would you mind asking the people in the village if any of them have seen anything strange recently?'

He continued staring at me. 'Ye mean more strange than dead bodies floatin' down the river?'

That made me grin. 'Something like that, yes.'

'Aye, well, I'll come an' find ye if we do.' He nodded. 'An' maybe that glove'll be of use to ye.'

I looked at the object, still dripping in my hand. 'Ah, so that's what it is.' I held it up. One of the fingers drooped, then another. It was rather disconcerting. 'You saw it two days ago? On the second of April?'

He thought about that. 'Aye, it was. The day after my grandson stuck a fish in m'boot. Thought it was a grand joke for an April fool.'

'Do you think the body might be held up anywhere down river?'

'There's always a chance, I suppose, but it woulda moved fast once it got caught up in the strin', and you're saying it has. The chance of anyone seein' it is thin. Did ye say it was a man or woman?'

'A man, he was bald.'

'Well, he'll be gone to the mountains so he will, and

then the sea.' He nodded. 'Now, I'll be biding ye a good day.' With that he turned and strode off.

I held the glove between my thumb and forefinger and walked it back to the castle, along with my dog.

CHAPTER 8

'April the second?' Swift had splayed the glove on a large square of blotting paper placed in the centre of a stained and battered worktable. Water had spread around the fingers and thumb to form a strange and rather unnerving shadow. 'Did you see the hands of the corpse in the river?'

I'd been thinking about that. 'I didn't have a clear view, but I'm certain the hand closest to me didn't have a glove on.'

Swift leaned over the glove once more. 'This is the left hand, and that was the hand we could see from the boulder...' He shifted in his seat. 'When he was carried past us, I thought his right hand had been cut off, and I've been trying to tell myself it was just an illusion. But if he'd been wearing a black glove like this, it might have given that impression.'

'That makes more sense than someone hacking his hand off,' I said.

'Yes, and it's a relief. I was worried we had a monster on the loose here.' He glanced over at me, a furrow of worry on his brow.

We were in the gunroom, which was the old Laird's private domain. Swift had commandeered it for use as an incident room. It was marvellous. I'd dangled the glove in front of him when I'd found him in the hall and he'd marched me off to this room packed with treasures.

Hoppe's Number 9 was the predominant smell, sweet and musky with undertones of ammonia. It was the best gun cleaning solvent ever invented, to my mind. I was holding a beautifully crafted Holland and Holland Royal Side by Side rifle. Its burr walnut stock gleamed with linseed oil, the intricately engraved metal work showed a fine stag with a magnificent head of antlers standing proudly on a rock. It was perfectly balanced and I'd never wanted to own anything so much in my life.

'Lennox, will you put that gun down and come here.'

'Swift, it's—'

'I know what it is, we use similar ones for deer stalking on the mainland.'

'What! And you've never invited me to join you?'

'We go in the season when the weather allows, and that is decided on the dawn. I can hardly call you in the Cotswolds and wait days for you to arrive.'

'We'll come and stay in the season.'

'Fine, but will you come here and sit down.'

'Why?'

'Lennox!' he snapped.

I sighed and put the rifle back on its rack in the felt-lined gun cabinet. I was tempted to pick up the Mauser M98 stacked below it, but satisfied myself by running a hand along its sleek steel barrel instead. Then I went to sit at the battered worktable opposite Swift. 'What?'

'If this truly is Douglas Brodie's glove, then he was probably killed two days ago. The day Sullivan was found at the bottom of the stairs.'

'It's quite an assumption,' I said and picked up the magnifying glass to peer at the finely cut leatherwork.

'I called Billings back and asked the Yard to track down Douglas Brodie's last known movements. According to Fitzroy, the man lived in Stirling. I gave Billings the address.'

'What did Fitzroy say about Brodie?' I put the magnifying glass down; there wasn't really much to see. Swift, or someone, had lit a fire of sticks and logs in the simple stone fireplace. A stack of rough-cut blocks of peat was arranged on a pile next to the hearth, the earthy scent mingled with all the other wonderful smells typical of a well-stocked gunroom.

'He'd written to him over six weeks ago, along with the other potential heirs. Brodie had replied informing Fitzroy that he knew the Laird had died, having seen the notice in *The Oban Times*, and that he intended coming to claim the estate. Fitzroy wrote back informing him his claim was equalled by a number of others and that he would be allowed to attend on the assigned date, which was the beginning of April.'

'Wasn't the date more specific?'

'Some of the heirs were coming from across the Atlantic; Fitzroy doubted they'd all get here on one particular day.'

I nodded. It was reasonable, given the unpredictability

of travelling even short distances. 'Did you find anything on any of the ladies' shoes?'

'No.' He shook his head, his lean face solemn. 'But whoever had been out this morning may have gone barefoot, or hidden whatever shoes they wore.'

'Or tossed them in the river.'

'Yes, that had occurred to me, Lennox.'

A knock on the door was followed by Greggs bearing a tray holding steaming plates of breakfast, which we'd missed amid all the excitement.

'Lorne sausages, black pudding, bacon, eggs, sautéed mushrooms, and tattie scones fried in butter, sirs, with a pot of strong tea,' he intoned. 'Mrs Craggie and Lady Peggie have prepared a traditional Scottish breakfast for you.'

Fogg had settled by the fire where Tubbs had already made himself comfortable, but they were both on their feet in an instant. Swift moved the glove and blotting paper over almost as quickly.

'Perfect, thank you, Greggs.' I gave him a grin.

He smiled as he set our plates in front of us, then picked up the teapot. 'Shall I pour, sir?'

'Please,' I replied.

I hadn't had tattie scones before. I sliced the corner from one and tried it; it was crispy with a soft inside and utterly delicious.

'What are tattie scones?' I indicated them with my fork.

'Mashed potato, a little flour and cream, patted together to form a pancake and fried in butter,' Swift explained. 'They're a special treat.'

'Which you've never treated me to,' I replied.

'Reserved for honoured guests,' Swift replied with a grin.

'Are you ever going to take your coat off?'

The grin vanished. 'Fine.' He stood up, pulled off his trench coat and gave it to Greggs, who went and hung it from a nail hammered into the back of the door.

'*Ahem.*' Greggs cleared his throat. 'Is there anything else, sirs, because Lady Persi said I could help with the detecting and I understand another body was discovered this morning.'

'It wasn't exactly discovered,' I said. 'It raced past us and down the river.'

'What do the heirs know about the body?' Swift asked him.

'Sir Richard Fitzroy explained to them what he and Lady Peggie witnessed this morning,' Greggs replied. 'Lady Peggie insisted. She said it was only reasonable after your search of the shoes this morning.'

'How did they see the body?' I asked and cut into another tattie scone.

'Lady Peggie saw it from her window and sent Mr Craggie for Sir Richard, sir.' Greggs placed steaming tea cups in front of us. 'Mr Craggie was then sent for you and the Inspector.'

'Well done for that, Greggs,' Swift commended him.

'And sit down,' I told him as I sliced a piece off a Lorne sausage to drop down for Foggy, and another for Tubbs because he was trying to climb up my trousers.

'Sir, I couldn't,' he quibbled.

'You're officially designated a deputy detective,' I told

him, then dug into my pocket for the notebook I happened to have brought with me. I put it on the worktable in front of him.

'Sir!' His eyes rounded in delight. 'A notebook.'

'And a pen.' Swift passed him a fountain pen.

'Oh, oh, sirs, this is…this is…quite overwhelming,' he burbled. 'A deputy detective.' He sat down, his fingers fumbling as he opened the notebook. It was brand new. I'd purchased it recently in Stow-on-the-Wold when Persi and I had gone in search of wool and tiny bootees and bonnets and the sort of things one buys for newborns. I had to put my fork down for a moment as thoughts of the baby washed over me.

'Lennox?' Swift said.

'What…?' I snapped out of my momentary stupor. 'I'm fine,' I said, then speared the last mushroom on my plate.

'Start with the date, the place, and list of suspects,' Swift told Greggs.

'Suspects,' Greggs repeated, a hint of relish in his voice. He began writing. I should have warned Swift that Greggs could be quite precise in his endeavours, and very slow. He ferreted in his waistcoat for a folding pair of pince-nez; there was a long black cord attached and he placed it around his neck, and then perched the glasses on the bridge of his nose. Then he put them on the end of his nose, then somewhere in between, before moving them back and forward until he could focus on the page. Finally he wielded the pen. *April 4th,* Greggs wrote in a fine copperplate. *Castle McFee…Scotland.*

'You'll have to speed it up, old chap,' I told him. 'Particularly if you're taking statements.'

'Oh!' He stopped writing. 'Will I be interviewing murder suspects, sir?'

'No, you'll merely be taking notes,' I replied. 'But only if you get on with it.'

'Very well, sir. I will endeavour to do my best.' He continued to write at the same rate, the letters formed in beautiful curls across the page. It was like watching paint dry.

Swift was more patient than I was, so I decided to go and ring Persi. Foggy decided against coming with me while there was still the possibility of food to be had. Tubbs followed me into the hall, then hopped up on a chair, then a cupboard, and from there made quite a leap onto one of the high window sills, where he sat to stare out at the courtyard.

Swift had said the telephone was in a room somewhere off the hall. I wandered about opening doors to find a disused parlour and a small scullery, also disused, until I came upon the glorified cupboard which housed the telephone.

'Ye want the polis?' a Scots' voice asked; male and gruff.

'No, I'd like you to put me through to Braeburn Castle please.' I sat down on the hard wooden seat.

'The one wi' the malt whisky?'

'Yes.'

'Och, it's braw stuff is the malt.'

'Yes, I know, would you please put me through–' The line suddenly crackled and scratched, then a soft voice sounded at the other end. 'Braeburn Castle.'

'Florence?'

'Oh, Lennox, we were hoping one of you would call. Did you arrive without any problems?'

'Yes. Swift will telephone shortly, he's busy making lists.'

She laughed at that. 'He will be in his element then. Just a moment.' The line went quiet.

'Lennox?' Persi said, her voice full of laughter in my ear. 'How is it, have you discovered some dreadful conspiracy?'

'No.' I grinned even though she couldn't see me. 'Well we might have, it's all a bit confusing,' I said, then asked how she was, which was fine, of course, then told her all about the inmates and the two murders.

'If the body in the river was Brodie's, where has he been for the last two days?' she asked.

'Perhaps he was caught up on something in the water and then the body was dislodged for some reason?' I replied. It seemed the obvious explanation.

'I suppose that would explain the glove…' she mused. 'Would someone have killed him as soon as he arrived at the castle? They'd have barely met him.'

'I suppose the killer must consider all the other heirs to be rivals.' Tubbs had appeared and decided to join me. He jumped up on my lap and began kneading my trousers with sharp little claws.

'Aren't you worried that there may be more deaths?'

'Yes, we both are. It's indiscriminate and dangerous.'

'Have you really no idea?' Her voice lowered to a more serious tone. 'The motive isn't a personal grievance; the murderer must be practically unhinged.'

I thought back to the killers who Swift and I had uncovered in the past. 'Murderers are surprisingly good at hiding their true natures.'

'Well, I suppose they would be,' she replied. 'Have you thought about names?'

'Of the culprits?'

'No, the baby,' she laughed.

'Erm…' Was I supposed to do that? It hadn't even occurred to me.

'Don't worry, it's a bit soon. The little one isn't due for five months yet.' She spoke softly, a gentleness to her voice as though murmuring to a child.

It made my heart lurch to hear the mother's voice within her.

She quickly reverted to her usual self. 'Is Greggs helping with your detecting?'

'I gave him a notebook, he's having a wonderful time.'

'We'd already given him one.'

'Really? He didn't let on,' I said.

She laughed. 'He probably wanted to show you his appreciation. I think he's been missing the simple life when it was just you and him together.'

'Nonsense.'

She became more serious. 'Make sure he's included, Heathcliff.'

'That's what I've been doing,' I protested. 'We can call the baby after him if you think it would help.'

That brought her laughter back. 'I'm not terribly keen on Norman.'

I opened my mouth to respond with something light, then realised that in all the time I'd known my old retainer, I'd never once called him Norman. I'd almost forgotten it was his name.

'Lennox?' she said.

'Sorry old stick…I mean Persi, dear.' I took a breath to stop myself from babbling.

'Who would you nominate as the most likely suspect?' she continued.

'I…wait.' I'd left the door open and leaned forward to peer round into the hall from my seat at the small table. There didn't seem to be anyone about. 'I'd have put money on the irritating American, Mick Malone,' I whispered. 'But I don't think he has the brains for it. And Swift believes there are two of them working together, so does Fitzroy, although that doesn't make sense either because the heirs don't know each other, so they haven't had time to form a pact.'

'Are you sure?'

I considered that. 'Actually, no. We don't know very much about them.'

'If you took a wild guess, who do you think it may be?' she continued.

'Daniel Addison.'

'Really? Not Professor Coltrane?' She sounded surprised.

'What? No. Why would I think it was him?'

'Because his partner died in such a strange way,' she replied.

That stumped me. 'Did he? How do you know?' Tubbs

decided to abandon me and jumped from my lap to scamper back into the hall.

'I know his reputation. He's a professor of Anthropology at Boston University. He and a colleague called Professor Pierce had a falling out over a book they were writing together. Pierce was found dead a few days later, having fallen out of a window. It was in the papers.'

I frowned at that. 'Which papers?'

'Oh.' She paused. 'The academic ones mostly. Sorry my love, you probably wouldn't have seen it, though *The Times* may have mentioned it.'

'A penny a minute.' A loud voice suddenly jolted me upright. Craggie was in the doorway.

'What?'

'It costs a penny a minute to talk on the telling phone.' He was holding the umbrella again.

'Fine.' I rooted in my pocket for a handful of coins and put them on the small table. 'This is a private call.'

'An' this is a private castle,' he replied, then stomped off muttering about ootlanders and murderers.

'Actually, I changed my mind,' I told Persi. 'I'm putting Craggie at the top of my list.'

CHAPTER 9

'Fitzroy wants everyone to meet in the drawing room,' Swift said. He'd donned his trench coat, ready for action.

'Did you call Florence when you went to telephone Billings?' I asked him.

His lean cheeks reddened. 'I…um… I was going to, but things…I'll go and do it now.' He stood up and made a dash for the door.

Greggs was still writing copious notes in perfect copperplate. We were in the gunroom, or rather the incident room, as Swift now termed it.

'Come on Sherlock, they're gathering upstairs.'

'Pardon, sir?' He looked up, blinking behind the pince-nez.

'Bring the notebook and pen, we're going to join the suspects,' I said.

'Oh, sir! This is really quite marvellous.' He took the spectacles from his nose, unhooked the black cord, folded them, carefully wrapped the cord around them and tucked them in his pocket. Then he screwed the lid on the fountain pen, put that into the same pocket before carefully blotting the page he'd been writing on. I thought back to the lively Miss Busby, with her quick mind and movements, and wished for a moment that she was back with us. Greggs stood up, placed his chair precisely against the table, tugged down his waistcoat and prepared to follow.

I strode out and up the stairs as he puffed behind me. I had to open the door to the drawing room myself.

They were all gathered by the fire again in much the same places as yesterday.

'Major Lennox.' Lady Peggie approached, hand outstretched. 'Thank you so much for your prompt actions this morning. It was a shocking discovery.'

'Did you notice if the man was wearing a glove?' I asked her.

'I…' She hesitated, then turned to Fitzroy.

'Yes, on his right hand.' Fitzroy had also stood up to greet me. No one else had.

'Sir, Inspector Swift found the maker's name in the glove from the river,' Greggs helpfully told me. 'It was manufactured by Hexham's of Stirling.'

They were all watching, and listening.

'That would indicate it could have been Douglas Brodie,' Fitzroy said.

I glanced at Greggs, then stepped over to him. 'We don't share details of evidence,' I hissed.

'Oh. Oh, sir, I do apologise,' he said, his chins wobbling. 'Although you really should have warned me.'

I bit back a retort and went to stand in front of the fire to address the heirs. 'Who went outside earlier this morning?'

'Before you, do you mean?' Professor Coltrane said.

'Yes, obviously,' I replied, trying to keep any hint of tetchiness from my tone.

No-one said a word, which was hardly a surprise really.

'Who was this Brodie guy anyway?' Malone broke the silence.

Greggs sat on a distant chair and arranged his pen and notebook.

'He was another potential heir,' Fitzroy said.

That caused a babble of questions; I quickly cut them off.

'How did you all get here?' I asked a question that had been bothering me.

'On the train,' they replied, then all started talking over each other.

'One at a time please.' I held up a hand. 'Which train, and when?'

'I reached here on the afternoon of March thirty-first,' Susannah replied. 'I had travelled from London after arriving on the ship from New York two weeks earlier. I stayed at the Ritz to recover and have fun. It's my first time in Britain and it's been quite an adventure!'

'I came over a week ago and stayed in Southampton, then took the overnight train,' Molly said. 'I arrived here early on the morning of April first. Lars and Daniel were on the same train.' She looked over at them on the opposite sofa; they both nodded.

'Me an' Sullivan and the Prof were on the noon train,' Malone said. 'April first.'

'He is correct,' Professor Coltrane added. 'I had travelled

from Boston the week before and stayed at The Berkeley before coming here.'

'On the same ship as Miss Susannah?' I asked. 'Or anyone here?'

'I believe not,' he replied.

'I was on the same ship as the Professor.' Belinda spoke up. 'But I was in first class. I saw him on the lower deck, but we didn't cross paths.'

'Nor did we have any reason to,' Coltrane added dryly.

Belinda was unperturbed but threw a haughty glance at him anyway. 'I stayed at Claridge's then travelled here alone on the early train on March thirty-first. I was the first to arrive. I had to be driven from the station in a grubby little cart by that awful little man.'

'Which man?' I asked.

'You should know which man if you're a detective,' Belinda retorted. She was dressed in something warmer today, a pale yellow frock of thick silk crepe with a drop waist and pearl buttons on the long sleeves. She actually looked quite attractive, in an expensive, showy way. Everyone else was dressed as they were yesterday.

'She is referring to McDuff, the station master.' Fitzroy answered the question. 'He lives at the station house and brings post or produce destined for the castle. People too, should there be any. He has done so since the train track was installed.'

'We need to speak to him,' Swift said. He'd walked in a few moments ago, nobody but me had noticed. 'Did anyone see Brodie? Did he come on the same train as any of you or join you in the cart? We'll find out from this man, McDuff, what date he came, so you may as well tell us now.'

Lars fixed pale blue eyes on Swift. 'How can this man be here since some days, and be killed, then be flushed down the river today?'

'Not flushed, Lars,' Daniel Addison told him. 'It's not the right way to phrase it.'

'It would be *swept* down the river,' Molly corrected.

'Like as a brush?' Lars looked at her, then shrugged. 'Very well, but how was it to happen, that he was swept?'

'That is still under investigation,' Swift replied.

Fitzroy stood up. I'd remained in front of the fire because it was nice and warm there, but stepped aside to allow him to make an address.

'Douglas Brodie was another heir.' The lawyer spoke carefully and gravely. 'He and Sullivan may have had the strongest claims to Castle McFee and the estate. This was perhaps a coincidence, but whatever the motive for their deaths, I implore the person who carried out these appalling deeds to reveal themselves to the detectives, and stop this murderous campaign. The estate can never be yours under such a circumstance. You risk the noose if you are caught.'

We all waited. Everyone's eyes flicked around again, waiting for an admission of guilt. It didn't come. The seconds ticked by, tension rising in an unnerving silence.

Swift stepped forward. 'If you give yourself up now, a case might be made to avoid a hanging.'

This didn't help. There was still no sound, no movement. It was as though everyone had frozen, holding their breath as the tension ratcheted tighter.

'Arghhhh.' A sudden cry from the back made everyone jump and swivel around. Greggs had leaped up from his seat, his glasses sent flying, pen and notebook tumbling from his lap. Tubbs had jumped onto the back of his chair and put a friendly black paw on his shoulder.

'Oh, it's a cat,' Susannah said. 'How adorable. I have one just like him at home.'

'I adore cats,' Molly said. 'Does he live here?' Tubbs jumped off the chair and came sauntering between sofas and chairs, tail in the air, to join the group around the fire.

Greggs fumbled for his glasses and stuck them back on his nose, then picked up his notebook and pen, muttering under his breath.

'Oh dear.' Susannah went over. 'Poor Mr Greggs, did the cat startle you?'

'I…erm, *ahem*,' he mumbled. 'Mr Tubbs merely took me by surprise.' He straightened the glasses which were perched   precariously at a drunken angle.

'Is that his name?' Molly had picked up the little reprobate and was cuddling him. I could hear him purring from where I stood.

Lars came to stroke the cat's head, and most of the others crowded round, murmuring how sweet he was. Poor Greggs *hummed* and *hawed* as loudly as he dared, but was forgotten in the cuddling of the cat. Even Lady Peggie was extending a hand to rub his head.

Fitzroy had not joined in, and now loudly addressed the room. 'As the guilty party has not come forward, I suggest each of you keep in mind the situation. Be vigilant. Now we will all move to the library. Please follow me.' He went out onto the landing where the sun had risen high enough to throw bright rays of light to dispel the gloomy shadows in the hall.

They were chattering to each other as we followed, Molly laughing at something Lars said. I could understand their apparent lack of fear. Trying to imagine a murderer in their midst was difficult. Nobody seemed dangerous, or aggressive; they were mostly quite friendly towards each other, apart from Belinda. Nor had they witnessed the body at dawn. It must have sounded such an extraordinary event that it was hard to believe.

I stopped to wait for Greggs to catch up.

Malone paused in passing. 'Lady Peggie said he was your cat.' Somehow he'd ended up with Tubbs in his arms and was gazing down at the sleepy animal with something like adoration. 'He's a nice little guy. I never had a cat before. When I get this place, I'm going to fill it with cats and dogs and make it into a proper home.'

'Where are you from Malone?' I asked him.

He glanced up at me; he hadn't had a shave and looked more grizzled than ever. 'A place called Hell's Kitchen, and I ain't never goin' back there,' he said then went down the stairs after the others, Tubbs still cradled in his arms.

Swift joined me. 'What did you make of that?'

I shook my head. 'They don't want to register the reality.'

'No,' he agreed. 'But it's one of them, or more likely two. A few of them travelled together, they could have formed alliances then. Or even known each other before, for all we know.' He turned to Greggs who was now emerging from the drawing room. 'Did you list which of the suspects came here on the same train together?'

'I…erm, I believe I did, sir. Perhaps we could review their positions when we interview them individually.'

Swift bit back a sigh and we all walked down the stairs and into the hall.

The loud bang caused by the front door being flung open gave us pause. A woman, short and stocky, with a chubby face red from exertion, walked in. She was carrying a large basket full of peat turfs in her arms.

'One of 'em fell out on the step,' she puffed. 'This creel is rotten. I'm ready for burnin' it wit' the mòine.' She was a Scot with a very broad accent, wearing a long beige uniform under a washed-out apron and a linen mop cap trimmed with lace.

All three of us moved to help, Greggs was first to her side.

'May I take the basket, Mrs Craggie?' he asked.

'Ye can Mr Greggs and I thank ye for it. Can one of ye's fetch the lump of mòine from yonder?' She nodded toward the open door, then bustled past us and dropped the basket, or creel as she termed it, into Greggs' arms. He puffed out a breath as he took the weight.

I went to pick the peat block up. I'd never actually seen them in use before coming here, Swift and Florence always had logs. The peat was densely compact and lighter than expected, and larger. Fragments were crumbling off, so I carried it carefully to Mrs Craggie, who was now leaning over the massive fire and placing the peat over the top of the logs. Greggs had put the basket down and was trying to catch his breath.

I handed over the peat to her. She took it, laid it over the others then straightened up to wipe her hands together.

'His name was Douglas Brodie,' Swift was questioning her.

'He was the dead 'un in the water that Craggie and the Lady saw this morning?' she asked.

'Yes,' Swift replied. 'He must have arrived around a few days ago.' He was being deliberately vague about the day of Brodie's arrival as we had no real facts to go on. And it would have been sensitive information too.

'I wouldn't know, such a crowd as they are,' she replied. 'The name doesn't mean nothing to me.' She put her hands on hips and looked up at Swift with narrowed blue eyes, her skin creased at the corners. 'You're the polis, then?'

'Yes,' Swift replied. 'The man had been murdered with a knife in the back, then put in the river. There must be somewhere he's been these last few days.'

'How many days ago?' she asked.

I cut in. 'Where do you think his body may have been hidden?'

'Is this for a fact then?' she questioned.

'It is,' I assured her.

Creases formed on her forehead as she considered it. Her hair was grey and peppered with white, curling in short locks around her cap. 'I can't ken what dead men do,' she said, then leaned forwards to peer more closely at me. 'What type o' knife was it in his back? I'll search me kitchen, see if we're missin' one.'

'It had a black handle,' I replied. 'Wooden probably.'

'And the blade?' Her blue eyes were bright with a gleam of sharp intelligence. She was weighing me up.

'It wasn't visible,' I replied. 'I imagine your knives are blacksmith made.'

'Aye, course they are,' she said. 'Where else would ye find knives?'

I didn't answer that as it was obvious there weren't any shops in the area. This glen would have been as self-reliant as Braeburn, but without the benefit of the whisky distillery to bring in outside funds.

'They'll be hefty then,' Swift said.

'Aye, those that are fer cuttin' meat,' she replied. 'Now, I've work waitin'. I'll be goin' back to it.' She stomped off, pausing only to nod to Greggs in passing.

'A formidable lady, sir.' Greggs had recovered himself. 'But she has been kind enough to save scraps for Mr Fogg and Tubbs, and her cooking is really quite commendable.'

Swift glanced at me. 'Come on, we should be watching the suspects. They're presenting their personal documents to Fitzroy.'

'Fine,' I said and we all trooped off to find the library. I'd wanted to go outside and search the outhouses for signs of where Brodie's body may have been stored before he was tossed in the river, but that would have to wait.

Greggs knew the way. I noticed as he walked ahead of us that he had a bit of a spring in his step, as though his new, and very temporary, position as a deputy detective was something of a promotion.

'The library, sir,' he intoned, and swung open the door to reveal a raucous shouting match between the potential heirs.

CHAPTER 10

'This is not valid proof,' Fitzroy was saying, his finger resting on a handwritten sheet of paper placed on a corner of a very long reading table set in the centre of the library. Other papers were spread around it, but were almost eclipsed by an ornate piece of stitched parchment laid down the centre. It was nearly as long as the table. Tubbs was, inevitably, curled up asleep in the middle of it. Fogg was near the fire with Malone, who was bent over him ruffling his ears and telling him he was a good doggie.

Greggs went to a very old desk in austere style set back a distance from the fire. He settled himself with notebook, pen, spectacles and all the rest of it. The place was typical of a man's private library; walls covered in shelves full of books, the smell of old leather and mouldering paper, stale tobacco, woodsmoke and a hint of whisky. It felt very like home.

'Why do you not think my paper is valid?' Lars was speaking to Fitzroy, his pale eyes glittering from under lowered brows. They were both facing each other, the others gathered around, watching and listening intently, apart from Malone who seemed to prefer the company of my dog.

'To begin with, it isn't in English.' Fitzroy's voice was calm and reassuring, the sort of tone he probably used with juries or nervous witnesses. 'Any document that was produced by any member of the McFee clan would be written in English.'

'It was writ by my grandmother, Alma Olafson, in 1846,' Lars retorted. 'Her memory telling of our ancestor Wendlyn McFee who was born 1796. Wendlyn is a big name in our family. She was my grandmother's grand-mother. She told the story herself. A story how she married my many great grandfather at this castle and they went to live at his home in Denmark. How can this memory not be true?'

'I am not disputing what your grandmother wrote.' Fitzroy spoke evenly. 'But it is not a legally recognised document, nor is it one that arose from this castle.'

'Are you saying this is an untruth?' Lars' anger was rising with his voice, his cheeks suddenly flushed dark.

'No, I'm saying that it is not a legally recognised docu-ment,' Fitzroy repeated. 'A certificate would be accepted, such as one for marriage or a birth. A formally stamped and witnessed will, or a death certificate. Anything that has been endorsed by someone in authority, which cannot be the person who wrote it.'

'I got a photo of my great grandmother McFee, it's got her name written on the back.' Malone came over and butted in. 'I dunno why you're being so nitpicking. I reckon you've already decided who you wanna win and you're just playin' around with us.'

'Mr Malone that is utterly untrue,' Lady Peggie said. 'Sir Richard has explained it a number of times. You must have a legally recognised document.'

'Which is what I've got.' Belinda spoke triumphantly and waved an elaborately signed and stamped paper in the air.

'Wait a minute.' Malone wasn't giving up. 'Great Grannie's name was Hortense McFee and she was born here in this castle in 1793. She was 90 when the photo was taken, and that's me standing next to her. I was 17.' He went to stand next to the parchment and banged a stubby finger on it. 'See! That's Hortense right there on the clan tree.'

Swift and I joined the crowd around the table. I managed to get a look at the photograph Malone was waving around. It was silvered and curled at the edges, but I could make out a very old lady seated upright on a chair. She was dressed in typical dark Victorian clothes with a lace cap tied under her chin. The young man standing to her side was grinning broadly; he wore a butcher's striped apron over a thick cotton shirt and dark trousers.

'Mr Malone, you must understand that anybody could have written that on the photograph you possess,' Professor Coltrane said, his chin drawn in, almost meeting his red bow tie. 'The identity of the individual remains unverified.'

That lecture did not go down well. Malone turned puce, his fists bunching.

'Now, Mr Malone,' Susannah Bellamy tried a calming

voice. 'I believe the professor was merely voicing the possibility of doubt, and not doubt itself.'

'No, I was not,' Professor Coltrane said, which didn't help.

Daniel Addison stepped forward. 'I think this is best decided by Sir Richard Fitzroy,' he said diplomatically.

'Exactly,' Fitzroy said. 'Now we will go through each of your documents one at a time. Mr Addison, would you please begin?' He turned to him, then held a hand up. 'And no-one is to interrupt.'

'Right.' Addison drew himself upright, his Adam's apple bobbing. He was wearing the same smartly tailored suit with white shirt and navy silk tie. I wondered how he'd managed to carry his suitcase along with the case of fine wine, then realised he'd probably paid the porters a handsome sum to do it for him. 'I have the official copies of the registered birth of Margot Balfour. Her mother is listed as Alisa McFee, born 1790, of McFee Castle. Alisa McFee was my great, great grandmother.' He handed the certified papers to Fitzroy. 'I have other records, and a number of certificates for births, marriages and deaths, including my father's. He was a direct descendant of Alisa McFee, who was the eldest daughter of Nial McFee.'

'Through the female line,' Lady Peggie said.

Swift cast a sharp glance at her as Fitzroy scanned the documents.

'There's a discrepancy here,' Fitzroy said and pulled a pair of gold-rimmed spectacles from his jacket pocket to peruse them more closely.

'What?' Addison said, uncertainty in his voice. 'There can't be. My father hired a company of expert genealogists to find these documents, and had them legally copied and certified. It took months, and it was extremely expensive.'

'Why?' I asked.

'What?' Addison spun round. 'What do you mean?'

'Why would your father have had these documents found?' I asked.

'Because Sir Richard contacted him some years ago when the question of inheritance was first raised,' Addison replied. 'You should know that.'

I didn't see why I should, but turned to Fitzroy with brows raised.

Fitzroy sighed. 'When the Laird began having health problems, he asked me to list the potential heirs and assess their claims to the estate. I contacted those I could find and asked them to confirm their identities and whatever claim they thought they may have. Fortunately the Laird rallied and we took no further action.'

'Could you tell me what the problem is with my papers?' Addison was becoming agitated.

Lady Peggie answered, her face stern and serious. 'Your antecedent grandmother cannot be Alisa McFee. Alisa died shortly after her birth, but her sister Fenella McFee married a man named Balfour. This is made more complex because their line devolves from Nial McFee. He was the most prolific of the McFee's, he had four sons and five daughters by three different wives. And we do not have any record of Fenella's offspring, or indeed any other female born on the outer edge of the hereditary line because their children were not born in McFee Castle – they were born wherever their mothers went to live after their marriage.' I had the impression Lady Peggie knew a great deal more about the McFee ancestry than anyone.

Shock registered on Addison's face, and confusion on everyone else's. I was as used to calculating hereditary lines as the next nobleman, but even I'd got lost among the names.

'But…but…how can it be wrong?' Addison stuttered, his Adam's apple gulping in his thin throat.

Fitzroy sighed. 'I'm afraid it will be the transfer of kirk registers. Your "experts" would have garnered the information from the General Register Office in Edinburgh. This was only begun in 1855, but the government demanded it hold all previous records. A clerk was sent to travel the glens to copy the ledgers kept in the local kirks. It is known that transcription mistakes were made.'

'Or your documents are fakes manufactured by an unscrupulous fraudster who took your father for a ride,' Belinda said matter-of-factly.

'But some of the facts are correct,' Molly reminded her. 'And it's a bit far-fetched to assume someone would fake a copy of an old birth register.'

'It depends how much was offered to them to find it,' Belinda retorted. 'Some people will stoop to anything for money.'

'Do you know this because you live among thieves?' Lars asked.

'I do not live among thieves!' Belinda snapped in irritation.

Molly laughed. Even Professor Coltrane grinned.

'Enough,' Fitzroy said sharply. 'I'm afraid it makes very little difference as the connection to the direct line is not established.'

'I beg to disagree.' Daniel wasn't giving up. 'If my line is to Fenella, I still have a legitimate claim and can have the genealogical experts prove it.'

'May I say something, Sir Richard?' Susannah began. 'I have spent some time researching how to discover one's ancestors. Births, weddings, and deaths are all written in the church records, as you just mentioned.'

'They are,' Lady Peggie said. 'And we have the original registers. I will bring them.' She went to a low book-case below the tall window, where sunshine was falling in slanted rays through small panes of lead-lined glass. She picked up three large ledgers, each bound in tan leather, peeling and stained with age. We all stood back as she brought them over and put them down carefully on the very end of the long reading table. I don't know why she hadn't just showed these to everyone to start with.

She opened the first ledger. 'Our registers start in 1759, no records were kept before that, other than the hereditary tree,' she said, turning the thick pages. We shuffled down to watch. The first pages were decorated with a pen and ink drawing of a crest and shield and the name McFee of the Clan McFee inscribed on an elaborate scroll. Then an inscription of a Latin prayer, then a blank page to show the family could afford to waste expensive handmade paper. 'This is the register of births,' she continued.

We realigned ourselves into a semi-circle behind her as she continued to turn the pages. 'You can cross-reference the names to those on the parchment.' She pointed over to the hereditary tree.

Molly moved to go and gaze at the names. The same image of the crest and shield was drawn at the top, coloured with vibrant inks typical of the time. She read out the first name on the parchment: 'Laird Duncan Robert James McFee, 1479 ~ 1532. That was long before the kirk records began.'

'Yes, this is when the Laird won over the feuding clans and was recognised by the King of the Scots,' Lady Peggie replied, still leaning over the ledger.

'What about Alisa and Fenella?' Addison was at Lady Peggie's side.

Lady Peggie turned more pages then stopped and ran a thin finger down black-lined rows of names written in different hands and faded ink. 'Now here is the list of Nial McFee's offspring.' We shuffled closer behind her. I could see how long the list was. 'Fenella was born in 1799, and poor Alisa was born in 1790 and died the same year. There's a tiny 'd' next to her name, as you can see.' She placed her forefinger on the name written in faded ink.

Molly had remained gazing at the parchment, her auburn hair falling around her pretty face. 'The McFee wives' maiden names are not listed,' she remarked.

'No, and the daughters' husbands were not listed either,'

Lady Peggie replied. 'But we can find those records in the kirk marriage register.' She pushed the births ledger aside and opened the next to turn the thick pages yellowed with age. 'Look, here is the record of Fenella McFee's marriage to James Balfour in 1818.'

'But…' Addison tried in confusion. 'Where does that leave me?'

'Nowhere,' Malone replied. 'My Hortense was older than your Fenella, so I win.'

'Oh, do shut up, you dreadful little man,' Belinda said. 'I have these papers—' she was cut off by Fitzroy.

'Miss Molly next please,' the lawyer said sharply. 'And I will remind all of you to behave respectfully towards each other.'

I straightened up as everyone went over to join Molly. She picked up a sheet of thin paper glued to a larger piece of white card. Lady Peggie remained where she was, leaning over the ledger.

Molly smiled, the excitement clear on her face as she held the card out to Fitzroy. 'I have had a facsimile made of our family bible, and I asked our Reverend father to sign and date it to prove its truth.' Her Canadian accent was pleasantly lilting.

Fitzroy's face drooped in disappointment as he read the document. Molly was too busy explaining the list of names and her relationship to the McFee line to notice.

'And you can see we go back to Nial McFee's daughter, who was also called Molly,' Molly said, her smile growing wider. 'She was born in 1818. The line is totally clear, and we've had lots of Molly's in our family because of her. It's a tradition!'

Fitzroy nodded solemnly. 'Thank you Molly–'

'You can see her name here.' She put her finger on the parchment where a crowded list of names was written under that of Nial McFee and his three brides. 'And she must be in the births register.' She looked at Lady Peggie. 'Isn't she?'

'She is,' Lady Peggie replied, turning back to the register. 'Her mother was Nial's third wife. Molly was his last child because he died shortly after her birth. He was 74 years old.'

'Really!' Molly's eyes flew open. 'Wow, well, that makes him, um…'

'A randy old goat,' Malone said, grinning.

'Mr Malone, you will not use such language in this house,' Lady Peggie rebuked him sharply.

'Sorry, ma'am,' Malone said, entirely unrepentant.

'Very well,' Fitzroy said. 'Now may I ask Miss Susannah to present her case.'

'I have a complete family tree back to Nial's younger brother,' Susannah said. 'He was called Iain, and Iain's daughter was my great grandmother. She was called Greta and she was born in 1769.'

Lady Peggie was still studying the register of births. 'Greta McFee was indeed Iain's daughter, and she was born here in the castle…but,' she paused then added, 'Iain was not wed when the child was born. He never married, actually.'

Everyone fell silent for a moment to take the implications of this in.

'That means…' Susannah said, then hesitated as she tried to make sense of it.

'Like I said, Nial McFee was a randy old goat and he wasn't the only one–'

'Enough Malone,' Lars told him. 'You are a bad person to use this language. I will toss you in the river if it is said again.'

'You will not!' Malone blustered, pushing his shoulders back.

Lars laughed.

'Quiet,' Swift suddenly snapped. 'We need to listen to this.'

'Thank you, Inspector,' Lady Peggie said. 'Now, Lars, I believe I have found your predecessor. She is indeed Wendlyn McFee, born to Nial McFee. She was his third daughter.'

'Except your papers are not legally authorised,' Belinda instantly reminded him. 'Whereas mine are,' she added in triumph and thrust them into Fitzroy's hands.

He sighed as he took them. I could see they were certified and stamped copies of birth, marriages, and deaths. Fitzroy leafed through them to find the oldest. 'You are descended from the daughter of Nial McFee's older sister, Elsie McFee.'

'Which puts me ahead of everyone else!' Belinda said triumphantly.

'We have not heard from Professor Coltrane, yet,' Fitzroy reminded her tersely, and turned to the professor.

'I believe my documents are similar,' he replied, offering a handful of the now familiar-looking papers. 'I think we must have had the same person acting as our genealogist,' he said to Belinda.

That took the wind out of her sails. 'Well who are you descended from then?'

'My great grandmother was the daughter of Elsie McFee's eldest son,' he said with a hint of pride. 'And I believe that puts me ahead of everyone.'

'Except for the law of primogeniture,' Daniel Addison said. 'And I believe that would count in this circumstance, wouldn't it Sir Richard?' He turned to Fitzroy.

'Mr Addison is correct. It's a complex legal argument, but ultimately the daughter of a son would outrank the son of a daughter, even if the daughter was older than her brother.'

That confused everyone entirely.

'Wait a minute, will ya.' Malone wasn't giving up. 'My great grannie was come down from Nial McFee's oldest surviving daughter, so that puts me on top.'

'You must prove it,' Fitzroy warned him.

'I'll use the same people they used.' Malone pointed at Belinda and Professor Coltrane. 'They'll find those papers and that'll prove it. I got Grannie McFee's marriage certificate, and her birth certificate, and her death certificate back home.'

Fitzroy frowned at him. 'If so, why didn't you bring them as requested?'

'Didn't think you'd take me for a liar, did I?' Malone

retorted. 'And there's something else I got that none of you have.'

'What?' Fitzroy demanded, his patience patently worn thin.

'I've got a gold coin,' Malone said with a grin and dug into the sporran hitched around his waist. He held whatever it was in his clenched fist, then when he was sure we were all looking, he opened it to reveal a large gold coin. 'It's got the crest on, the same one like on the family tree.'

He was right, we could all see the crest stamped onto the gold. It was a pretty piece, thicker than most coins and about two inches across. It gleamed with the rich yellow hue of pure gold; the rim was reeded and the details finely rendered.

'What is on the other side?' Professor Coltrane was the first to speak.

Malone turned it with stubby fingers. 'Initials. There's an H and a B, with some flowers and stuff round them.'

'Oh!' Lady Peggie had rushed over and now held her hand out. 'May I?'

'Sure,' Malone said genially, enjoying his moment of triumph.

Lady Peggie turned it over, gazing at it intently. 'It's one of the dowry coins. My husband spoke of them, and there are images of them on some of the portraits. When the gold mine was still productive the Laird had a coin struck for each of the daughters when they wed. They continued the practice until the mine was exhausted. I've never actually seen one.' I could hear the emotion in her voice, she seemed awed. 'I think most of the coins were sold eventually,' Lady Peggie said as she carefully passed the coin to Fitzroy to examine. 'They were not legal tender of course, their value was in the weight of gold.'

'Were some melted down?' Susannah asked.

'I believe some of them would have been.' Lady Peggie nodded, a gleam of what could be a teardrop in her eye.

'Whom do the initials represent?' Addison asked Malone.

'Hortense McFee and whoever,' Malone said. 'It must be in that register of yours.' He indicated the marriage register.

Molly was closest to it and she began to flick through the pages.

'Wait,' Fitzroy said. 'The initials are not H and B, it's A and B.'

'No it ain't,' Malone argued.

'May I?' Swift held his hand out. He held a magnifying glass in the other.

Fitzroy gave it to him and leaned in as Swift peered at it.

'It is an A, not a H,' Swift confirmed.

'Well, whatever.' Malone shrugged. 'I'm still the top of the list. Hortense was legit and she was born 1793. None of the rest of 'em count.'

A hushed silence fell as the terrifying vision of Malone as the new Laird began to fill their minds.

'See?' Malone was gleeful. 'I'm gonna be in charge of the clan now, and live in the castle.'

'You will need more proof,' Professor Coltrane said.

'Yes, and you could have found that coin in the sporran

when you stole it from William Sullivan,' Daniel Addison said, a hint of anger in his voice.

'Maybe you killed him for that coin,' Lars accused him.

'I didn't kill no-one,' Malone yelled, which led to more high words, and they all joined in.

'Quiet,' Fitzroy called out, then addressed Malone. 'There must be no illegitimate descendants in your lineage, or your claim will be voided. Are there any?'

'No, of course there ain't,' he retorted defiantly. Except there was a hint of uncertainty in his voice that we all heard, followed by the inevitable outbreak of demands and questions.

'Hold your wheest,' Craggie shouted, breaking up the argument as he arrived under his umbrella. 'There's lunch in the drawin' room. Ye'd best be movin' if ye want yer tea hot. Come on now, and less of this hollerin'.'

CHAPTER 11

'One moment,' Fitzroy said to us as the heirs crowded out, all of them still arguing with Malone.

'Yes?' Swift said once they'd gone.

'I had letters from William Sullivan before his arrival,' Fitzroy explained. 'As you'll realise, I've received correspondence from the potential heirs on and off since they were first approached. Most of them had the decency to hold off until the Laird died, but Sullivan was very persistent. He wrote that he was descended from Annette and Bruce McFee. Bruce was Nial McFee's youngest brother, and Annette was a second cousin twice removed. It would have put Sullivan above the others. Sullivan insisted that he had papers and a gold coin bearing their initials.'

'So Malone did steal the coin,' I said.

'And Sullivan's papers by the sound of it,' Swift added. 'Which he probably burned. You should have mentioned it earlier.'

'I agree, although I have only just seen proof of the coin that was mentioned,' Fitzroy replied.

'What about Brodie?' I asked about the dead man, presumably still floating down towards the loch, and sea.

'As I said, quite a lot of correspondence but no actual proof from him, other than a letter to say he was confident of his claim and would see me shortly.'

'As he's dead, would any descendants of his now have a claim?' I asked.

Fitzroy shook his head. 'He did not have direct descendants, nor did Sullivan to my knowledge.'

'Keep Malone busy and we'll go and search his room,' Swift told him.

'Very well, I will do so,' Fitzroy replied.

'And save some lunch for us,' I added as the lawyer walked out of the door, papers tucked under his arm.

Greggs came over. He held the notebook in one hand, pen in the other, his spectacles still perched on his nose. He'd taken on the air of a fussy schoolmarm. 'I have taken considerable notes, sirs,' he began. 'Although I may need to revise the names of the McFee antecedents, as there were rather a lot mentioned. It was really very complicated. I shall have to refer to the family tree and cross-reference to the kirk registers.'

'There's no need to bother about those, they're Fitzroy's problem,' I told him.

He stopped, chins wobbling as he pulled in his jaw. 'Really, sir. I have filled many pages with who was descended from whom, and the dates of birth, and the details of illegitimacy and the brothers, sisters, and cousins. It would have been helpful had it been mentioned that it was of no importance to the investigation at the beginning of the session.' He sounded quite peeved.

'Greggs, you don't have to do this–' I began, but was interrupted.

'Hurry up,' Swift said, holding the door open. 'We don't have much time.'

We followed him out. 'You can always just go back to butlering,' I said to Greggs.

He puffed out his paunch. 'It was merely a polite reminder, sir. And quite reasonable in the circumstances.'

'Shush,' Swift said as we crossed the hall and started up the stairs.

'We don't always know what's going to happen, or what's important,' I hissed.

'Given that I'm newly deputised, I would have thought a little consideration would be extended,' he hissed back.

Swift had been stalking ahead of us. 'Will both of you be quiet.'

That made us shut up.

Malone's room was even more of a mess than when I'd been in earlier. Clothes on the floor and tossed over furniture, the bed unmade, his suitcase open on the floor with items half dragged out of it. Greggs tutted.

Swift began rummaging among the mess. I leaned against the door with my arms folded.

'Do you think perhaps you should look under the bed, sir?' Greggs suggested.

'No, but you're welcome to.'

'*Ahem*, my back, sir. As you will recall…' He indicated his spine as though I might not be sure of its whereabouts.

'Lennox, you can look behind the curtains, under the bed and on top of the wardrobe,' Swift called to me from where he was kneeling on the worn rug, searching among the clothes in the suitcase.

'I will look behind the curtains, sir.' Greggs swung into action.

'Fine,' I said and went to the damned bed. There was nothing under it other than a thick layer of dust, an empty chamber pot and mouse droppings. I stood up, sneezing.

'There's no papers among his belongings.' Swift stood too, brushing off the knees of his trousers. 'And nothing incriminating, as far as I can see.'

'Sir! Sir! I have discovered something! A clue!' Greggs was holding a crumpled piece of paper.

'What?' Swift was instantly at his side.

'A sales ticket, sir.' Greggs beamed as he handed it to Swift. 'It is from a tailor in Newcastle for making up a kilt in the McFee tartan, along with a sporran, Argyle jacket, kilt hose and belt and buckle. It is made out to Mr Sullivan for twenty guineas.'

'That's expensive,' I said.

'Indeed, sir.' Greggs raised his brows at the sum.

'Fitzroy said Sullivan was wealthy, although not how he made his wealth,' Swift said. He read the details of the tailor's receipt, turned it over to find there was nothing written on the reverse, then folded it up and slid it into his trench coat pocket.

'No, and I'd say Malone has very little money. He was dressed in a butcher's apron in the photograph he had of his grandmother.' I moved to the wardrobe. It was a short, squat affair made from old pine. There was nothing in it nor on top of it. 'Was there any mention of a dirk in the items Sullivan bought?'

'No,' Swift replied. 'You're thinking of Brodie's body in the river?'

'Yes, and the knife in his back,' I agreed.

'Was there truly a body in the water this morning, sir?' Greggs asked. 'None of the guests really seemed to believe it.'

'Lady Peggie, Craggie, and Sir Richard Fitzroy all saw him,' I said with a degree of exasperation.

'Of course, sir,' Greggs replied. 'But it does seem very peculiar…'

I was in no mood to argue. 'Come on, we'll go and search outside. I want to know where that body has been these last few days.'

'What?' Greggs instantly baulked. 'But it is freezing, sir.'

'You can stay here if you prefer.' I was already heading out of the door and down the corridor. Swift was striding with me and we were down the stairs in no time.

I opened the front door.

'Hey!' A grizzled old man stepped back from the doorstep. He wore a railwayman's cap, stubble on his chin, and a dark blue uniform, frayed and worn. 'Whit ye doin' there then?'

We came to an abrupt halt.

'I might ask the same,' I replied.

'Ach, ye's one o' them sassenachs,' he replied in a thick highland accent. 'I dropped a letter in th'box.' He indicated a black metal box marked 'post' fixed to the granite wall.

'McDuff?' Swift guessed.

'Might be,' the man replied. There was a fat piebald pony attached to a trap near the bridge, which I assumed to be his – the trap that is, not the bridge.

'You bring people and provender back and forth from the train station,' I said.

'Might do,' he replied. The top of his cap barely reached my elbow. He raised his chin high and tried to stare me down. It would have helped if he could actually see out from under the cap, the peak was almost resting on his nose.

'Did you fetch the guests here from the train station earlier in the week?' Swift asked him directly.

'Might 'ave.'

'This is Detective Inspector Swift of Scotland Yard.' I decided some authority was needed. 'Answer the question.'

There was a moment of silence while he chewed that over. 'Aye, alright, I did bring 'em. Is that it?'

'No. Come with us.' Swift took charge. 'We'll interview you in the incident room.'

'I'll no step into the Laird's hall,' McDuff objected. 'It's nae for the likes o' me. In the back only, and then only if I'm deliverin' summat.'

'Right, fine,' I said. 'Who did you bring from the station and when?'

'Ach, there was too many t' say.'

We were standing on the doorstep in the central court-yard, the sun hadn't yet reached it and it was distinctly chilly.

'Do you remember a man called Brodie?' Swift asked.

'The Scot,' McDuff replied. 'Only one among 'em. Frae Stirling he came. Said t' me he were the new Laird.' He gave a grin, his teeth the colour of old tobacco. 'He wisnae the only one as said it.'

'Which day did you bring him here?' Swift continued.

'The one after all the others,' he replied.

'April the second?' I said.

'Might be,' he replied. 'Were it Wednesday?'

I thought about it. 'Yes.'

'Aye, it were then.'

'What did he look like?' Swift asked.

'Didnae ken,' McDuff replied, then raised his cap to show misted irises. 'I got cat-a-rats. Doctor says he could take 'em oot, but I'll no be havin' 'im messing with me eyes. I can see whit's needed. Like youse being a stranger, and so tall as y'are.'

'How do you manage to get around?' I asked, thinking it a shame for the poor chap.

'It's no so hard. Been here all m'life an' I ken every stick an' stone. An' Meggie too.' He pointed a thumb over his shoulder to indicate the fat pony cropping the grass.

'Did Brodie say anything else to you?' Swift had moved into full police mode.

'Ha, a mumpin' man. Tells me he should 'ave a motor pick him up. A motor!' He shook his head. 'Whose havin' a motor oot here in the mountains?' McDuff grunted, or possibly chuckled, it was hard to say. ''Cept that one.' He pointed at my Bentley. 'Big 'un, that is. Bet it's fast.'

'It is, it's mine,' I said.

He nodded. 'A sassenach an' all.'

'Brodie,' Swift reminded him.

'Aye, he were the last one. Came by his'sen on the milk train, arrived at four o'clock in the afternoon. I left 'im over by the bridge cos' there was'nae post, nor provender to leave off. Them's been havin' baskets o'food brought from the town. Back an' forth most days I've been these last few weeks.'

'What time was it when you dropped Brodie off here?' Swift continued.

'Dunno,' he replied. 'It depends on Meggie, sometimes she'll go at a trot and sometimes she'll only go at a slow walk.'

'Was she trotting or walking that day,' Swift asked, a hint of tetchiness in his voice.

'I don't rightly recall, but if she were trottin' it would be half past four, if she walked, it'd be later.' He thought about it. 'Rainin' it was, hard and cold. Ice in it. Had to wear a cloak and hood, so did yon fella. Mumped all the way.'

Swift frowned. I stifled a grin.

'Right,' Swift said. 'Did you notice what colour Brodie's hair was?'

'Didnae have a hair on his head,' McDuff replied. 'And I could see that even with me cat-a-rats. He wore a hat comin' off the train. Only one got off. His hat got blown off and he ran for it. Shouted at me to help. Called me porter. I told him I weren't, but I helped 'im get the hat. Didn't stop him mumpin' though.'

That was at least useful, because it confirmed the dead man in the river was indeed Brodie.

'What about gloves,' I said. 'Was Brodie wearing gloves?'

McDuff nodded. 'Aye, an' never took 'em off, clutchin' his fist like it were aboot to come off. Said I should carry his bag. I told 'im he could carry his own bag, and he could walk an'all, if he mumpted on more.'

'What was his bag like?' Swift continued.

'Suitcase, made frae dark leather.'

'He's dead,' I said. 'We saw him float down the river this morning. He had a knife in his back.'

He opened his mouth, let it hang agape for a moment, then said, 'A knife?'

'Yes, we think he was killed the day you dropped him off,' I said. 'We saw him in the river this morning, but we don't know where he's been in the meantime.'

'Lennox,' Swift hissed at me. I ignored him. These sorts of secrets never stayed secret for long, and this man might provide an insight.

'Well, I'll be beggared,' he said, then chewed his jaw for a moment. 'Mae'be he were caught on the stank stones. Them's the ones that hold back the river to make the braid-water.' He pointed to the broad expanse of water in front of the castle. 'Come. I'll show ye.' He turned to trudge along the bank, going upstream, ahead of the bridge.

We followed, not having explored the area beyond that end of the castle yet, or indeed much of the surrounding countryside. There was a little kirk some way back, and a graveyard studded with leaning stones around a squat mausoleum. We walked the wide stretch of grass between its low wall and the riverbank.

He stopped when we reached an area curving out into the water. 'You should look for ye'selfs.'

A line of rocks like ragged black teeth ran from one narrowed bank to the other, forming a dam of sorts. Foaming white water flowed through the narrow gaps between them and over their tops. Swift and I stared at the dark pool where the river was held back, then along the tree-lined channel to where it emerged from between more trees growing amid the high hills.

'It's filled with meltwater,' I said.

'Aye, so it will be.' McDuff nodded. 'The stank stones was put in when the castle was built. All tumbled in till the mouth was shut. There's said to be a cave below the stones that stirs up the undercurrent. We call it the wyrms-hole where the water-dragon lives.' He grinned. 'Used to tell it so to frighten the bairns an' keep them away.' His grin faded. ''Tis deep and dangerous. If yon man was killed and shoved in, he might have been held, then washed over the stones when the melt lifted 'im up.'

I walked to the edge of the dark water and gazed into its depths. Swift joined me.

'Nasty,' he said.

'Hum,' I muttered agreement. The surface appeared almost glassily still, but there was a shimmering tension below it, the deeper turbulence sensed rather than seen.

And the frothing water pouring between the stank stones was a giveaway too.

Swift bent to peer at the damp grass. 'If Brodie was stabbed here and pushed in...' He moved a few steps forward, then stood up. 'How would any of them know about the pool? And why would he come here with them?' He was talking quietly, as though to himself.

McDuff pulled the cap back down over his brows. 'I'll be away now.'

'Wait,' Swift said and went after him. 'Did Brodie say anything else? Was he expecting anyone to meet him?'

'Nae, the rain comin' doon stopped him talkin' after a bit,' McDuff said, and reached a hand out for the pony. 'Miserable beggar and cheap with it. Didnae give me a farthing for me trouble.'

I dug into my pocket for a shilling and held it out to him.

He frowned. 'What's this for then?'

'For Meggie,' I said.

He nodded. 'Aye, she'll be needin' new shoes.' He shoved it in his pocket. 'I'll thank ye.'

We watched him go. He plodded alongside the pony rather than ride in the trap. There was something of the land about him, as though he'd grown from it, and given his bent legs and shrunken frame, was slowly sinking back into it.

CHAPTER 12

'Do you think that's what happened?' I asked Swift as we entered the courtyard, our footsteps echoing on cold cobblestones.

He sighed. 'It's possible, I suppose.'

I didn't say anything, but the whole scenario seemed strange to my mind.

We returned to the gunroom, or incident room as Swift now called it. Fogg came to greet us with a yip; Tubbs was nowhere to be seen. There was a tray on the worktable with a teapot and the rest, along with a plate piled high with cheese and ham sandwiches and three scones. I think it meant we'd missed lunch.

Greggs was fussing with the fire but stopped and went to pour tea into cups, then the milk. The homely act brought instant comfort and Swift and I sat down in a lighter mood.

'Do you believe Mr Brodie came straight to the front door upon his arrival, sir?' Greggs said after we'd told him what McDuff had said.

'Probably.' I picked up a sandwich and bit into it. The bread was crusty and dense, the cheese tangy, the ham salty with an excellent pickle spread on it. It was all utterly delicious.

'Assuming he was killed shortly after he arrived.' Swift reached for his own sandwich. 'But it would also mean the killer was waiting, and watching for him. Apart from Fitzroy, who knew he was coming.'

Greggs gasped. 'Sir Richard Fitzroy is the primary suspect! Should I write that down, sir?'

'Yes, and help yourself to tea and whatnots, old chap.' I was feeling a tad guilty after snapping at him earlier.

'Thank you, sir.' He sat down and opened the notebook on a fresh page. He wrote 'suspects' at the top of it, and then, 'in order of suspicion', which didn't make much sense but I didn't say anything.

'Brodie would have been killed the day after Sullivan,' I said between eating another excellent sandwich.

'Who'd only been found that morning…' Swift said.

'Yes, we've already established that,' I said.

He mumbled something then carried on eating in silence.

'Should I add Mr and Mrs Craggie to the list of suspects, sir?' Greggs asked.

'Yes, near the top,' I answered because Swift was now staring into space. 'But Malone should be above them.'

He carefully ripped the page from the book, muttered to himself, crumpled it up, tossed it in the fire, then started again. Foggy watched him, then turned back to watch me as I finished the sandwich. I gave him a piece of ham.

Peace reigned as we ate our way through the food. There

was one scone each. I snaffled the largest; it was thickly buttered and layered with raspberry jam and yellow cream. Greggs scratched away with his pen, the fire crackling in the grate. Swift absentmindedly picked up a scone. Foggy drooled onto the moth-eaten rug.

'Sir,' Greggs broke the comfortable torpor. 'Where should I place Lady Peggie in the list of suspects?'

'With Sir Richard,' I replied.

'Really sir!' His brows rose and he added a note.

'Swift,' I said.

'Hmm?' His gaze had settled on the dancing flames in the hearth.

'The glove.' I'd been giving it some thought. 'Brodie was clutching his fist tightly, McDuff said, so how did the glove fall off?'

'He was clutching *something*…' He jerked upright. 'A dowry coin.'

'That's what I was thinking,' I agreed. 'The killer was searching for it and must have felt it inside the glove.'

'And pulled the glove off to get the coin, then tossed it into the river.' He pulled the glove towards him where it had been pushed aside to make way for the tray. It lay on its blotting paper bed, a little drier but still shrivelled and curled. It looked even more like a mummified hand, which I found unsettling.

'If he had gripped it tightly enough there might be an imprint.' Swift was trying to turn the glove inside out.

Greggs stopped writing to observe. 'I have a loupe, sir, which has ten times normal magnification.' He rooted in his jacket pocket and extracted a black metal loupe which looked similar to the ones I'd seen jewellers use. It was rather attractive, with etching around the circle holding the glass.

'Why have you got that, Greggs?' I asked him.

'I collect stamps, sir,' he replied. 'They are an investment for my old age.'

'Really?' I was astounded. He'd never mentioned it before.

'I have only recently taken it up,' he intoned. 'Lady Clementine advised that stamps could prove most gainful, sir, and made me a gift of the loupe.'

'Did she really?' I frowned. Lady Clementine was a feisty lady of a certain age who had settled in our village of Ashton Steeple. She was as eccentric as she was kind. She and Greggs had recently begun attending afternoon tea dances in nearby Burford. I was becoming concerned she was giving Greggs ideas.

'I can't see anything.' Swift was squinting at the inside out glove, the palm uppermost. He held his hand out for Greggs' loupe.

'I would also suggest a torch, sir,' Greggs said as he handed it over.

'Yes, thank you Sherlock,' I said. I'd already pulled mine out and was trying to push the rubber button to switch the damn thing on. It finally flickered into life.

'Move the beam closer, Lennox.' Swift was now scrutinising the glove through the loupe. He let out a sigh. 'I think I can make out an indent of the rim, but it's very faint.'

'Let me look,' I said. He gave me the loupe. It was quite fascinating to see the raised skin of the leather, where it had been worn smooth, and areas where it had been creased. 'There is an indent,' I agreed. 'The top section is a semi circle, but we need to define it more clearly, and then put Malone's dowry coin over it to see if it's the same size.'

'I have chalk, sir,' Greggs offered.

I looked at him. 'Greggs, why do you have chalk?'

'Milady mentioned chalk might be useful if there should by chance be a blackboard here.'

'Lady Persi said that?' I asked, just to be clear.

'Indeed sir, and she also said I should bring the loupe.' He gazed back at me with an air of innocence, plus a simper of pride that he'd outfoxed us.

'So she knows about your stamp collecting too?' I said.

'Naturally sir. We have discussed it while dusting.'

Sometimes I think I have absolutely no idea what goes on in my house.

'Chalk would be perfect, Greggs,' Swift said.

He dug in yet another pocket and produced a box of white chalk. 'It is from young Angus' playroom, sir. Lady Florence gave it to me before we left.'

Swift smiled at mention of his lovely wife. 'She's always very thoughtful.' He began slowly stroking the end of the chalk across the surface of the leather. He had to blot off the damp areas that were catching too much, but between the dabbing and stroking, he managed to clearly expose the indentation made by the rim of the coin that Brodie must have been clutching inside the glove.

'And that's the reason we saw him in the river with only one glove,' I said.

'Exactly,' Swift agreed. 'And possibly the reason he was killed.'

'Greggs,' I said. 'Would you go and find Malone and ask him to come here.'

He sighed, as though I were being somehow unreasonable. 'Very well, sir.' He got up and went out, muttering something about deputies' duties.

I glanced at Swift. 'Could Brodie and Sullivan have been killed for the coins?'

'If they were, why didn't the killer keep Sullivan's coin, rather than leave it in the sporran for Malone to find?' he replied.

'You're assuming Malone isn't the murderer?'

'If he was, why would he show everyone the coin?' Swift said.

'He only showed us Sullivan's coin.'

'But we can't be sure it is Sullivan's coin,' Swift continued.

'Fitzroy told us Sullivan's McFee predecessors had the initials B and A, and that makes the coin more likely to be Sullivan's,' I persisted.

'But we don't know what initials were on Brodie's coin,' Swift countered.

I was becoming confused, so I shut up.

Swift mused for some moments. 'Brodie was clutching the coin inside his glove. It was important to him. What if Fitzroy answered the door, or was outside waiting for him. Brodie might have shown it to him to prove who he was.'

'It was pouring with rain,' I said.

'Then he came to the door. He may have shown it to whoever opened it to prove his claim,' he countered. 'It wouldn't have to be Fitzroy.'

I shook my head. 'I doubt he'd show it to another heir… unless the killer pretended he was Fitzroy and was waiting for Brodie in order to murder him.'

'How would another heir know he was coming?'

'I've no idea. Perhaps some of them knew each other, or of each other.'

Swift frowned at that. 'What about the knife?'

'The killer was already armed with the knife so was ready and prepared,' I said. 'Unless whoever it was intended killing someone else, but Brodie came along with the coin and was murdered for it.'

'Lennox.'

'What?'

'You might as well pick a name out of a hat, because it'll have the same odds as your meanderings.'

'They are not meanderings,' I retorted, stung, then thought some more about it. 'We should find out who else has a dowry coin.'

'Obviously.'

I was coming to the conclusion that it wasn't necessarily helpful having Greggs take notes because it meant Swift wasn't taking them. Swift was at his best when following procedure: filling pages in his notebook, listing suspects, interviewing them, finding clues and drawing on a blackboard – which was his most favourite process. When he wasn't doing all of that he was really quite irritating.

Foggy yawned by the fire, then rolled over on his back and started snoring.

'I'll go and find out where Greggs is.' I stood up.

'You'll probably miss him—'

'Sir, sir…' Greggs came in puffing and out of breath. 'Sir, it's Mr Malone…I think he's dead!'

Swift was instantly on his feet.

'Where?' I demanded.

'His room…' Greggs puffed and tottered to a chair to slump into it.

Swift and I raced out of the gunroom and upstairs, and along the passage. Malone's door was open; he was lying face down on his bed, a nasty gash and noticeable swelling on the back of his head. Blood had matted his hair and run down his neck.

Swift pulled his cuff back, muttered, 'Two o'clock', then went to lean over Malone, feeling for a pulse. 'Damn it,' he swore, moving his hand under the man's stubbly chin.

'Ow,' Malone grunted, voice muffled by the quilt he was lying on. 'Whatta you doing?' Then he let out a long groan.

'What happened?' I asked.

'Dunno,' Malone said, still muffled. He put his arms underneath him and tried to push himself up, but collapsed almost immediately. 'My head hurts.'

'You've been hit by something,' Swift told him. 'Stay where you are.'

'I ain't plannin' on goin' nowhere,' Malone said, sounding a little more like his usual self.

'Lennox, can you find a bowl of water and a towel?' Swift asked me.

My answer to that would normally be no, but I could see a jug and towel on the washstand by the window, so I went to fetch them over.

Swift wet the grey towel then dabbed at Malone's head. 'Did you see who hit you?'

'No, I walked in here, then *bang*. I didn't see nor hear a thing. It's gettin' as bad as New York.'

I'd been looking around to see if there was an obvious weapon left in the room. There wasn't. 'Do you still have the dowry coin?' I asked him.

'I dunno,' Malone said, then shifted on the bed to fumble in the sporran around his waist.

Swift stood back as Malone moved to sit up. He raised the flap and peered into it. 'God damn it, it's gone,' he swore, then groaned as he clutched his head. Fresh blood began to trickle down the back of his head.

'You need stitches,' Swift said and gave him the towel to hold over the gash.

'What was I smacked with?' Malone asked.

'Something blunt, luckily for you,' Swift replied.

'What is gone wrong with him?' Lars came in through the open door.

'I got hit,' Malone said. 'And robbed.'

That made Lars open his eyes. 'Hvad? You was attacked? Min Gud, how can this happen?'

'There's a killer running round the castle trying to murder people,' I said with a touch of irony. We had actually been trying to drum this into them almost since we arrived.

'Ah yes, as you say. This is now becoming very serious. You must exert yourselves, gentlemen.' Lars moved to lean over Malone, still sitting on the bed. 'Remove the towel, please.'

'No,' Malone replied.

'You do as I say,' Lars ordered.

'Have you seen anyone with a weapon of any sort?' Swift asked Lars.

'No, why would I?' He had tugged the towel from Malone's hand to gaze at the wound. 'You need stitches. I will bring my kit.'

'What kinda kit?' Malone demanded.

'My medical kit, of course, what other?' Lars handed the towel back to him and headed for the door.

'You're a doctor?' Swift asked him.

'I am a veterinarian,' Lars replied. 'For big animals. It will be easy, we do not have to tie him like an ox.' He went out.

'He's a vet?' Malone was unimpressed. 'I ain't gonna be sewn up by no animal doctor!'

'I wouldn't argue with him. He'll tranquillise you if you do.' I grinned.

'It ain't funny,' Malone grumbled, his shoulders sagging.

'What time did you come into your room?' Swift reverted to the policeman.

'After I left the drawing room,' Malone replied. 'We'd had lunch, just sandwiches, and then scones and tea an' coffee. We were all chatting, and arguing over that old goat Nial McFee, but it was mostly kinda friendly…. Fitzroy gave us a lecture, he said we were kin, members of the clan, y'know. We should start to get on with each other. He went off with Lady Peggie and we all stayed until Craggie started tidying away. Me and the prof left together. The prof said he was going to explore the old part of the castle, and I came back here. Daniel said he'd been looking around, there was passages and old staircases all over the place.'

'Was anyone left in the drawing room by then?' Swift asked.

'I dunno.' He shrugged.

Lars returned with a leather bag slung over his shoulder. 'Do you want pain killer?'

'Now just you wait a minute. How do I know you ain't the maniac who bashed me on the head?' Malone held his hands up, but the action caused the blood to start running from the gash again.

'You can wait for the doctor if you want,' Lars said. He had rummaged in his case and brought out a tin, which showed a neat sewing kit when he opened it. 'I can brush the skin with ethyl chloride, this will make it numb for you. Do you want to try it?' He pulled out a small bottle and some cotton wool balls.

Malone rubbed the blood from the back of his neck with the towel, wincing as he did. 'Alright then, but I'm watchin' everything you do, and so's these cops.'

'We're detectives,' Swift said.

'Yeah, whatever,' Malone muttered.

Swift oversaw proceedings at Malone's insistence. I wandered the room looking for any clues we may have overlooked. There weren't any.

'I thought your family were wealthy, Lars?' I asked the Dane.

'They are,' Lars replied, his pale eyes narrowed on the curved needle he was using on Malone. 'But I am not idle. We have three farms in our land, with many hundreds of cattle and pigs. I like to tend to these; I do not like them to become sick.'

'Won't they miss you if you come to live here?' I continued.

'Ja, they will, but my sister is also a vet, and my two younger brothers like the farming. I would like to raise the highland cattle here. They make good beef. Then maybe I will breed them with the Rød Dansk Malkerace. I can sell these mixes to Sweden and Norway where they have cold winters in the mountains.'

'Do you have one of the dowry coins?' Swift asked him.

'Yeah, like mine, which has been stolen,' Malone instantly added.

'It was not yours, it was the dead Sullivan's,' Lars reminded him. 'And I have one. It is very precious to our family.'

'Can we see it please?' Swift asked.

'Ja, when I finish this work,' Lars replied and picked up a small pair of scissors from the tin containing the sewing kit.

Greggs arrived, slightly breathless but more composed. 'I was on my way to return here, sir, but Mr Craggie had some information to impart.' This was delivered with a sense of drama.

'What was it?' Swift instantly responded.

'It was…um…' He paused, noticing the minor surgery Lars was making to Malone's skull.

'He's a vet,' I said. 'What did Craggie want?'

'To complain that a cudgel was missing from the umbrella stand in the hall, sir. He is now searching for it,' Greggs said. 'I asked what it looked like and he explained that it was a simple piece of hardwood shaped into a cudgel.'

'Very useful of him,' I commented dryly.

'Apparently there's a brass band around the neck, sir, with an inscription on,' Greggs continued. 'It had been gifted to the castle by a visiting Irish chieftain some centuries ago when they held highland games in the glen.'

'It'll be a shillelagh then,' I said. I didn't comment on the fact they had a shillelagh in their umbrella stand because I kept a long sword in mine, and Swift had a double-headed battle axe in his.

'Indeed, sir,' he intoned. 'I believe it may have been used in the attack upon Mr Malone, although I did not impart this thought to Mr Craggie.'

I didn't reply because it seemed a pretty fair bet he was right.

'And it is good he has a thick skull or he might now be a corpse,' Lars said, straightening up.

Malone didn't respond, he was trying to feel for the stitches Lars had just completed.

'Do not touch,' Lars ordered. 'Or I fit you with a shade, like a dog.'

'Haha,' Malone said sarcastically.

'Could you fetch the dowry coin?' Swift asked Lars.

'It is here.' Lars reached inside his case and pulled out a small brown leather box of noticeable age. He pressed a brass button and it opened. 'This is mine, and it will be my son's one day.' He handed it to Swift.

'W and A,' he said.

'Wendlyn McFee and Anders Olafson,' Lars said. 'This coin she brought with her from this castle. It has the McFee arms on its behind.'

'Why didn't you show it to Fitzroy this morning?' I asked.

'I did not like his insulting of the letter written by my grandmother,' he replied. 'But I will talk with him later on it. Alone.'

'May we borrow it for a short while?' Swift asked.

'Why?' Lars asked. The afternoon sunlight lit his blond hair and threw shadows over his face. His expression was mostly impassive, with occasional flares of anger or irritation. There was something of the Viking about him and he was strong enough and broad enough to do any amount of damage he chose.

'As part of our investigation,' I said. 'It's quite safe, and will only take a few minutes.'

He thought about it. 'Very well, but I want it back in quick time.'

CHAPTER 13

Swift was already heading out of the door; Greggs puffed after him. I followed more slowly, listening as Malone asked Lars if he'd throw some logs on the fire.

'Very well, old fellow,' Lars replied. 'And now you must rest on your bed in quiet, or your head will break again.'

'You won't leave me alone, will you?' Malone said. 'They might come back.'

'I will not allow anyone to hit you. Now rest,' Lars ordered.

Swift and Greggs had beaten me back to the gunroom. Foggy hadn't moved from his spot by the fire, Tubbs had now joined him and neither bothered to raise their heads when we walked in. The lunch tray had disappeared, I assumed Craggie had been in to remove it. We really should lock the door, although the old butler probably had spare keys squirrelled away somewhere so it would hardly stop him.

'The circular imprint in the glove is the same size.' Swift was sitting at the worktable holding Lars' dowry coin against the damp palm of the dead man's glove.

I nodded, not in the least surprised. 'Greggs, could you make a pencil rubbing, please?'

He too was sitting, slightly breathless from all the rushing about.

'Like a brass rubbing?' he asked. 'Indeed, sir, but I am afraid I do not possess a pencil.'

'Here.' Swift instantly produced one from his trench coat pocket.

Greggs took on a determined air. He placed the coin under a page from his notebook and began shading it with the pencil held aslant and was making a good job of producing a copy.

'I'll stand guard shall I?' I said and folded my arms.

'That will not be necessary, thank you, sir,' he said, po-faced. 'We will not possess the coin for long, so we cannot be in any danger.'

'But others might be,' Swift said.

'Malone could have died.' I turned serious. 'We could be standing over a corpse right now.'

'I know.' Swift shook his head. He'd taken a seat opposite Greggs and was watching him, a deep frown between his dark brows. 'It may have been provoked by the body in the river this morning.'

'Out of frustration, you mean?' I asked.

'Yes. The killer wants to frighten everyone into leaving, and Brodie's death two days ago failed to register because the body wasn't seen.'

I pondered that. 'If they killed Brodie to frighten the heirs, why was Sullivan's death made to appear an accident?'

That caused his frown to deepen. 'Hmm…you think it is about the dowry coins?'

'It would seem so,' I said.

'That means they did not intend anyone to see Brodie's body,' he said slowly as he thought it through. 'They must have thought he would be washed away down the river the day he was stabbed to death.'

'It was probably not long before five o'clock, so dusk would have been gathering, and it was raining,' I mused. 'But I don't understand why they failed to set Sullivan's murder up as an accident. It was so poorly executed.'

'Perhaps it was a chance opportunity,' Swift said.

'How?' I was skeptical. 'He'd have had to be leaning over the bannister at that exact spot when the killer just happened to be with him and decided to drop the chandelier on his head.'

'But there may be two culprits, sir,' Greggs reminded us, his voice slightly muffled because he was bent over his notebook.

'Or the killer threw something over the bannister and Sullivan went to lean on the rail and look down,' Swift continued.

I nodded, thinking this was a very real possibility. 'Are you writing this down Greggs?' I asked him.

He looked up, blinking. 'Sir, I am occupied in making a pencil rubbing of the dowry coin.'

'Fine, but we need these theories noted,' I said.

He huffed. 'Very well, sir. If you will give me a moment.'

We waited while he finished his rubbing and solemnly

handed the dowry coin back to Swift. Then he turned to a fresh page, exchanged the pencil for his fountain pen and began to write in laborious copperplate script.

I took a breath and remained determinedly silent until he'd filled a page. 'If the motive isn't to create panic, it's to steal the dowry coins.'

'We've already said that,' Swift replied tetchily.

'Then why attack Malone in such an obvious way?' I remarked. 'Because it seems reckless to me.'

'Or demented,' he said.

'Hm.' I couldn't see any madness, or such desperation, or really any guile in any of the people here, although the actions pointed to it.

'Major Lennox?' Daniel Addison had walked in behind me.

'What?' I turned around to face him.

'I just called in on Lars, he said Malone was attacked. Is it true?'

'Yes,' I replied.

'You mean, there was actually an attempt to murder him?' He looked astounded.

'Yes,' I repeated.

'But why?' He'd come further into the room. 'I mean, he's an irritating little oik, but he isn't going to become Laird. Fitzroy said his claim wasn't strong enough.'

'Do you have one of the dowry coins?' Swift asked him.

His gaze slid away. 'No, I don't, actually. It was sold when Great Grannie McFee married my predecessor. The money was used to build the Addison fortune.' He focused back on me. 'I've spent some time exploring the oldest part of the castle, it's a bit of a wreck but it's quite fascinating. I found something there the other day. Could I show you?'

'What was it?' Swift instantly demanded.

'Just old clothes,' Daniel replied, then shrugged. 'I suppose it's nothing.'

'I'll come.' I'd thought to go outside and make a wider search but it was all rather chaotic. And I wanted to question Daniel about his father's murder.

'Lennox,' Swift began, then lowered his tone. 'I'll return the coin to Lars before I telephone Scotland Yard again. Then I'll ask Fitzroy to call the guests together in the drawing room. You and Addison need to be there, too.'

'Fine,' I agreed. 'Come on, Addison,' I told Daniel. 'Lead the way.'

'The entry is behind one of the tapestries in the dining room,' Daniel said, trying to match my pace.

'Really? How did you find it?' I asked as we strode across the hall.

'I noticed it the other night at dinner. It was before you and the inspector arrived. I was sitting facing it and the cloth was rippling from a draught and I couldn't understand why. I had a look next day and saw it was an entrance.' He opened the dining room door; it creaked as he pushed it aside. He led past the huge fireplace where the smouldering remains were damped down with peat turfs. 'Over here.'

I followed him beyond the long oak table, cleared of all but a white linen cloth. We stopped at one of the hunting scenes and he pulled it aside.

'An old servants' entrance,' I said as he pushed against the panelled opening.

'Yes, I think half the houses and castles in Britain have hidden doorways,' he agreed. 'I've seen a few that have priest holes too.'

'And some that lead to dungeons,' I said.

He grinned, lifting his long face and serious demeanour. 'I believe there aren't any here.' He lit his torch, which almost everyone seemed to carry, given the lack of modern electric lighting.

'Too close to the river,' I said.

'Exactly,' he agreed. 'They'd only flood, although it would save the trouble of executing prisoners, I suppose.'

'If they hadn't already frozen to death,' I replied.

The cold was bitter here and there was very little light. I switched on my own flashlight and ran it over the stone walls and floor. Everything was mottled black and grey with traces of green algae. It smelled of damp and something deeply earthy—like the lingering trace of centuries of toil: men and women hurrying up and down with platters of roasted meats, flagons of ale, whisky, steaming broths, bread, puddings, and all the fare that once filled the tables.

'What did you do after lunch?' I asked him.

'Are you asking if I hit Malone over the head?' he called back lightly. 'I went for a quick walk then returned to my room. I'm going back over my documents from the genealogists and finding out which need revision. My father did all the work initially, but I'll have to write to the company he used and ask them to take a closer look. I think my claim is valid, actually.' The passage had widened then formed a fork. 'The kitchens are off to the left,' he said and took the one on the right. 'When I came here earlier it was a bit scary on my own, I almost gave up and turned back. The professor has been doing a lot of exploring, he says he's mapping the place out. I think it's a good idea.'

We carried on and came to some steep stone steps, the treads worn smooth in the middle.

'They must have had a great many servants in the past,' I remarked.

'Yes, they even entertained Kings of Scotland.' Daniel was forging ahead of me. 'The McFee's had grown wealthy from the gold.'

'So Fitzroy said,' I called back. 'Do you know anything more about the gold mine?'

'No, only what was told to us.'

The steps had wound up and around a corner, then stopped at a narrow landing. Dimmed sunlight fell through an open doorway, dust swirling languidly in the pale rays.

'Here we are.' He walked across the threshold, the simple plank door pushed aside where it was leaning on its hinges. 'Most of the rooms are empty.' He raised an arm to indicate a lofty chamber.

Our feet echoed on bare floorboards, grey dust rising in soft plumes as we crossed the vacant space. The rough-hewn walls were unadorned and held in place by thick lines of pale mortar. The ceiling high above was beamed and laced with dust-encrusted cobwebs; they hung eerily in long grey strands, swaying slowly in the chill draught. There was a fireplace as large as that in the dining room we'd just left, but the work was more crudely carved and had the look of the truly mediaeval about it.

'There was a leak in the corner.' I'd paused to look up at the ceiling then down to the floor, where a tell-tale dark stain showed water had dripped in from above.

'I think it's been fixed, but a couple of the glass panes are broken.' Daniel pointed to one of the narrow windows.

There were only four windows let into the thick walls, and they were the source of the filtered sunlight.

'It's a tower house,' I said.

Daniel grinned. 'I know. Isn't it marvellous? This must be the original part of the castle. It would have been a tall rectangular building with great wide walls and no opening on the ground floor. The door was way above ground and everyone would have had to come in and out using a ladder.'

'Which they'd have pulled up if they were attacked. It was a simple form of a drawbridge.' I was familiar with the history of Scottish castles, Swift would lecture on it every so often, and I knew a fair bit too. History had been the only subject that had interested me at school, and I was also keen on novels featuring war, daring deeds and bloody battles.

'Come on.' Daniel walked towards a doorway opposite. 'I'll show you the room with the clothes.'

'What happened to your father, Daniel?' I asked him in conversational tone.

He didn't reply, just carried on walking.

'Swift will ask Scotland Yard the same question,' I added.

'I doubt they'll tell you,' he said and shoved his hands in his pockets. 'It was all kept hush-hush. There are only a few people who know how he died.'

'Are you one of them?'

He let out a sigh. 'Yes, I am.'

We'd entered another empty room, smaller than the other but otherwise of the same design and in the same state. I could see there had been footsteps back and forth, although they were made indistinct by the powdery dust. Another door led out onto a wooden staircase. We took the worn planks, our boots echoing in the closeted space created by the granite walls.

'Do you know who killed him?' I asked.

'Yes…' He lowered his head, his thin shoulders stooped. He entered the doorway first. 'Here.'

I stopped in my tracks. We were in the very top of the old castle, the dark-beamed ceiling above reaching into the shadowy peak of the roof. Dressmaker's dummies, headless but the height of a man, stood along the back wall. They were arranged in the form of a marriage ceremony. On each outer edge were a 'man and woman'. The 'men' in full ceremonial Scots' style with a doublet jacket, white dress shirts, lace cravats and the gathered plaid draped over their shoulders. The one on the right was in the McFee tartan, I didn't recognise the other clan colours.

Their 'wives' wore long Victorian frocks, boned and corseted, though with the slightly thicker waist of the more mature woman. The one on the left in purple taffeta, the bodice complete with a full row of black buttons, high-necked lace, a large cameo and a bustle at the rear. The 'lady' on the right wore dark yellow crepe with a frill neck, a fringed shawl and a parasol propped against an empty sleeve. Shoes were placed on the round wooden stands holding up the canvas dummies; the men had ghillie brogues, the women had single-strap shoes in black leather, sturdy but elegantly designed.

Between them were two 'bridesmaids' in pale rose satin dresses with puff sleeves, their forms slimmer and less formal than the matrons, with slender silk shoes and pointed toes.

In the centre was the bride and groom. He wore the unknown tartan, she wore white silk under a full-length veil of finest tulle. The veil had been placed over the neck of the dummy, a ring of dried rosebuds held it in place. There wasn't a speck of dust in the room, nor on the clothes, although some of the fabric showed signs that it was slowly perishing.

'Do you think it's Lady Peggie and the Laird's wedding attire?' Daniel asked me.

'I don't know,' I said, nonplussed at the sight.

'I'm not very up on ladies' fashions.'

'No...' I replied. My mother had adored clothes and would come into the breakfast parlour most mornings in some stunning frock and ask what I thought. 'Very nice' was my usual reply, and she'd then go on to tell me the type of fabric, the cut, the lace and all the rest of it. I'd barely given it half an ear, but I had learned something of ladies' fashions as a result and knew these were older than the style my mother wore. 'Have you touched anything?' I asked him.

'No, I didn't like to.'

Neither did I, there was something strange and disturbing about it. I'd felt the same about the whole place actually, and this display just added to it. I switched tack. 'Who killed your father?'

The look he flashed me was haunted. 'My girlfriend's father. He was head of security at the embassy – a local man, not a Brit. I won't tell you his name, nor hers.'

'And I won't ask, but I need to hear the story.'

'It was in Hyderabad. My father was…greedy. Avaricious. It's a family trait. One that I haven't acquired,' he added hastily. 'I was stepping out with the girl, she was nineteen, I was twenty-two. It was just light-hearted. We liked each other, we had fun. I squired her around, followed by a chaperon of course. Shopping, wandering around the markets, that kind of thing. It was innocent – I was too scared of her father for it to be anything more.' He tried a grin, but it failed to come off. 'My father liked to take things from other people, and he had an eye for young ladies.' He took a breath to control his voice. 'It had been the source of terrible arguments with my mother. That's why she wasn't with us on the posting. She'd refused to come. I was supposed to be learning about diplomacy and the system, you know, so that I could join the foreign office one day. That's a day that's never going to dawn,' he said, his eyes shifting back to the wedding party in their decaying finery. 'Father cornered her in the salon. She had come early to meet me, the chaperon had to wait outside. I was held up in the office by one of the staff. I think he'd arranged for that to happen. I didn't hear her cry out, but I heard the sound of running boots along the marbled hall. I realised it meant trouble. I raced out, so did other people, but they stopped when they heard the gunshot. My girlfriend ran from the salon, her hair dishevelled, she was sobbing with fear.' A calm seemed to fall over him as he told the tale, as though it were some sort of catharsis. 'Her father had shot mine. It served my father right. He was lying on the floor. He held his hand out to me, calling for me to send for a doctor. I didn't move. He tried to crawl towards me but he was bleeding badly. He'd been shot in the chest. I took the gun from the man responsible, and told him to leave, and remove his family from the area as quickly as he could. Then I waited for the doctor. My father died before he could get there.' He turned his glance to me. 'The upper echelons know. They covered it up. He was guilty of far more than assault, he was an embezzler. Just a rotten thief. They were glad to wipe their hands of him.'

I nodded; there wasn't any remark worth making. It made me all the more thankful for the loving parents I'd had and the happy home I'd grown up in. Until my poor mother died.

We gazed at the dummies for moments more, then I asked, 'Did your father write to any of the other heirs?'

'Yes,' he replied. 'But I don't know which. My mother destroyed many of his papers when she'd heard he'd died.

She was frightened there was evidence of his crimes and burned them.'

'Then how did you discover your lineage?' I asked.

'I'd heard him talk about it. He mentioned the name of the group of genealogists he'd employed and I went to see them when I returned to London.'

'What is this group called?'

'The Collegium of British Genealogists.' He grinned. 'Rather a grand name for a couple of elderly ladies in Knightsbridge who spend their days among dusty old registers.'

I grinned too. They sounded an interesting pair. 'Good. Swift will have called everyone to the drawing room,' I said. 'Come on.'

CHAPTER 14

'Lennox, I had to start without you,' Swift said as I joined him in front of the small crowd gathered near the fire in the drawing room. Malone was sitting centre front, his head bandaged as though wearing a turban. I assumed it was of his own doing as I doubt Lars would have made him look quite so ridiculous. Everyone else had taken the same armchairs and sofas of the evening before.

A pot of tea and an empty cake platter was placed at one side of the fire. I realised it was after three o'clock. Everybody seemed to have already eaten judging by the crumb-covered plates and empty cups left on elbow tables.

'Fine,' I said and went to sit down in an armchair. Foggy must have followed Swift and came to greet me by leaping about my knees. Tubbs was already ensconced and sitting on Malone's lap.

'As I was saying,' Swift continued. 'Someone here has attacked Mr Malone. This could have been fatal. If any of you has any information, or thinks they may have seen something, you must come forward.'

Necks craned as they looked around at each other in expectation. No-one said anything. Nothing happened.

'Are they killing rivals, do you think?' Professor Coltrane asked. He held a journal open on his lap, it seemed he'd been making notes. I could see a neat ink drawing made of a dowry coin on the facing page.

'Yes, of course they are,' Belinda said sharply. 'Why else would they kill any of us?'

'Maybe for the dowry coins?' Molly said. 'Mr Malone had the one he found in Mr Sullivan's sporran. There's a link right there.'

Swift's eyes narrowed as he turned towards the Canadian. Her auburn hair gleamed, her fresh face avid. It was astute of her to have made that connection.

'What about the man floating in the river this morning?' Daniel said. 'Does anyone know if he had a coin?'

More muttering and shakes of the head.

'Nobody met him,' Susannah said. 'We didn't even know he existed until today.'

'Is that correct?' I asked the room in general. 'Did any of you know of the other's existence?'

None of them replied.

'I want each of you to tell me where you were at two o'clock today,' Swift said.

'I went for a stroll, then returned to the castle through the old stable door,' Professor Coltrane said.

Swift motioned to Greggs to write that down.

'I went for a quick walk for some fresh air,' Daniel said. 'I followed a path alongside the bank of the river, then returned to my room to go over some papers.'

That was consistent with what he'd told me.

'I went to the library to look at the registers and the tree of McFee,' Lars said. 'I need to make a copy of my ancestor line for my family.'

'Oh what a good idea,' Susannah said. 'I will do the same.'

'Could you tell us where you were at two o'clock please?' Swift asked.

'I sure can.' She smiled. 'I had a hot bath. It took such an age to fill, but I was just cold all the way through and I felt so much better afterwards.'

'Fine,' Swift said. 'Belinda?'

'I was reading my magazine in bed with the fire blazing. It was the only way I could warm up.'

'It's hardly cold,' Molly said. 'This is spring weather. I wrote a letter to my folks telling them what was said this morning, then I went for a walk across the bridge. I didn't see anyone while I was outside.'

'Can I ask again if any of you saw or heard anything? Please think carefully.' Swift wasn't giving up.

Nobody replied. Greggs finished writing and looked up, pen ready, then put it down with a sigh.

'Lennox,' Swift said.

'Right.' I moved in front of the fire. 'The genealogists employed by Mr Daniel Addison's father were called the Collegium of British Genealogists. They provided information to more than one family,' I stated. 'Who else used them?'

Swift frowned as I hadn't had a chance to tell him this yet.

Belinda flushed. 'We did.'

'Did you or your family contact any of the other heirs through information provided by this organisation?' I felt quite the detective using such formal language.

'There was some correspondence between Daniel's father and mine,' Belinda admitted, 'but my father's secretary managed most of it.'

'Have you seen these letters before coming here?' Lars demanded.

She scowled at him. 'Oh, very well, yes, I did. But I did not write to anyone.'

'Maybe your father did, or his secretary,' Molly said.

'Why would they?' Belinda retorted. 'They would be rivals.'

'I had a letter from your father,' Professor Coltrane told her. 'He informed me that he had the greater claim and would not hesitate to prove it through the courts.'

Gasps were heard at that revelation.

'Well if he says he has a better claim than you, then he will have, and we have some of the best lawyers in California,' Belinda answered hotly.

'You did not tell this to us,' Lars called out. 'You lie by leaving out these facts.'

'Well the professor didn't tell you either,' she retaliated.

'Enough,' Fitzroy shouted. 'Any of you who have been in correspondence with any other claimants should please inform us of it.'

Needless to say, none of them admitted to any such thing.

'Please tell us what happened when you first contacted the potential heirs,' Swift asked Fitzroy.

He was seated next to Lady Peggie, who turned an intent gaze at him. It made me wonder if there was any attachment between them.

'I had just retired from my firm in London,' Fitzroy said, 'and returned to Edinburgh to close down my deceased father's legal practice there. He had a few family clients that had been held for many years, this clan was one in particular. Because of the long history between our families, I came here to discuss a continuation with the Laird.' He returned Lady Peggie's gaze for a moment then focused back on Swift and the room. 'The Laird was not in good health and fearful for his future. I agreed to track down the most likely heirs, and their whereabouts, and write to them. This took some considerable time, and fortunately the Laird improved and lived another eight years. But, as I'd requested legal proof of each claimant, it triggered some to track down their ancestral history and use a genealogist. This could have led some claimants to know who other likely candidates would be.'

Swift nodded.

'Sir.' Greggs was seated a little way behind everyone and had been making determined notes while bent over the page. He now put his hand up. 'My understanding of those who used the Collegium of British Genealogists is Miss Belinda's father, Mr Addison's father, and Professor Coltrane. Is this correct?'

'I did too,' Susannah Bellamy admitted.

'Thank you,' Swift said dryly as Greggs duly wrote that down. 'You should have told us that before. Did any of you correspond with any others – apart from Belinda's father and Professor Coltrane,' he added as Belinda opened her mouth.

'I did not,' Susannah said.

'Did any of you contact Sullivan or Brodie?' I asked. 'Or did either of them contact any of you?'

No one said a word in answer to that, which I suppose was to be expected.

'Would any mention of the dowry coins have been made?' Swift asked.

'I've no idea,' Fitzroy replied.

'Who has one?' Swift asked.

Molly held up her hand, then Susannah did the same. I gave Professor Coltrane a hard stare and then he too held up a hand.

'You know I have one,' Lars said.

'Why did you not show them to us this morning?' Lady Peggie demanded, a shrill tone of anger in her voice.

'I wanted to discuss it privately with Sir Richard,' Susannah said.

'And I,' Lars said.

'Me too,' Molly added.

'As did I,' Professor Coltrane admitted in his precise tone. 'I considered it a card up my sleeve and did not want to play it too soon.'

'I think they should all be put together for safe keeping,' Lady Peggie said.

'I agree,' Swift said.

'Should I take them?' Fitzroy suggested.

'Yes,' Swift agreed, 'and lock them away somewhere safe.'

'I will do so with Lady Peggie's assistance,' Fitzroy said. 'And I would like to make an announcement.' He raised his head to address the room. 'I am sorry to advise that there is no clear cut heir to the McFee estate, nor the title. You are all of one blood, however diffuse it may be. You are the clan McFee, and so are your families. I have given this considerable thought, and I have discussed it with Lady Peggie. I believe it best that you all decide who should become the new Laird, or the new Lady, between you, as in the days of old.' He held his hand up, as loud muttering was raised. 'Doing so will help rebuild the clan, rather than divide you all. You have seen that the estate requires funds, it requires skills and passion to renovate the castle. It requires people to fill its empty rooms. I would like you to cooperate now, and work together to find a solution that you can all agree on.'

'But *we* have the best claim,' Belinda instantly objected.

Malone disagreed. 'No you don't, I do.'

'You can't prove it,' she retorted. 'And you've all got to be legitimate.'

Lars stood up and spoke out. 'I agree with what Fitzroy has said. It is the best way.'

'I, too, agree,' Susannah said.

'And I,' Daniel added.

'And me,' Molly sang out, a delighted smile lighting her pretty face. 'It's a great idea!'

Professor Coltrane was the only one who hadn't spoken. All eyes turned to him.

'Very well,' he said, stretching his turkey neck to give him a little more height. 'I accept that this would be a democratic solution, and I hope it works for the best, but it may be overturned by the legal process if one of us can prove their claim beyond doubt.'

'Exactly,' Belinda said and crossed her arms.

'And such a victor would win the castle and lose the clan,' Fitzroy warned. 'And the goodwill of the villagers, and the neighbouring clans round about.'

'My family is my clan,' Belinda said, her eyes cold and hard. 'We don't need a bunch of locals, we have servants of our own.'

Susannah gasped at that piece of arrogance. 'Well I hope you know what you're doing because I believe this will be a cold and lonely place if you ever need a helping hand.'

'Yeah, and you just put a target on your back too,' Malone added. 'Cos whoever's doin' the killin' will be goin' after you next.'

'Absolute rubbish,' Belinda snapped back and stood up.

If she intended stalking out, her intent was interrupted. Craggie had entered the room behind us, his umbrella held high.

'I found the shillelagh,' he called out from the rear of the room. ''Tis in the braid water. Sum' un will have to go swimmin' for it, or it'll be lost to the river.'

'What is this shillelagh?' Lars asked as everyone rose to their feet.

'The thing I was probably hit over the head with,' Malone said.

'A shillelagh is an Irish cudgel,' Professor Coltrane explained.

'Craggie, what is this?' Lady Peggie went to ask her butler.

'I saw it, milady,' he replied, looking up at her. 'I searched all aboot, then I thought it might be in the water like yon man this mornin'. An' I was right.'

'You had better show the detectives where it is,' she said with an irritated sigh, then added bitterly. 'Another monstrous act perpetrated in this domain.'

I went over to him.

'I'll show ye now,' Craggie said to me as Swift came over too.

'Come on,' Daniel called out and the room emptied to loud chatter and the clatter of feet, rather like a bunch of school children being released from class.

Craggie led outside and onto the middle of the bridge to stand and point into the broad stretch of water where it was at its widest. 'There ye go. I thought it might be here, and I saw a flash o' light from where the sun caught at it.'

We all crowded round to peer into the crystalline water and its stony bottom. It was fairly easy to spot – should you be looking for such a thing. The shillelagh itself was black, but the brass ferule fixed around the end was bright and clear.

'Did you see who threw it in there?' Swift asked, leaning on the cold stone parapet.

'Nay, course not, or I'd tell ye if I did,' Craggie replied.

'Someone needs to dive in and fetch it up,' Swift decided, then looked at me.

'Absolutely not,' I said. 'The water will be freezing.'

'You're a strong swimmer, Lennox,' he said, then lowered his voice. 'We should set an example.'

'By *we* you mean me,' I replied.

'You know I'm not very good in water,' he replied.

'Well here's a chance to practise,' I replied.

'I go,' Lars said as he pulled his sweater over his head and laid it over the coping of the bridge wall. 'I swim most days in the rivers at home. It is good for the blood.' He took his thick vest off too and put that on top of the sweater.

'Oooo!' I heard some of the ladies behind us exclaim as Lars bared his broad, muscular chest.

I looked around: Susannah, Belinda, and Molly were grouped together, watching quite intently.

Lars yanked his belt undone, unlaced his boots, kicked them and his socks off, then his trousers. We all took a step backwards. He laid the trousers with the rest then placed both thumbs into the top of his undershorts.

'Keep your pants on, Lars,' I told him.

'Ohh,' a groan came from the ladies. Swift and I turned to frown at them, so did the professor. They straightened their faces, assuming an air of innocence.

'I do not like to get my clothes wet.' Lars was still poised with thumbs at the ready.

'There are ladies present,' Daniel told him. 'You can't strip to the buff in front of them. It's not done.'

Lars looked around at the bright-eyed women watching closely. 'They are grown, it is nothing they do not know of.'

'No,' I insisted. 'Just keep them on. Craggie can go and find a towel.' I turned to the old butler.

'Can't,' Craggie replied.

'Craggie, will you please do so,' Lady Peggie told him. He didn't move.

'Are you goin' in or not?' Malone said.

'Lars, no–' Swift ordered, but too late, the Dane had dropped his last vestige of decency, stepped onto the parapet and dived into the water.

Giggling broke out behind us.

'Lady Peggie,' Fitzroy said to her. 'Perhaps you could escort the ladies inside?'

'Indeed, I shall do so.' Lady Peggie was straight-faced, but the others, including Belinda, were all laughing. 'Mr Greggs, perhaps you can come with me to retrieve a towel?'

'Certainly, milady,' he offered, and put his hands out as though to shoo the women indoors.

They went in as Lars broke the surface, the shillelagh held high. He spluttered water from his mouth. 'It is more heavy than I thought.'

'It's made from a root ball.' Swift leaned further over the parapet. 'Try not to hold the end.'

'Ah, you think of fingerprints.' Lars was treading water. 'I have read of it.' He laughed suddenly. 'I must swim like this every day now. Like back home in Denmark. The water is exhilarating.' He let himself drop below the surface, rose again to take a breath, then swam arm over arm for the shore.

CHAPTER 15

'Whose fingerprints are they?' I asked, and leaned forward to make out the swirls and whorls picked out by Swift's assiduous dusting of powder. We'd returned with the shillelagh to the gunroom, and Swift, along with Greggs, had gently dabbed the wooden club dry. It was now laid on the worktable, a thin towel laid beneath it, and generously daubed with grey-white powder.

'No idea,' Swift said.

'Are we going to take everyone's fingerprints, sir?' Greggs asked, anticipation in his voice.

'Yes.' Swift was just as excited, but better at hiding it. 'Lennox, can you ask Fitzroy to call everyone together?'

'They are all in the drawing room admiring Lars' heroics,' I said and stood up. 'I'm going to walk Foggy.'

He frowned, but didn't try to stop me. 'Fine. We'll go and find them.' He was always a man on a mission, whereas I needed some quiet time, away from the chatter and the undercurrents swirling below it.

'I won't be long,' I said and left as he and Greggs were gathering the usual requisites: ink, foam pad, a stash of paper. Greggs was having a wonderful time, he had found an old leather game bag and now filled it with the items, plus more as he and Swift thought of them.

Foggy raced off ahead of me, tail high, ears flapping as he ran across the hall. He stopped at the front door, eyes bright, black nose twitching and tongue already hanging out. Tubbs had decided to attend, though he insisted on being carried. I put him down once we were on the track leading to the bridge, then paced behind them as they scooted off with tails high and paws bounding on the stony surface.

The track wound around a high hill, it was the route I'd driven in on, as had McDuff with his pony and trap. It had seemed to be the only road into the glen, but I'd noticed a grassy path leading off and up the hillside. I aimed for that and quickly found myself under the heavy shade of closely grown trees. It was cold out of the sun, but it condensed the sharp scent of pine sap oozing from the trees.

I walked steadily upwards, fallen needles crunching underfoot, long grass brushing my boots along with fronded ferns reaching out from black earth, their delicate tendrils uncoiling in bright green tips.

A red squirrel, its fur russet and black, chittered a warning from a cone-laden branch. Fogg stopped to give it a *woof* then ran on. I could hear lambs bleating in the distance. A horse neighed, a cockerel crowed, cattle bellowed somewhere on a hill and the sound of running water underscored it all. A peaceful corner of heaven, wild and tranquil and undisturbed by man.

That was an illusion, of course. Man's hand pervaded everything. The sheep had been brought here, as had the chickens, cows, and horses, and the round tower that I was aiming for was another sign of man's endeavours.

Tubbs decided he had walked enough and stopped to lie down in my path. I scooped him up and carried him in my arms. Foggy reached the tower before me and ran barking around it for no good reason. I scanned it as I moved closer; the dry stones forming it were rough, and bound together in interlocking form. It was a skilled job made by people who knew the ancient ways. It was half buried in the hillside and I was able to climb behind it on an earth beaten track liberally dosed with rabbit droppings.

It wasn't very high, around twenty feet or so. The top seemed unfinished, with loose stones around its brim, indicating it was not a lookout tower. I gazed down into it; it was around three quarters full with large stones. Mostly they were flat, or flattish, rather than round. They appeared to have simply been dropped in and had scattered within the confines of the thick round walls. Lichen in brown, black, and green stains had spread across the walls, moss filled many of the gaps, bright green and sponge-like with small yellow flowers sprouting amongst them. Bees were already busy gathering their pollen.

I was above the trees and had a fine view of the glen from here. The castle dominated the scene although the grey stone walls gave it a more natural air – actually it reminded me of a huge man-made cave. The river sparkled in the sunshine. I could see white-painted cottages beyond the promontory and the narrow gap where Swift and I had tried to intercept the body. I looked back to where the stank stones held the inflowing water. Strange how the pool of water looked black, even from here. The small kirk was set back some distance from the castle, the cemetery and leaning gravestones set before it in grassy turf. Outhouses were ranged behind the castle, though I could barely make them out from here. Framing the whole were more dark pine trees, masses of them, rolling back towards the high hills and higher mountains beyond.

Who wanted this so much that they were prepared to kill three men for it? Or was it the dowry coins? Or both?

I sat down on a pale rock protruding from the thick grass. Tubbs purred in my lap. Fogg lay panting at my feet. Brodie was the true mystery. Who had known he was coming? Fitzroy had, but the heirs had been contacted eight years ago when the Laird was first taken ill. Some had used the same genealogists to uncover their claims for the estate. How many had really made connections with the others? Daniel Addison's father was dead, we only had Daniel's word for how he'd died. Persi said Professor Coltrane's partner had died in strange circumstances…but there was nothing to point in anyone's direction. If Brodie had been killed the day he arrived, where had his body been left? And was he killed because he had the strongest claim, or for the dowry coin? But the coins weren't worth a huge amount, a few hundred pounds at most. And the estate was a money pit; without deep pockets, anyone inheriting the place would quickly find themselves paupered.

I'd given Greggs my notebook and didn't have a use for it anyway. A list of suspects would simply be the names of people here in no particular order. I had no idea who was behind the murders. Belinda seemed the grasping type, although that may be because she wanted to impress her father, or prove herself. If she was an example of her family, they'd be a disaster for the place. Molly was the antithesis, but she could hardly manage everything alone, even if she did have inherited wealth of her own. Lars might succeed, Susannah was too old, in my view, as was Professor Coltrane. And what of Lady Peggie? She had upbraided Fitzroy for inviting the heirs to come to the castle. Did she really want to move to a cottage in the village?

I stood up, brushing my trousers down. Fitzroy had proposed an intelligent solution to the problem – let them decide the Laird, or Lady, for themselves. I decided to retrace my footsteps down the track and see how Swift's endeavours were going.

'We have discovered the owners of the fingerprints, sir,' Greggs confided when I came across him in the hall. 'Mr Lars and Mr Craggie's.'

I eyed him. 'Has Swift arrested either of them?'

'He has not, sir. Lady Peggie forbade it, as did Sir Richard. Apparently Mr Craggie had picked up the shillelagh only a short time ago when he was told that the putative heirs would be gathering.'

'That doesn't mean he didn't hit Malone over the head with it.' I took off my coat and handed it to him.

'But Mr Craggie was with Lady Peggie and Mrs Craggie

during the period Mr Malone was attacked, sir.' He folded my greatcoat over his arm, like the good butler he was. 'Therefore it must be assumed he could not be the party responsible for these heinous crimes. We have, however, taken the prints of the entire household, despite their many objections.'

I glanced at him; he had a simpering smile on his face. And I'd also noticed his sudden switch into the lyrical. 'You're not planning on writing about this, are you Greggs?'

'Certainly not, sir,' he spluttered. 'I would not dream of doing so.'

'Not for the parish magazine, or one of your theatrical journals?' I asked because Greggs was fond of dramatics, and attention. 'Or is it for Lady Clementine?'

His cheeks turned pink. I'd hit the nail on the head. 'She is the soul of discretion, sir.'

'No she isn't.'

'She has given her word, sir,' he quibbled. 'And I must inform you that the heirs are still in the drawing room. They are writing statements of their movements since they arrived, at Inspector Swift's behest. If you will excuse me.' He made a rapid escape with my coat.

I headed for the drawing room, where the sound of muted voices greeted me through the open door. Foggy had beaten me to it, so had Tubbs. They were both curled up on the hearthrug in front of the blazing fire. I wove between the sofas to the front where Swift was standing. Everyone else was sitting ranged in front of him, their heads bent over papers. They were all writing. Lady Peggie wasn't there, nor was Fitzroy.

'Lennox,' Swift said in a low tone when I reached him. 'We've taken prints and the heirs are writing statements.'

'I know.' I extended a damp boot towards the yellow flames. 'Greggs told me you only found Lars' and Craggie's prints.'

'Yes, we know Lars touched it. It's possible the killer wore gloves, so it doesn't give us definitive proof. Lady Peggie confirmed both he and Mrs Craggie were with her at the period in question. That means we can eliminate the three of them,' he said, bright-eyed and happy now that he was doing proper police work.

'Why throw the shillelagh into the water then?' I asked. 'If no incriminating prints had been left on it.'

'Caution, I suppose,' he said.

'I've finished writing,' Daniel called out and held up his piece of paper.

'And me,' Molly said.

'I have also,' Lars said.

'Wait where you are, please.' Swift went to gather the statements from them.

Craggie tottered in, rattling tray in hands. It held a steaming cup and a plate of biscuits. He advanced slowly towards me. 'Ye missed the tea and cake. The Lady said I should bring some for ye.'

'Thank you,' I said appreciatively.

He put the tray on a worn leather stool by the fire. I sat next to it.

'I walked up to the tower on the other side of the bridge,' I told the old butler, thinking to find out more.

'It in't a tower,' Craggie said and shuffled off without further explanation.

'Craggie is correct,' Professor Coltrane said. He was sitting closest to me and had obviously been listening. 'It is the McFee Cairn, it commemorates the clan's fallen heroes.'

'Ah.' I picked up my plate of Victoria sponge, wielded the silver fork accompanying it and waited for enlightenment while eating. The sponge was so light it almost melted in my mouth, along with the cream and jam filling.

'I discussed it with Lady Peggie the other evening,' he continued. 'Each stone is dropped in there for a life lost for the clan. It is in remembrance of those who died before their time. Mostly men who were killed in battle, but there are some who died in a collapse of the gold mine.'

Swift had finished collecting statements and came back to the fire and sat down, papers firmly clutched. I'd finished the cake and was now finishing my tea.

'Was that why it was closed?' Molly was openly listening.

'Not quite.' Coltrane began a lecture, apparently in his element. 'The gold had run out and the Laird at the time was convinced they only needed to dig deeper to find a fresh seam – but it was a desperate act. There were not the funds by then to buy suitable supports or the machines needed to pump out the water that collected as they dug deeper. A sudden downpour caused a spate of water to fill part of the mine. Some drowned, others were buried. They were dug out but the collapse left two dozen men dead. Lady Peggie said those that drowned remain buried in the mine to this day. The entrance has since been filled and covered with turf. It is no longer visible, nor accessible.'

Greggs meandered in quietly then went to sit at the rear and begin his preparations for note taking.

'What happened to your partner, Professor Coltrane?' I asked.

He almost choked.

A number of heads went up.

'What?' he said.

'Your partner died after you'd had a falling out,' I repeated.

'How did you find that out?' Coltrane lowered his voice, the geniality suddenly gone.

'They're detectives,' Molly said, and sat up, eyeing the confrontation with sharp interest. 'They're supposed to find things out.'

Coltrane fumed for a moment. 'It wasn't how it sounds. He did it, he killed himself. I tried to stop him.'

'That's your story,' Molly said.

The others were now all ears.

'What do you know of it?' Belinda asked her.

'Nothing, it's what they say in detective novels.' Molly grinned. 'I thought I'd give it a try.'

'You shouldn't be so nosy,' Belinda replied.

'We are now to agree on the new Laird, or Lady, between us.' Lars came to Molly's defence. 'There cannot be secrets of such importance if we are to do this.'

Susannah sighed. 'I guess you're right about that. Professor?'

He hesitated, his lips pursed thin.

'You should explain yourself Professor,' Swift said.

Coltrane blinked, then nodded. 'Very well. I was a senior lecturer of Anthropology at Boston University. Professor Gavin Pierce and I were commissioned by the University to write a book titled *Primitive Society: A Study of the Origins of Custom and Belief among the Races of Man*. It was to discuss societies' progress from primitive to civilised stages. We had framed this into sections on savagery, barbarism, and civilisation. We worked well together until it came to biological determinism and hierarchical racial categories. This was an area Pierce and I had argued about before, but I thought he had realised that the principle of racial hierarchy was utterly flawed—.'

'Wait,' Malone cut in. 'What does that mean?'

'It's the presumption that some people are naturally superior to others,' Susannah said with distaste, her southern accent more clipped than usual. 'A popular ideology among those who want to think they are somehow born superior because of their birth. It is contemptible, in my view.'

Malone was still wearing his turban of bandages although it had slipped sideways now. He nodded, then pushed it back when it fell over one eye. 'I lived with just about every type there is and they're all exactly the same underneath, some folk are clever, some ain't. Some are lazy, some real hard workin'. Some are honest, but a lot aren't, not when they're dirt poor, anyway. Everyone does whatever they gotta do to survive.'

Coltrane shook his head and carried on. 'This book was very important to Pierce, he was ambitious and wanted to become President of the University. I was on the point of retiring, but hoped to leave with my good reputation intact.' He stared at the flames cracking in the hearth for a moment. 'Pierce had been approached by The Eugenics Record Office and offered funding to promote the theory of eugenics in the book. I refused absolutely. I knew the funding came from wealthy people with their own agendas. I told Pierce I was pulling out. He declared he'd go ahead with a junior man, and informed the sitting President. I'd discussed this previously with the President. He was of the same mind as I and told Pierce that he was out of order. He threatened him with the loss of his tenure. Pierce had already taken some of the funding, and spent it. He was rather foolish in that regard. A few days later he came into my office and exploded, ranting at me that I'd poisoned everyone against him. He shouted that I'd be sorry, then he ran to the window. It was summer and wide open. We were only four storeys up, but when he jumped it was high enough to kill him. I had run after him, but he was too quick. A student saw him fall, and saw me leaning from the window a moment afterwards. I was accused of pushing him, or not stopping him. Rumours flew around, most of them ridiculous.' His eyes hadn't lifted from his hands held in his lap. 'I was acquitted through lack of evidence, but it finished my career. I have not been able to publish articles or collaborate with my colleagues since. The book was never published.'

The general feeling seemed to be of commiseration and I felt sorry for the chap, assuming him to be innocent, of course.

Lady Peggie and Fitzroy came in together, breaking the strained atmosphere.

'Are we disturbing you?' Lady Peggie asked.

'No,' the professor replied. 'We are having a heart-to-heart.'

Fitzroy waited for Lady Peggie to sit, then settled next to her. 'I think that advisable given that you must choose your own clan leader now,' he said.

Susannah put her hand up.

'Yes?' Swift said.

'There is something I must admit to,' she replied.

We all sat up with a gleam of expectation.

'You killed Sullivan?' Belinda teased with a mocking tone.

'Don't be ridiculous,' Susannah retorted. 'It is not of a death, it is a birth.' She paused to take a breath. 'The birth of my dear son.'

'Well that's surely...' Daniel began in positive tone, then stopped, presumably recalling Miss Susannah Bellamy was a spinster.

'Y'all will realise that I was unwed at the time,' she continued. 'And I never did wed because I was made almost an outcast. My dear parents stood by my side, but our close-knit society didn't want anything to do with me. So I left. I went to live in Arizona where no-one knew me. I did good works, and made friends with folk who were enlightened. Now I run a charitable foundation, and my boy is grown up and getting along just fine.'

'I don't understand,' Lady Peggie said. 'Was your community so harsh as to condemn you for a youthful indiscretion?'

'They were,' Susannah replied. 'When that indiscretion was with a coloured man.'

Most of us had guessed the connotations of what she'd said, but Lady Peggie had probably lived a very sheltered life here in the highlands. Her eyes flew open. 'But how awful for you,' she said. 'I am so sorry to hear you were persecuted in such a way.'

'I think Daniel may want to explain the death of his father,' I said and gave him a meaningful look.

He reddened instantly. 'I…um…this is very painful for me,' he stammered, 'but I agree that we must all be honest.' He explained in very broad terms the facts of his father's death, and skimmed over the abuse of diplomatic privileges.

Shock and very little sympathy followed the revelation, but there was no condemnation of Daniel, who was visibly upset at having to recount the tragic event.

Professor Coltrane spoke up. 'Sir Richard, have you placed a time by which we must decide who should be the next Laird, or the Lady?'

Fitzroy glanced over at us. 'I believe we cannot do so until the person responsible for the deaths of Sullivan and Brodie is discovered. And the attack on Mr Malone,' he added, then held up a hand as questions were called out.

'But as I have every faith in our detectives, I do not believe this will be long in coming. Until then I must again press upon you not to wander about alone, and to ensure the ladies are always escorted wherever they wish to go.'

'I'll look after you, Miss Susannah,' Malone instantly offered.

'As will I,' Professor Coltrane said.

She smiled sweetly at them in turn.

'Molly?' Lars turned to her. 'If I am allowed?'

She beamed, her whole face lighting up. 'Oh, Lars that is just dandy!'

Daniel shifted in his seat, disappointment clear on his face.

'Well?' Belinda turned to him.

'I…*ahem*. May I be your escort, please, Belinda?' he asked politely.

'Yes…but then again you might be the maniac attacking everyone.' She eyed him.

'But I'm not,' he stammered. 'And it would give me away if I attacked you, so I wouldn't anyway.'

She opened and closed her pouting lips as she considered that. 'Well I'll tell you now, I have a gun and I know how to use it.'

'Good, that's good,' he said, then tried a smile. 'I think you're rather nicer than you pretend actually.'

'Do you?' She seemed surprised by that. 'So where are you taking me?'

'I…um…would you like to go and see the cairn Professor Coltrane was talking about?'

'I guess,' she said.

'The cairn's across the bridge?' Daniel asked Coltrane.

'It is,' he replied. 'Take the track then look for the grassy path.'

'We will see you all later then,' he said and waited as Belinda rose to her feet, adjusted her dress, then walked ahead of him, her back very straight and her nose in the air.

'Lennox.' Swift held me back as they all trooped out.

'What?'

'This Collegium of British Genealogists, where is it?' he asked.

'Knightsbridge,' I replied. 'Run by a couple of old dears, according to Daniel Addison.'

'I'll call them,' he declared.

'Fine,' I said, and he went off.

Greggs sat blinking for a moment and then came to pick up my tray and tottered away with it, so I left too.

CHAPTER 16

I headed for the gunroom and found Fitzroy sitting at the worktable frowning at the shrivelled glove.

'Major Lennox.' He looked up as I entered. 'I am deeply disturbed by the events in this house.'

I pulled a chair from the table to sit opposite him. 'You wrote to Brodie, you had correspondence with him, could anyone else have known he was coming?'

'Yes, it is possible, and I imagine you must have already come to that conclusion.' There was something reassuring about him. The Scots accent, the rounded vowels picked up in London, a deep mature voice. The kind of chap you'd definitely want on your side in a courtroom battle.

'Was Brodie's claim strong enough to have made him the new Laird?'

'I cannot say, I have never seen his documents,' he replied.

'What about Sullivan?'

'Judging from some of the facts stated in his correspondence, I believe it's possible.'

'You said Sullivan was wealthy,' I reminded him, and I

was thinking of the photograph we'd found and how he looked like a labourer. 'Did he inherit money?'

'No, he was in construction. A builder, he was apparently quite sharp. He grew his business and made his own money, or that is what he informed me of when he wrote to me.'

'Right. And Malone, does he have money and a valid claim to the title?'

'I doubt he has money.' He frowned. 'And despite his bravado, I do not believe he has any proof of lineage. There is also the question of legitimacy. One cannot accept any lineage that includes illegitimacy along it. Personally I'd be surprised if he had a clean line; indeed, I would not be surprised to hear if he weren't some sort of felon.'

Neither would I, though I didn't say so. 'Concerning a "clean line" – you heard Susannah, her son is illegitimate. Would he be able to inherit?'

He looked away. 'Probably not.'

'So, who now has the best claim?' I asked.

'Daniel Addison…' He paused. 'But I made enquiries after the death of his father. There's a lot of ambiguity there.'

'Which the others now know about.'

'Indeed,' he replied gravely. 'And Professor Coltrane has explained the unfortunate experience in his past too. I have collected all the dowry coins, as I pledged to do, and have placed them in the castle safe-box… Major Lennox, I must admit that this situation is testing my resolve. I truly think we should allow the claimants to leave. Another death would be too appalling.'

'It is not a decision for us, it is a matter for Scotland Yard, and I doubt they would agree.'

He looked upset at that, his eyes momentarily closing. 'Do you have any idea who is behind it?'

'No,' I replied, then felt sympathy for him and added, 'Not yet.'

Swift came in with Greggs on his heels, and my dog. Foggy *woofed* a greeting then lay down to roll over onto my feet.

'Sir Richard,' Swift said and came to sit with us.

'Sir.' Greggs bowed in greeting then took a seat by the fire but within earshot.

'Sir Richard has collected all the dowry coins,' I said then let Fitzroy give them the details, and explain all he'd just told me.

'Have any of the heirs ever visited Castle McFee in the past?' Swift asked him a question we should have raised earlier.

'Not to my knowledge,' Fitzroy replied. 'Daniel Addison's father declared he would come, and I informed him very firmly that he must not.'

'Presumably McDuff or the villagers would know if anyone had attempted a visit,' I said.

'Yes, naturally,' Fitzroy agreed.

'You must know this castle and the estate quite well,' Swift said.

'I do. My father was a very close friend of the Laird's. I often stayed here with my parents as a child.'

'Why are there wedding clothes in the tower?' I asked him.

Swift looked up sharply at that. This was something else I hadn't quite found time to mention. 'What?'

I explained as succinctly as I could.

'Strange…' Swift turned to Fitzroy. 'Why are they there?'

'It is an…' He struggled for the word. 'An eccentricity of Lady Peggie's,' Fitzroy said, then sighed. 'I believe it is better I tell you the tale, rather than her. The Laird and Lady Peggie had a daughter, Fiona. It was a difficult birth and Lady Peggie very nearly lost her life, as did the child. Fiona was…' He hesitated. 'Not quite as developed as she should have been. Forgive me,' he spread his hands. 'I have never wed and so do not have direct experience of raising children. Fiona grew physically as she should, but her wits did not. She was slow to learn and very naive. She was given to terrible tantrums when frustrated, and through these tantrums she ruled her poor mother.' He shook his head. 'Lady Peggie was devoted to her regardless, although the Laird was less tolerant…' He paused a moment then continued. 'There was a boy from the neighbouring village whom Fiona would play with, and she grew very fond of him. She remained fond of him as she reached her majority, at which point she declared she would wed him. He was not enamoured of her, but he saw the opportunity that marrying the Laird's daughter would present. His name was Callum. He agreed to marry Fiona and the date was set for early spring. This was almost thirty years ago now,' he added. 'Fiona was never in good health. She would become overexcited, which quickly brought on fatigue. However, she was determined to make all the clothes herself – she was particularly adept at dressmaking. It was her only talent and her mother had always supported her enthusiasm for it. Once the wedding was agreed, Fiona and Lady Peggie purchased the fabrics for themselves and for Callum and his parents. Callum's family were poor and would have barely been able to provide suitable outfits. Fiona worked endlessly, cutting, sewing and tailoring the cloth. She enjoyed it, but she would work into the night and often forget to maintain her fire, or eat her meals, even though they were left for her. She would often fall asleep over her work. Her mother tried to intervene and help, but there were times Fiona grew frustrated and demanded she be left alone.' His eyes focused into the distance. 'Some days before the wedding, Fiona caught a bad cold, which turned into a cough and settled in her lungs. She was feverish, the doctor was called, but the illness overcame her very quickly. She died of pneumonia the following week.'

We remained suitably silent; the only sound came from the scratching of Greggs' pen and the clock on the mantelpiece.

'The young man, Callum,' I asked. 'What became of him?'

'He married another girl some months later and moved south with her to Cumbria. They are still there,' Fitzroy said. 'I should mention that you have met Callum's father. He is the railwayman, Jock McDuff.'

'Really?' That made me sit up.

'As I said, Callum was a local boy,' Fitzroy replied.

'I didn't see Fiona's name on the family tree,' Swift said.

Fitzroy glanced up. 'No, the Laird would not allow it.'

'Why?' I demanded.

'The Laird said Fiona was a simpleton, and unless she bred an heir, could not be added.' Fitzroy spoke heavily. 'He was a harsh man, and Lady Peggie argued with him, as did my own father, but the Laird was the ruler of his own domain. His word was final.'

'What was Lady Peggie's life like here?' I asked quietly, angry at the treatment of the girl, and her mother.

'She was expected to work,' Fitzroy replied. 'There was neither money nor adequate staff, and the Laird handled his resources carefully. You should not judge him on this, he had no choice in the matter. Lady Peggie was from a minor line of nobility and came without a dowry. The Laird was quite a few years older than she, he was titled and head of a once powerful family with a long lineage. It was considered a good enough marriage and Peggie had no other options, as far as I am aware.' Fitzroy shook his head. 'Fortunately times have changed over the last fifty years, although too late for her. Now if you will excuse me. I will take some time before we gather for drinks and dinner.' He nodded to us all and went off.

'Sir!' Greggs said once the door had closed on Fitzroy. 'It could be the railwayman. He would have been ideally placed to murder Mr Brodie.'

'Why on earth would he?' I asked.

Greggs didn't have an answer for that, but it didn't stop him trying. 'From spite, because his son missed an opportunity to become Laird, or to stop strangers taking the castle. Perhaps the villagers want to thwart outcomers from taking control, and McDuff is their modus operandi.'

'A modus operandi is the method killers use, not the killer,' I said. 'And it still doesn't make sense, because he couldn't have killed Sullivan or attacked Malone.'

He *harrumphed* at that.

'Exactly where is this wedding party?' Swift asked. 'It sounds almost deranged.'

I told them both in more detail about how Daniel Addison had shown them to me, and I described the clothes.

'A tragic tale,' Greggs declared. He'd come to sit at the table with us. 'Almost Dickensian.'

'I agree,' I said. 'But it paints Lady Peggie in an unexpected light. She'd seemed quite upright and stable to me.'

'The loss of a child, Lennox,' Swift said and shook his head. 'It doesn't bear thinking about.'

We remained silent for moments.

'Was there anything useful in the statements?' I asked.

'No. We already know they'd all gone to bed when Sullivan was killed. Brodie would have arrived…' He paused to check his watch. 'Around now. It's always a quiet hour before drinks. They said they were all in their rooms, or using the bathrooms. Some were reading. They'd all just had tea together and wanted a break. It's been quite intense.' Swift sighed. 'Malone was attacked after lunch. They repeated the stories they'd already told us. I sometimes wonder why we take statements. Nobody ever admits to anything incriminating.'

'Well why do you?' I asked.

'Because it's procedure,' he replied. 'It's really of more use when there are innocent bystanders and they describe what they saw at the scene of crime or an accident.'

'Could a lady be the culprit, sir?' Greggs asked. 'Including the attack on Mr Malone?'

'Possibly,' Swift replied. 'And there may be two working together.'

'They'd be taking quite a chance walking through the men's quarters,' I said. 'It would be remarked on.'

'Particularly if they were carrying a shillelagh,' Swift said, then grinned.

I glanced over to it; we'd left it on the window sill, the fingerprint powder still visible. 'It's not even the length of my arm, it could easily be hidden under a coat, or jacket.'

'If there were two heirs working together, as has already been discussed,' Greggs said ponderously, 'it may indicate a man and woman.'

'Fine,' I said. 'We haven't questioned Mrs Craggie about the knife yet.'

'Should I go and ask the lady to come to the incident room, sir?' He had picked up the hint.

'Yes, please,' I replied.

He went off and I turned to Swift. 'Did you call the old ladies in Knightsbridge?'

'The Collegium of British Genealogists.' He grinned. 'Talk about eccentric. Yes I did, they vaguely recalled the search for the McFee line. They couldn't find any files or correspondence. I had the impression they're in their dotage. They promised to look through their archives, but

I called Billings after that and he agreed to send a sergeant down there to help them along.' He raised a brow. 'I didn't think we'd get anything from them otherwise. And Billings has sent a man to Brodie's flat in Stirling. We should receive a report on that later today, or tomorrow… What did Daniel tell you about his father's death?'

I gave him the full facts that Daniel had related to me up in the tower.

He thought about it. 'A harsh and traumatic childhood may have brutalised him. He could be capable of the murders here. It's possible his father had acquired information on the castle and the McFee's.'

'He said his mother burned most of the papers,' I added.

'We don't know that is true though, do we?'

'Sirs,' Greggs announced as he opened the door and stood aside. 'Mrs Craggie has refused to be interviewed. She is preparing dinner.'

Swift looked up, then yawned. 'Might be a good time to take a break, and I'd like to speak to Florence.'

'Fine,' I said. 'I'll see you for drinks in the drawing room.'

CHAPTER 17

Drinks were a jolly affair, given the events of the day. It was helped by Daniel Addison's offer to open a couple of bottles of the superlative Chateau Margaux he'd brought with him.

'Now this is really quite excellent, young man.' Professor Coltrane raised a glass to him.

'It's the Pavillon Blanc du Château Margaux from 1912,' Daniel replied. 'It's still a little fresh, but 1912 was an excellent year.'

We were gathered in the drawing room for the usual pre-prandial noggins. Greggs wasn't there so I'd grabbed a glass of the white wine from the tray of glasses Daniel had arranged a little way from the roaring fire.

'We have some first-class wines in California,' Belinda said, then sipped hers. 'But I admit this is almost on a par.'

'Damned by faint praise,' Susannah said with a cat's smile.

Daniel smiled back and raised his glass.

'I am terribly impressed,' Molly called over to him. She'd been sitting stroking Tubbs on a sofa. 'Even I can tell this is great quality.'

'Yeah and I'll bet it cost a packet,' Malone added. He was slouched in an armchair, the ridiculous turban replaced by a large plaster fixed over the wound. I could see it was still swollen.

'I would be interested to hear more about your whisky distillery, Inspector,' Daniel said to Swift.

This began a long lecture from Swift in unnecessarily pedantic detail, although Daniel, Lars, Fitzroy, and Professor Coltrane all took a great interest in it.

I went to chat to Molly, who was still cuddling my cat on her lap.

She beamed up at me as I sat down. 'Micky Malone says he's going to turn the castle into a refuge for abandoned animals. He's sure got my vote!'

'Really?' I said. 'You wouldn't want the place for yourself?'

'Oh, maybe.' Her smile dropped away into seriousness. 'I didn't think it would be so big, or so run-down.' She lowered her voice as she said that, glancing over at Lady Peggie, who was talking to Susannah nearest the fire.

'You have family don't you?' I sipped the exquisite wine, hoping that Daniel had more squirrelled away.

'Sure, I have my mom. She'd love it, and I have two younger half brothers, but...' She paused. She raised her wine glass and took a sip. 'It would be amazing fun having our own real castle to live in, but it's even more remote than our ranch in Calgary.' She plucked with her free hand at the long woollen skirt she'd changed into for dinner; it was russet with flecks of purple and dark orange and suited her auburn colouring. The cardigan she wore over a white high-necked lace blouse was the same hue. She looked exceedingly pretty, and very proper in a country kind of way. 'We're only three miles out of the town and I've got a truck now, so it doesn't take long, not like when we only had the buggy.'

'I imagine it would be very expensive to repair the castle too,' I prompted her.

'Yes, that was my thinking. My pa left me a ton of money, and we've got cattle and horses… We have a great guy managing it all. I mean, it's not that I'd leave home and come live here all the time. That wasn't what I thought. I talked it over with my family and we just reckoned on vacations, but it needs more than that. It needs dedication. Like your friend, the inspector, does with his castle.'

We both looked over at him: he was expounding on types of casks and the aging process, and all things in between.

'What if you were to wed, and your husband wanted to run it with you?'

'And what do you mean by that, Major Lennox?' She raised auburn brows at me, a hint of mischief in her blue-grey eyes.

Lars hadn't looked over at her once, but I'd noticed she'd glanced at him a couple of times, and she did so again now.

'Lars wants to breed cows here,' I said. 'You said you have a ranch and cattle, you must know something about them.'

'Oh, I do.' She laughed. 'Calgary is known for cattle. We have the stampede every July. It's a celebration of our lives out there; rodeos, wagon racing, steer wrestling, wild bronc riding. Just all-round country living – and a huge pancake breakfast, that's my favourite.' She looked me in the eye. 'Yes, I know all about cattle, horses, and ranch life. So maybe Lars and me could make a match, if he's of a mind, but I've only just met him, so it's not something I'm planning on right now.'

'Which brings us back to the question,' I said, then emptied my glass.

'If I'd like to become Lady of the Clan?' she replied, then stopped to think about it. 'I guess I would…I don't know… When I look around, and see the reality of what it would take. It's a big job and a bit overwhelming. I think it might be too much for me.'

That surprised me, and gave me pause. I hadn't imagined her as a suspect, there was something too honest about her, although I know Swift would warn me to keep an open mind. 'So you have no motive for murder?'

Her eyes flew wide at that. 'You bet I don't, and I just don't get it.' She leaned forward to speak more quietly. 'Is this place really worth killing for?'

'Plenty of people fought over it in the past,' I said, thinking of the cairn on the hillside.

'That's because it was their home,' she replied. 'You have to fight for that because without it, you've got nothing. No shelter, no way to grow food, nowhere to keep live-stock. Without a home and land you and your kin would be dead pretty quickly. We're not living as pioneers in Canada any more, but we still have our feet firmly in the soil.' She finished her glass too, then held it up with a big smile at Daniel. He must have been aware of her because he instantly excused himself and came over with the bottle.

'Top-up?' he asked, then filled her glass before turning to me. 'Major Lennox?'

'Yes, please.' I raised my own glass and he dribbled the remains into it.

'Oh, I am sorry,' he said as the wine barely rose an inch. 'I could fetch some more–' he offered, then stopped. Greggs had arrived and now announced in portentous tones,

'Ladies and gentlemen, dinner is served.'

I drank the dregs in one mouthful and put my glass down. I was about to offer my arm to Molly, but Daniel beat me to it.

'I can carry the cat, if you like?' he told her.

'No, he's coming with me.' She held Tubbs with one arm and slipped her hand under Daniel's elbow. She realised Lars had risen to his feet and was now watching her. She gave him a big smile, and walked off with Daniel and Tubbs.

Belinda raised her chin defiantly and waited as the big Dane came over to her. 'Are you going to escort me?' she demanded.

'No,' he replied. 'Unless you act as a lady, I will not act as a gentleman.'

She flushed, her chin held a little higher as though trying to look down her nose at him. That failed of course as he was head and shoulders taller than she was. She eyed him, then dropped the attempt at imperiousness. 'Please would you escort me?' she said, a faint crack in her voice.

'I will,' Lars replied, then held out an arm. 'Come,' he said, and she slipped her hand through his, her head now tilted up to gaze at him, and they went out.

The professor had arranged to escort Lady Peggie, and Fitzroy had Susannah on his arm. Malone ambled behind them, and Swift brought up the rear. He was grinning.

'What's so amusing?' I asked him.

He frowned. 'Nothing, I was just explaining to them about the whisky process, that's all.'

'Molly doesn't think she wants to be The Lady of the Clan,' I told him as we followed the procession down to the dining room.

He eyed me sideways. 'Lennox, you must not accept everything people tell you as the truth.'

'I wasn't,' I countered. 'I was simply informing you. Did you find anything out?'

'I…well, we were discussing distillation and madeira versus sherry casks for maturation.'

'Diligence, Swift, and process, and procedure,' I intoned.

'Yes, very amusing, Lennox.'

I grinned.

I was seated next to Lady Peggie for some reason, and Swift was stuck between Belinda and Malone, which served him right.

It was venison stew tonight, with dumplings.

'There must be some interesting stories from the clan history,' I said by way of conversation to Lady Peggie.

'There are,' she replied.

I speared a dumpling then sliced it in half. I was pretty

hopeless at small talk; I was wary of mentioning the wedding party and the tragedy attached to it, so had tried fishing for a topic to set her off. 'Battles, and all that. I visited the cairn today.'

'Yes.' She was picking at her food. 'Laird Fergus started it after he and his men slaughtered the McDuffs to the last man in 1368.'

The dumplings were pretty solid and I was in danger of glueing my teeth together. I took a swig of red wine before answering. 'The chap with the pony and trap is McDuff.'

'The McDuff clan beyond the mountains, not from the glen,' she replied.

'Right.' I ate some more stew, which was swimming in a rich sauce and smelled of brandy and spices. It was excellent, despite the chewy dumplings.

'Fergus kept the head, of course. It was a terrible insult but there were none remaining to object,' she said then ripped a bread roll apart to dunk in the remains of her stew.

'What head?' I asked.

'The head of the Laird McDuff,' she replied.

That made me sit up.

'An actual head?' Malone asked. 'Like a real head?'

'Yes,' Lady Peggie replied. 'It was hung by the hair from a ham hook in the chimney for six months.' She waved a hand in the direction of the crackling fire blazing in the hearth.

Silence followed as we all stared at the ornate clan arms carved and painted above the mantel shelf.

'What did they do with it once it was dried?' Professor Coltrane asked.

'Placed him behind the shield hewn in the stone,' Lady Peggie replied without any emotion. 'There are two eye holes bored into it so he could watch the clan celebrate his defeat every year, and all that he was missing in this life.'

'Is he still there?' Belinda said with horror in her voice.

'Of course,' Lady Peggie replied.

Malone was the first on his feet and shoved his chair aside to go and peer on tiptoe at the carving. 'There are holes…' He reached up and tried to push a pudgy finger into one of them.

'Please refrain from disturbing him, Mr Malone. It is better not to wake the dead,' Lady Peggie told him.

Daniel had hesitantly pushed his chair back to join Malone.

'Sit down, please,' Fitzroy ordered.

Daniel shuffled his chair back into place and Malone reluctantly came away.

'Are there ghosts in the castle?' Molly asked.

Lady Peggie gave a dry laugh. 'In every corner, crevice, and corridor, but they are generally harmless.'

Greggs came in, pushing the trolley. The room was deathly quiet so he called out, 'Ladies and gentlemen, dessert is served.'

'Oh, thank goodness,' Susannah said. 'What is it, my dear?'

'Individual baked apple, stuffed with plums, cinnamon, nuts and molasses. Each is topped with double cream and honey sauce, madam,' Greggs told her with a happy grin. He placed the first plate in front of Lady Peggie; she thanked him, and picked up her fork.

'You could stick a couple of plums on the apple and call it McDuff's nut,' Malone said and laughed as everyone realised the baked apple, slightly shrivelled and browned, could actually resemble a head.

'Quiet, Malone,' Lars told him. 'You upset the ladies.'

We all ate in silence, apart from Belinda who gave her apple to Malone. She shouldn't have been so fastidious because it was exceedingly tasty, and the honey sauce was excellent.

'Now please remember to take a chamber candlestick to bed with you tonight,' Lady Peggie reminded us as we filed back into the drawing room for a bedtime brandy. 'Craggie will douse the candles early as we are running rather short.'

Murmurs of acknowledgement followed and she then bid us goodnight. Fitzroy also decided he was in need of an early bed. I had the impression he wanted a break from the fractious gathering of heirs.

'Do you think there really is a skull in the fireplace?' Daniel was the first to ask as we all sat on the sofas and chairs grouped in front of the fire.

'Possibly,' Swift said. 'We found a walled up skeleton at Braeburn.'

I remembered that and I let him tell the tale of what happened. Despite the stories of ghosts and evil deeds it was an amiable evening spent chatting and laughing as everyone drank a little too much and relaxed. Plus none of us were too keen to leave the warm fug built up in the room.

'I brought a recording with me,' Daniel said. 'Shall I play it? I left it by the gramophone.'

'Oh, what a swell idea,' Susannah said. 'We have musical evenings back home and everyone brings a phonograph record for us to listen to. And sometimes we dance!' She laughed.

'I enjoy to dance,' Lars said. 'We have the landsbybal, I like the Schottische best.'

'I'm not sure if my recording is for dancing, it's an old folk ballad sung by Juliette Fairhurst.' Daniel went to set up the gramophone. 'She has a wonderful voice, she's very popular in England.'

'I'll help,' Molly said. 'I saw some highland recordings on the shelf next to it, we can play those too.'

'Right.' Daniel leaned over the player, his nose almost touching the conical horn as he lined up the needle. 'The song is called 'Oh, Sally My Dear'.'

We listened to the lilting tune. It was quite beautiful, and plaintive, although it had that typical earthy pragmatism of so many folk songs. I decided to remember Juliette Fairhurst's name. Greggs could order a copy for Persi; it might keep her in one place for a while as she listened to it.

'That was quite marvellous,' Professor Coltrane murmured from the deep cushioned chair he was slowly sinking into.

'There's a recording of 'The Bonnie Lass o' Fyvie', here.' Molly had taken a phonograph from its sleeve and held it up. 'We might be able to dance to that.'

And we did, and to 'The Skye Boat Song' and a few others we found, and we had a jolly good time of it before the fire burned down and we decided we'd better all head for our beds. The hall was in darkness but we all pulled out our torches. The ladies had grouped themselves closely together and set off along their passageway as we men turned into ours. We hadn't even reached the corner of the corridor before we heard the screams. Lars, Daniel, Swift and I raced back to the landing and continued to where they were standing huddled together staring about.

'I felt something! It brushed my head,' Belinda shouted. She was ducking down, her hands raised.

'What is it?' Lars demanded.

'There's something here,' Molly called, fear in her voice.

'Please shine your light,' Susannah cried out. 'We can't see.' She was bending down, scrabbling for the torch they'd dropped. It was lying on the floor near her feet.

'It's a ghost, I swear it's a ghost.' There was a note of hysteria in Belinda's voice.

We went to stand with them, shining our torch beams about.

Swift picked the one up off the floor and pressed it in Susannah's hand.

'Agh,' Malone shouted out. He and Greggs had lumbered up in the rear. 'It's flying round me. Get it off.' He flailed his hands out. 'What is it?'

'I think it's a bat,' I said.

'Ah, yes,' Swift agreed.

We carried on aiming our torches about but, needless to say, we couldn't see or hear a bat in the dark.

'Is that all. A little bat?' Lars said. 'You are scared by a bat?'

'I didn't know what it was,' Belinda said, then put a hand over her mouth to stifle a sob.

'Can I help?' Daniel offered, and put his hands out. She stepped forward and suddenly buried her face in his shoulder. He put his arms around her and held her to him.

That was a bit of a surprise and we all gazed at them for a moment. Then Foggy spotted the bat, and started barking, making everyone jump. He raced off along the corridor back towards the landing, presumably in pursuit.

'Come ladies, I see you to bed,' Lars decided while I shouted at Foggy to be quiet.

'And I.' Professor Coltrane gently took Susannah's hand.

Swift and I left them to it. Greggs came with us, as did Malone.

'You sure it was a bat?' Malone said, looking distinctly unhappy.

'Yes, you can adopt it,' I replied.

'We have quite a few bats at home,' Greggs remarked.

'I know,' I replied.

'We have a few hundred,' Swift said.

'So you got your own castle.' Malone looked at him. 'And it's full of bats?'

'No, only in the attics,' Swift replied as we walked back to the landing.

'I might be going off castles,' Malone said, shoving his hands into his pockets.

'May I ask, sir,' Greggs said. 'What were you referring to when you said two plums could be added to the apples for eyes?'

Malone told him. 'And it's probably just bits of skin and bones now.'

'A shrivelled head?' Greggs gasped, his chins wobbling. 'In the dining room?'

'It's behind the chimney breast,' Swift said.

'But in the dining room, sir.' Greggs was horrified. 'It is most unhygienic.'

'Better than mounting it on the wall,' I said.

CHAPTER 18

Morning dawned without cries of murder or any more screams in the night. It was quite refreshing actually. Swift had been up first and lit the fire. I lay in bed, thinking to leave him to it, although Fogg and Tubbs had their own agendas and sat on my chest until I gave in and got up. I put Tubbs under my arm, and Foggy scooted down to the hall and straight to the front door. I wandered out after them.

Dew lay on the grass, a cockerel crowed somewhere in the distance, and the fins of fat trout broke the surface of the broadwater. I'd seen fishing rods in the gunroom; I vowed to go and fetch one because it was the perfect day for casting a fly.

'Do you think his suitcase might wash up?' Swift came up to lean on the bridge beside me. He was already dressed, spruce in his city suit and tie, complete with trench coat. I was still in dressing gown and pyjamas.

'You mean Brodie's suitcase?'

'Yes, of course.'

'I'd put money on it being in the wyrms-hole.'

'I thought the same. You should have brought a rod, Lennox. Look at the size of that trout.'

'I am looking,' I said.

'Shame the Laird's rods are in such a poor state,' he remarked.

'Are they?'

'Yes, I checked.'

'Damn.'

'We need to search the outhouses, see if there's any sign of a place where Brodie's body might have been left.'

'I think he was dumped in the water just after he was stabbed,' I said. 'And I'm not dressed yet.'

'You could get dressed.'

'Fine, I'll do that, but I'm not going anywhere until I've had breakfast,' I replied.

'Right, come on then.' He grinned. 'I'll just go and call Billings.'

Swift in a chirpy mood was bad enough, but on an empty stomach, he could be really annoying.

Some half an hour later we were comfortably ensconced in a small breakfast parlour at a round table set by a sun-filled window. Greggs brought us blood sausage, pork sausage, eggs, bacon, fried bread and more of the potato pancakes, then beetled off back to the kitchen. I felt decidedly better after such a sumptuous meal. Foggy seemed quite happy; we'd shared quite a lot of sausage with him, and Tubbs was dipping his paw into the cream jug – a bad habit he refused to give up.

I sat back in my chair. 'I'm going to telephone Persi.'

'I've already called Florence,' Swift replied, putting his napkin on the tablecloth and rising to his feet. 'You'd best be quick, they're going to the mainland to view the old cairn today. The weather at Braeburn has improved.'

'Persi is supposed to be resting.'

'Well you'd better tell her that,' he said. 'I'll see you in the incident room. We're interviewing everyone today, I told Greggs to bring them in one at a time.'

I left the little duo to help out with the next set of breakfasters, crossed the hall and aimed for the telephone room. I didn't get very far. Mrs Craggie stomped into the hall and stopped in front of me.

'Yer man said ye'll be wantin' t' speak t' me.' She folded her arms, legs set apart and looking decidedly belligerent.

I sighed. 'Right, could I—'

'An' I'm busy. Just done breakfast an' I've fires to tend.'

'Then please come this way.' I wafted a hand and led her under the stairs to the gunroom where I discovered a card pinned to the ancient oak panel. It read, *Incident Room,* in fine copperplate script.

Swift had beaten me to it. He glanced up as I opened the door. The lady bustled in, took a hard stare at the fire as though to satisfy herself that we were feeding it properly, then went to sit opposite Swift and banged on the table.

'So have ye found oot what's all this aboot then?' she demanded.

'No,' he replied as I sat down next to him. 'We were rather hoping you may be able to help.'

'Doin' what? I don't know nothin' about polis' work,'

she replied. There was a grey smear of ash on her apron and across one creased cheek. She clasped her reddened hands in her lap, her long skirt draped over knees and down to her sturdy ankles and black lace-up boots.

Greggs slipped in the door behind us and tiptoed to the chair by the fire to take up his position as notetaker. Then he cleared his throat and took out glasses, then his pen, then he blotted the nib.

'Ready?' I glanced over to ask him.

'Indeed, sir,' he replied as he fixed the pince-nez on the end of his nose.

Swift straightened his back and launched into police mode. 'Mrs Craggie, have you checked to see if a knife has gone missing from the kitchen?'

'Yes,' she replied.

'And?'

'No.'

'No?' I repeated, disbelief in my voice.

'Aye, I said no,' she retorted. 'Ye're asking because of the man in the water?'

'Yes,' Swift replied.

'Don't know nothing about him,' she replied.

'He was killed the day after all the other guests arrived,' I said. 'Who came into your kitchen that day?'

'What time?' she asked.

I thought back to what McDuff had told us. 'Before afternoon tea.'

'Milady came, as always.' The habitual frown creasing her forehead deepened. 'Craggie, Sir Richard, and Miss

210

Susannah – she likes to bake and we spoke for a wee while.'
She sniffed. 'A nice type, so she is. Then the young lass with
red hair come to say hello–'

'Molly,' I said, just to be clear.

'Aye, Miss Molly,' she said. 'Not the painted one, she's
too full of herself to talk to the likes o'me.'

'Any of the others?' Swift asked.

'The tall one, a real foreigner he is, but a well-built lad,'
she replied, obviously meaning Lars. 'The slicht one came
by that morning, he's English, not much meat on his bones,
and wet with it.'

'Mr Daniel Addison,' Greggs murmured to himself as
he wrote the names down.

'Why did they come into the kitchen?' I asked, watching her, her eyes darting at us in turn, defensive in every
gesture. I could see she resented the intrusion in the castle
and was hardly surprised by it.

'The lasses came because they was curious to ken the
kitchen. The thin lad wanted wood for his fire, so did the
big foreigner. Ach, I forgot, the loud 'un came in too, he
just wanted grub. I gave him a slice o' cake and sent him
away because I were growing fou o'the grue with all the
comin' in and oot.'

'Fou o' the grue?' I looked at Swift.

'Irritated,' he translated, then asked, 'Would any of them
have seen the knives?'

'It don't matter if they did,' she replied. 'Cos there's
none gone.'

'Where are they kept?' I asked.

'The big 'uns are in the rack by the meat block.'

'You must have a lot of knives, given the age of the castle,' Swift said. 'I live at Braeburn. There's almost too much cutlery to count.'

'I've told yer, and yer not listenin',' she said very clearly. 'It wasn't one of my knives used to stickit the dead man.'

'Right,' I said, thinking I'd better change tack. 'Did you see the one who was "stickit"?' I asked. 'Before he died, I mean.'

'When did he die?' she asked, which I thought an interesting response.

'Sometime after half past four on April the second,' Swift explained patiently.

'No, I didnae see no more ootlanders that day, only the ones here now. I was gettin' the meal ready and the place was stappit full by then.'

'What about McDuff, the railwayman? Did he come into the kitchen for any reason?' I asked her.

'No, not that day,' she replied. 'He would if he had provender, but there weren't none, and he were fair puggled and wanting his hearth, so he told me the day next I saw him.'

'Puggled?' I looked at Swift.

'Weary,' he replied. 'So you didn't see either McDuff or Brodie that day?'

'I said so, din't I,' she retorted, her eyes flashing in anger. 'And I'd answer a guid bit quicker if ye put yer questions to be makin' sense.'

'Madam.' Greggs paused in his writing. 'May I enquire if any of the guests were outside during the afternoon in question?'

She smiled at him, or I think she did because her wrinkles shifted from a scowl to something less severe. 'Now I couldn't tell ye one way or another, but I like the way ye asked me.' She turned to us. 'It were rainin' bad. D'ye ken?'

'Yes, thank you,' Swift replied.

'Now, is there anythin' else?' she demanded.

I couldn't think of anything. Well, I could but thought we'd taken enough of her time.

'That will be all for now,' Swift said. 'And we appreciate your help, Mrs Craggie.'

'May I escort you back to the kitchen, madam?' Greggs stood and offered.

'Och, ye're a braw gallant gent, so ye are Mr Greggs.' She gave a coy smile and held her hand out.

Greggs duly offered an arm and off they went.

'You know, we might just have to take him on,' Swift said as he watched them go.

'No we're not.'

'Why?'

'He's my butler, and we're having a baby. I need him.'

'For heaven's sake Lennox, it's only a baby.'

I looked at him. 'Swift—'

He laughed. 'Really Lennox, you take things far too seriously.'

'What!'

He just carried on blithely. 'The knife could have been taken from the kitchen and she probably wouldn't have noticed, or she doesn't want to admit to anything.'

I was still thinking about the baby, and his ridiculous remarks.

He scratched his chin. 'Or the murderer could have brought the knife…' he mused.

'Make your mind up, Swift.'

He glanced at me. 'We don't know and may never know.'

'Unless we catch the culprit.'

'Yes. Billings was tetchy when I spoke to him before breakfast. I didn't want to speak in front of Greggs, but we'll have to let the heirs go if we don't solve this soon, Lennox. We can't have another death.'

I nodded, and understood. 'We'll have to keep that quiet or it'll be an incentive for the killer to murder again.'

'Exactly,' he said.

'Did he say anything else?'

'No, he was waiting for the police from Stirling to call.'

A knock sounded on the door. Belinda entered without waiting for a response, a frown marred her smooth forehead, her pouting lips painted the same colour peach as her stylish silk dress.

'I want to talk to you.' She came and sat down opposite us, a look of distaste at the stained worktable between us. 'I have sent a telegram to my father. I want some other policemen brought in. I don't think we are safe.' She eyed us with a shrewd look. 'And I don't think you can make us stay much longer either.'

Swift turned policeman. He picked up the statements and shuffled through them until he came to hers. 'Did you know Douglas Brodie, or were you ever in contact with him?'

'Don't try questioning me. I'm not answerable to you.'

'I can have you arrested,' Swift said.

'Try.' She glared at him.

He dug into his inside pocket of his trench coat, which he'd donned, and pulled out a pair of handcuffs. It was an endless surprise what Swift kept in his pockets. 'I'll walk you to the station and you'll be wearing these.'

She blanched. 'My father will sue you.'

I laughed. It didn't help.

'And you,' she snapped at me.

'You have a choice Miss Guthrie,' Swift said. 'Cooperate, or be held in the local station.'

She sat and boiled for a moment, arms crossed, her plucked brows almost meeting in the middle, then she let out a squeal of anger. 'You rats, I don't see why I should put up with this.'

'You aren't winning any popularity contests here,' I spoke amiably. 'You need to understand that trying to railroad people is only going to create conflict. And your fight against everyone is a lonely battle that you are never going to win.'

She threw me a scowl from the corner of her eyes. 'But I'm right,' she muttered.

'If you are,' I replied, 'you're going about proving it in entirely the wrong way.'

She sniffed. 'Nobody ever listens to me. I've got four brothers and they're all younger than me, and they do anything they want. I'm just patted on the head and told I'm going to make somebody a good little wife one day. Go get your hair done and pretty up. That's what they say.' A tear of self-pity rolled down one cheek. 'This castle is ours, and I'm going to prove it.'

'Then start earning it,' Swift said. 'Lennox is right, you can't fight everyone. That's not leadership, and this clan needs leadership.' He dropped his voice. 'And we have to put a stop to whoever is killing your clan members, and we can't do that without cooperation.'

She dashed away the tear with the back of her hand, sniffed once more and straightened her back. 'Right, I'll stay here and help. Tell me what to do.'

'Answer the question,' I said.

She threw a sulky glance at me but nodded acquiescence. 'I was telling the truth, I've never heard of him.'

'Where were you after lunch yesterday afternoon?' Swift snapped out the question.

'I told you. I suppose you're trying to figure out who hit Malone, and I just don't know. I don't think it was a woman because he was in the men's quarters.'

'There could be two people working together.'

Her eyes rounded. 'Really?…that's despicable.' She thought about it then jerked her chin up. 'You don't think I might be one of them, do you? Because I'm not–'

'I'm sure you aren't.' Swift moved smoothly into police mode. I think he'd decided to play the friendly one. 'Did you see anyone taking notice of the umbrella stand in the hall, or find anyone somewhere unexpected?'

'No…' She paused, raising one manicured fingernail to her lips. 'Although I think the butler is really weird. I'm always finding him in strange places. Susannah and the professor are real tight and they do go poking around. They said they're fascinated by the history…and you heard what he said about the guy at the university. Maybe he's got the killer instinct.'

'You came over on the same ship as him,' I said.

'I didn't meet him, he wasn't in first-class,' she replied as though I were being tedious.

'We only have your word for that,' I sniped back. If Swift was playing the nice policeman, I suppose I was to be the unfriendly one.

She glared, then shrugged. 'I promise I didn't, and why would I?'

'You might be paying him,' I said, then realised that sounded ridiculous.

So did she and laughed. 'Seriously? A doddery old assassin? How much do you think he might charge me?'

Swift grinned.

'Well, it was a long shot,' I agreed then smiled too. 'You were the first to arrive here,' I stated.

'Yes, I was. Susannah came shortly afterwards.'

'Douglas Brodie was the last to come, it seems he never entered the castle,' I continued. 'Had he been in touch with your family, or anyone, to your knowledge?'

'He's the man you said was stabbed,' she said. 'I just…I didn't see him. Not at any time, and I've never heard the name until you said it. I don't get it.' She shook her head, her reactions seeming more natural than the spoiled little rich girl she'd been acting before. 'Who knew he was coming?'

Neither of us answered that; it was the question we wanted the answer to.

'Were you outside on the afternoon of April the second?' Swift asked.

'God, no,' she exclaimed. 'It was freezing and pouring with rain. It's so cold here, even when the sun comes out. What time did he get here?'

'Somewhere after half past four,' I replied.

'We'd just finished afternoon tea. They have it every day, you know. Tea and scones or cakes. Most of us go freshen up or have some quiet time afterwards. It's a strain, being with a bunch of strangers in a place like this. And there are dummies up in the old part of the castle. Susannah took me up there. They were dressed in old clothes and one was a bride. It gave me the creeps. And that story about the head in the dining room. Ugh.'

'Do you really want to win this?' I asked.

She looked at her long slim hands. 'I wanted to prove to my family I could do something – that I wasn't just some sort of ornament waiting to be handed to a husband.'

'Like Daniel Addison,' I suggested.

She stared, then laughed. 'Don't be ridiculous.'

'You practically fell into his arms last evening,' Swift reminded her.

'So?' She shrugged. 'I was upset, he was being nice.'

'Your family doesn't have a dowry coin...' I said, leaving her to answer.

'No, it was lost, or sold.' Her face fell, her pretty lips turning down. The shingles in her blonde hair had softened, it suited her better than the rigid style. 'Nobody knows where it went. It's kind of a shame. We should have one.'

'What does your mother think about your trip here?' Swift switched tack.

'She wasn't in favour.' A flash of defiance glinted in her eyes. 'She thinks I should be grateful for what we have and leave it at that.'

'Do you really think the people who live here, and the families in the village, deserve to have someone use their home as a plaything?' Swift said. 'Because that's what you've been suggesting.'

'Swift married into the Braeburn clan,' I told her. 'He's worked hard to integrate and add some worth to the place.'

'I know, Sir Richard told us who you were.' She looked away. 'I'm sorry I can't be much help, but you must catch this evil person quickly, or let us leave, because you have no right to put our lives in danger.' She stood up and went to the door. Swift jumped up to open it for her. 'And I promise I'll think about what you said,' she stated solemnly, then walked out, peach frock flowing with her hips.

'Do you think she'll see sense?' I asked Swift once he'd sat back down.

'Difficult to say. It could just be a new tactic once she realised belligerence doesn't work.'

'If the motive for the murders is to remove the heirs with the best claim, why wasn't she targeted?' I mused.

'Possibly because her claim isn't as strong as the others.'

'If she can't win the title and castle, perhaps she'll settle for a dowry coin,' I said.

He frowned at me. 'You think she might have killed for one?'

'No, not really,' I admitted. 'But at least it would be a trophy or some such to return home with.'

He nodded.

'Should I find another suspect, sir?' Greggs had put his pince-nez away and now stood up.

'I suppose so,' I said. 'We'd better get it over with.'

'It is an essential part of the procedure, sir,' Greggs reminded me in a serious tone, and then went off with an air of intent.

I sighed. He was turning into Swift.

CHAPTER 19

Ten minutes later, Susannah entered like a breath of fresh air. Foggy and Tubbs bounded in with her and made a dash for the hearthrug.

'They followed me down from the breakfast room. My they can eat!' She smiled. 'Now your divine butler said y'all want to talk to lil' old me?' She exaggerated her southern accent, then laughed.

Swift smiled briefly then resumed his stern policeman face. 'We would like to interview you regarding the two murders, and the attack that have taken place here.'

Her own smile instantly died. 'I'm sorry, I was wrong to be flippant. And I will answer any questions that need answering.' She'd dressed in a mid-calf wool crepe dress in deepest plum, the sleeves tapered to the wrist with turned velvet cuffs.

'Are you fearful?' I asked her. 'Whoever has killed the two men here is very dangerous.'

She glanced at me. 'I should be, shouldn't I.' She let out a sigh. 'I've been locking my bedroom door at night but I'm still having trouble believing it to be true…do you really think this person means to kill us all?'

Swift shifted uncomfortably in his seat. 'Providing you all remain in groups, and continue to lock your door, I'm sure you will be safe.'

'Now one thing you can be sure of, Inspector,' she tapped a finger on the table, 'is that you can't be sure of anything. Not unless you know who did it, and I have to assume you do not.'

'You are correct, we don't know,' he admitted. 'But I can't allow you all to leave. It will be impossible to catch the culprit if we do so.'

'I don't believe that either,' she challenged. 'Whenever you figure out who it was, you and the rest of the police force will go find them and arrest them. You don't need us all here, held hostage just for that.'

She certainly wasn't the type to hold back, and she had a point. I tried a diversion. 'Why didn't you bring your son with you?' I asked.

She turned her blue eyes to me. 'Because he's away with the Army. He always wanted to be a soldier, and he joined the Buffalo Soldiers; they don't care what colour he is.'

Swift nodded. I assumed he knew about this regiment. 'Is he willing to become Laird if you become the Lady of McFee?'

'I think he would be,' she replied warily. 'I'll admit, I'm more keen than he is right now, but that's because he's out living his life. Once he's seen the castle and the land, I just know he'll adore it.' The question of her son's lack of legitimacy must be a subject hanging over any discussion on the clan leadership.

'And presumably he would inherit it from you when the time came?' I said.

'He would, and all the money I have, which I'll tell you now is a great deal,' she replied. 'Not that I'm in the habit of sharing that information with all the world, but I know it will be an important consideration.'

'Did you inherit this money yourself?' Swift asked.

'I did, and I've made a lot more since. I invested in the railroads, and oil. I always thought transport and energy was what America needed to grow, and we'd want to keep right on growing. I was proved right on that,' she said, then narrowed her eyes as though inviting us to challenge her. 'Is there any reason you think a woman should not be able to handle money herself?'

'None at all,' I replied. 'My wife's much better with it than I am.'

She laughed at that. She was a lively soul, and gave the impression of enjoying life, and her adventure here in the castle, despite the murders.

'Did you meet Brodie?' Swift threw in.

'No, I did not,' she replied, once again becoming serious.

'Where were you around half past four or five o'clock the day he arrived?' Swift continued.

'You'll have to remind me which day that was,' she said.

'April the second,' I said.

'It rained, we had afternoon tea then split up. I don't recall anyone going out, nor coming in with wet clothes.'

'What did you think of Sullivan?' Swift spun the conversation around again.

Her head tipped slightly to one side. 'A puffed-up fool tooting his own horn. Why he thought he would be Laird I just don't know.'

'Presumably he had papers to prove his claim?' Swift said.

'He said he had, and he said he would show us the next morning,' she replied. 'Richard asked if he'd prefer to give them to him then and there and Sullivan refused. He said he didn't trust anyone, including him.'

'Fitzroy was aware of Sullivan's claim,' I said. 'He was no higher up the list, nor more likely to inherit, than anyone else.'

'But Brodie was,' Swift reminded me. 'And he would very probably have been declared the heir.'

'Unless someone had documents proving they had a better claim,' Susannah said.

'Which they didn't,' I replied.

'But no-one knew that for sure at the time, did they?' Susannah said.

Which had taken us around full circle.

'If you weren't chosen as the Lady of the Clan,' Swift asked, 'who would you support?'

'Professor Coltrane,' she said without hesitation.

'Why?' I asked.

'He has a level head on him,' she replied. 'And he has no children, or family, and we have become friends. We are agreed that he will pass the estate to my son, and until then, I will supply the financing required to build the place back to its glory.'

That gave us both a moment's pause.

'Are you going to marry the professor?' I asked her.

She laughed at that. 'Dear Major Lennox, I have never wed, and my courting days are long gone. I do not want a husband, and I doubt a husband would want me.'

I didn't believe that. She could make some older chap a very happy man, and a wealthy one, too. 'But your son is not legitimate.'

'As I am quite aware, Major.' She suddenly turned very serious indeed. 'I have spoken to Sir Richard about this. He said that if Robert Coltrane were to adopt my son, then it would be possible for him to inherit from me. This is part of our agreement.'

'Did you know Professor Coltrane before arriving here?' I asked.

'I did not,' she replied. I wondered whether to believe her.

'Could you explain in more detail what happened on the afternoon of April the second?' Swift returned to the topic.

'Well, there was Sullivan's accident to deal with that morning.' She eyed him with an intent look. 'After lunch, Lady Peggie had asked us all to join together later in the drawing room, I think it was just to help comfort us. It was a very fine afternoon tea, with three different kinds of cakes. I went down to the kitchen before that to take a look; I just adore baking. Mrs Craggie was very kind, and I helped prepare the scones. Molly came too, and she set the trays up.'

'What time did you all commence tea?' Swift was eyeing her closely. This was the sort of detail that caught his attention.

'It was three o'clock exactly. Craggie had a bell and rang it in the hall. We all went. No-one was late or laggardly.'

'And you all left the room, when?' Bright morning sunlight suddenly cut through the grubby windows throwing shadows across Swift's lean face, highlighting his hawk-like features.

'Just after four.'

'Did everyone leave the drawing room at the same time?' I asked.

'They did.' She nodded. 'Craggie came in and started clattering around with the trays and made it clear he wanted to tidy up. We girls all returned down our corridor together. Lady Peggie went to the kitchen, and the men took themselves off.'

'You and the professor have been exploring the castle,' I remarked.

'We have. It has been fascinating, and I just loved the story of the mummified head last evening.'

'Really?' I said. It was the sort of thing to fascinate my wife, but most women would have been horrified.

'Yes, why not? It's true to the past,' she said. 'Times were hard and so were the people. We are blessed to live in an age of plenty, and to live in peace with our neighbours. They weren't so fortunate back then.'

'Would you leave it there?' Swift asked.

'I'd give it a decent burial in the churchyard, myself, but it would have to be a joint decision with the clan.'

I thought that was a sensible idea. 'You've seen the wedding party,' I said.

'I have.' She nodded, her silver blonde hair catching the sunlight. 'We came across it on our exploration. Robert Coltrane has been making notes and maps of the place. We asked Sir Richard, and he told everyone the story. He said it was better we knew and avoid upsetting Lady Peggie through unintentional ignorance. I feel for the poor lady, although I think it's time that tragedy was also buried.'

I wondered how Lady Peggie would react to that, and all the other changes a new Laird or Lady would bring to the castle.

'Is there a servants' staircase leading to the men's quarters?' Swift asked.

'Oh my! Inspector, do you believe I've been making illicit trips down there in the night?' She held her hand to her chest, mischief dancing in her eyes.

Swift grinned. 'No, but we haven't had time to survey all the nooks and crannies yet.'

'Well, of course there are passages going there,' she replied. 'And to the ladies' chambers and probably to places we have not yet had opportunity to discover.'

A light knock sounded on the door and Greggs came in. 'Ah, I do apologise, sir, I was rather delayed. The professor was not in his room. Should I…?'

'Oh, I think we're done here.' Susannah rose elegantly to her feet. 'Perhaps you can escort me, dear Mr Greggs?'

He raised a brow at Swift.

'Fine,' he replied. 'And thank you for your help, Miss Susannah.'

She beamed at him then slipped her hand under Greggs'

arm. 'Lead on, my dear. I think I will gather my wits in my room and then the professor and I will continue our explorations.'

They went out, perfectly comfortable with each other. It never ceased to surprise me how easily Greggs could charm the fairer sex.

'I'm going outside, Swift,' I declared and stood up. 'Then I'm going to ring Persi.'

'I'll come with you. We should take a look at the kirk.'

We managed to cross the hall and out the front door without being held up by anyone. Foggy came with us. Tubbs declined to leave the fireside.

The sun was relatively warm as we made our way around the castle towards the graveyard. It was a haven of peace and tranquility. We threaded our way through short, sheep-cropped turf, avoiding the many mounds lacking grave-stones and pausing to read those that did. Actually not many of the inscriptions had survived the harsh highland weather, and only a few could be made out.

'Dolores McFee, aged two,' Swift said. 'Infant daughter of Laird Gordon McFee and Lady Emma. *Suffer the little children to come unto Me. For of such is the Kingdom of Heaven.*' His voice cracked as he read out the words. 'Poor little mite.'

I couldn't reply, I had a lump in my throat. Impending fatherhood was beginning to spark all sorts of fears in my mind. I wondered if everyone felt the same way? Did my father worry about me? Yes, of course he did. And the war years must have been hell for him.

'Come on, Lennox,' Swift said quietly.

Foggy had run ahead, a bundle of joy full of brainless exuberance. He barked at nothing in particular and ran towards the trees planted along the rear wall of the graveyard.

We entered the chill of the kirk, the door creaking loudly. Our footsteps echoed on stone flags, the smell of mould and damp, wax and something earthy pervaded the place. Light filtered in through narrow lancet windows—some unglazed and shuttered, others holding panels of leaded green glass, uneven and imperfect. Simple benches stood in rows, a hollowed basin for holy water cradled in a niche near the door, rough walls in pinkish sandstone, an altar, plain and unadorned at the end.

'No-one's been in here for a while,' Swift said, his voice lowered to an undertone.

'Yes,' I agreed. 'Possibly not since the Laird's funeral.' The stone flags were worn, and clear of mud or stains. When we stopped to turn around they clearly showed our damp footprints.

Swift stooped down, gazing at the thin layer of dust gathered under the benches. He took out his torch and shone the beam across the surface of the flags. 'He wasn't brought in here.'

'No, let's take a look at the outbuildings,' I said and headed for the door.

Foggy was sitting in the low porch, his ears down, eyes round with that worried look only a small spaniel can adopt.

'What?' I said to him, rather pointlessly, but he did attempt to wag his tail.

'Something's wrong.' Swift stated the obvious.

'Phezzie,' I said to the dog. He knew what that meant: go and find the bird, or rather whatever it was that had frightened him.

We followed as he walked tentatively around the side of the kirk, following a path trod into the grass. We'd been in the shadow of the squat building but came into the sunlight again when walking beyond it. A band of dense yew trees ran behind the church; we could hear the sound of sobbing coming from beyond them. We lengthened our stride as Foggy hung back.

'Lady Peggie?' Swift called out as we emerged from the yews.

She was over in the far corner of the graveyard, kneeling over a mound, her hands covered in soil, frantically scrabbling at the earth.

We broke into a run.

'Lady Peggie!' I called out. She didn't look up, didn't seem to hear us.

We reached her in moments, slightly breathless.

'Lady Peggie.' Swift knelt next to her. She was bent over the grave, still ripping out the soil with thin hands. 'What is the matter?' He reached a hand to grasp her wrist.

'The coins. There are coins…' she gasped, her voice convulsed by sobs. 'Why? Why are they here?'

I saw them then. The dowry coins, the gold glinting through the dirt sticking to them. She had gathered what she'd found on the skirt of her dark blue dress. I noticed the wording on the simple headstone: *Fiona Emily Beatrice McFee. Beloved daughter of Lady Peggie McFee.*

'This is your daughter's grave,' I said to her, trying to sound kind though I was shocked.

'Let us help you up.' Swift put a hand under her elbow. I took the other, and realised just how thin the woman actually was.

We managed to lift her to her feet, the coins falling from her lap as we did so. She bent over again, scrabbling to catch them. 'Why?' she cried again. 'She never had a dowry. Neville wouldn't allow it. My poor girl, my poor girl.' She sobbed.

I'd leaned down alongside her and helped pick up the scattered coins, then took them all from her shaking hands and held them in my own.

'How did you find them?' Swift asked her.

She took gasping breaths, leaning on him for support. 'The grass was pulled out, I saw the gold. I couldn't understand it. Then I…' She took another heaving breath. I found a clean handkerchief in my pocket and handed it to her. 'Thank you,' she sniffed.

'Did you dig into the soil?' Swift asked her.

She nodded and blew her nose, trying to regain control over her distress. 'Somebody put them there, didn't they?' she said. 'The person killing them all.'

A cold shiver ran down my spine when she said that.

'Do you know anything, Lady Peggie?' Swift asked quietly. 'You know the castle well. Do you have any idea who did this? Have you seen anything?'

'No, no.' She had the handkerchief gripped in one hand, her fingers now claw-like and filthy. 'It's Richard's fault. I never wanted them here.'

'Where had the coins been placed?' I asked her.

'In the library, there's an old safe box,' she said. 'Nobody saw us put them there, we made sure of it.'

'Somebody must have done,' Swift said.

'Yes, yes, of course,' she muttered.

'How many are there, Lennox?' Swift turned to me.

I counted them in my hands, thinking of the heirs who'd admitted they had one. Molly, Lars, Coltrane, Susannah, the one Malone 'found' in Sullivan's sporran and was then stolen, and one more. Brodie's? 'Six.'

His frown deepened; he must have gone through the names just as I did. 'Six?'

'Yes.'

He didn't respond for a moment. Then put a little pressure on Lady Peggie's arm. 'Come, I'll take you back to the castle.'

She hung her head. 'Through the kitchen door, if you would. I don't want to see any of the heirs ever again.'

CHAPTER 20

I waited as Swift led her back between the gravestones, then gazed again at the coins. Most of the soil had fallen from them and they gleamed in the palm of my hand. They were heavy. I turned them over; they chinked against each other as I thought about their history and the making of them. The excited brides and grooms, the proud parents, the value of the gold…then I dropped them carefully into the recess of my inside jacket pocket.

I knelt to delve in the soil covering the grave, to ensure there was nothing else in there–apart from poor Fiona McFee, six feet below me. There wasn't, so I shoved the soil back in place and pounded the turf that had been ripped out of the ground. Foggy came to watch me. He still seemed forlorn.

I'd told Swift I'd see him in the gunroom, but I had to check the outhouses first – we couldn't leave any stone unturned, although we'd barely had time to identify half the damned stones. I brushed my hands on my thick tweed jacket as I walked in the shadow of the castle, my little dog at my side.

Swift and I were both shocked at the turn of events. It was cruel, and strange. What did the killer hope to gain? Fear, and then an exodus from the castle, I answered my own question

The outbuildings were behind the tower house, which was hardly a surprise as it was the oldest section of the castle. They were mostly low and of simple build; local stone interlocked in the same manner the cairn had been. No mortar, just man's skill at placing them one with the other. They were clustered around a spacious cobbled yard, weeds and moss growing between the stones. The longest building contained stables, row upon row of partitioned stalls, iron hooks fixed into the walls to tether the horses. Cobwebs hung from beams, shrivelled weeds and small twigs covered the cobbled floors.

I entered the attached barn. A chicken was scratching at a mouldy bale of forgotten hay. Foggy *woofed* and it flew up onto a roof beam, cackling in fright. It cheered the dog up at least, and he stood below it wagging his tail.

There was an air of desolation about it all, and abandonment. A rotted carriage stood alone in a coach house. There were sheep sheds, store houses, even a blacksmith's workshop full of rusted tools. A massive hearth, an anvil, a pile of horseshoes stacked in a corner and a tin barrel full of twisted scrap metal.

I gazed at the sunlight trying to break through the window; the panes were almost opaque with a thick layer of dirt – and decided to give up. There was no indication Brodie had been here, alive or dead, or indeed that anyone had been here for decades and more. I went back outside to breathe in the clear fresh air, my eyes on the steep hill rising behind the castle walls, the spreading trees that had invaded the paddocks, and buzzards wheeling high in the cobalt blue sky.

Foggy trotted alongside me as I walked, hands in pockets, back round to the front of the castle. I noticed Molly leaning over the bridge staring at the water, and veered off to see what she was watching.

It was Lars, swimming easily across the broad width of the river. I'd no idea if he was wearing any clothes or not.

'Molly,' I greeted her.

'Oh, Major Lennox.' She turned to smile at me. 'It's alright, he kept his pants on. And he's not going near the dangerous narrows at the end. I made him promise.'

'Have you been out here long?'

'No, less than a half-hour,' she replied then turned back to watch the Dane power arm over arm towards us. 'The water's freezing.'

'Hey there, Lennox.' Lars pushed wet hair back from his face. 'It's soft water, just like home.'

'I'll take your word for it,' I said.

'You should try it. Good for the blood.' He trod water, looking up at me.

'If you find anything down there, please bring it to the gunroom.'

'Like gold, maybe?' He laughed, then rolled to swim down to the clear depths.

'I'll see you inside,' I said to Molly.

'Will do,' she replied gaily.

Daniel and Belinda were walking out of the front door as I approached, seemingly comfortable with each other.

'Belinda has agreed to come and explore with me,' Daniel told me as I drew closer to them.

'I thought I should get to know the place,' Belinda said and forced a smile.

I can't say she was relaxed, or any friendlier, but she was trying to be agreeable.

'We'll be back in time for lunch,' Daniel promised.

'Fine,' I said and entered the hall, shutting the door behind me. It closed with a reverberating bang.

Greggs was in the gunroom, or rather the incident room.

'Sir!' He greeted me. 'I have prepared a "persona card" for each suspect. It was an idea miladies and I discussed at Braeburn before our departure. We thought it may aid in the investigation.' He had been sitting at the worktable, pen, ink pot and blotting pad before him, and now stood up with a small stack of cards in his hand. I could see he was rather pleased with himself, and he simpered happily as he placed the cards one at a time on the table.

'Very good,' I said and went to join him. I could almost feel the presence of Persi and Florence as he laid out the cards in rows; it's just the sort of thing they'd have loved to do themselves.

'I have sketched simple portraits for each suspect and written their names below the image, sir.' He pointed to the nearest one. 'This is the card for Professor Coltrane. I do not know his age, but imagine him to be in his late sixties.'

The ink drawing was actually quite good; it showed a simplified version of Coltrane's lean face, a few wrinkles, the wiry brows and thin grey hair behind his ears. He was depicted with spectacles and a bow tie.

We both turned around as Swift came in behind us. 'She's gone to her room. Mrs Craggie is preparing a tray of sweet tea and biscuits.'

Greggs raised sparse brows.

'Lady Peggie was upset,' I told him without going into detail.

He was too preoccupied with his cards to ask questions. He explained what they were to Swift.

'Excellent idea, Greggs,' Swift commended him. 'Let's see them.'

Greggs wafted a hand over the display neatly spread out on the table and explained in great detail.

'You have hidden talents,' Swift said as he took a closer look at the drawings.

'What does this mean?' I put a finger on a row of eight stars under Coltrane's face.

'This is the possibility that he may be the murderer, sir,' Greggs said.

I realised that he would never be the same after this. 'Eight stars out of how many?'

'Twelve, sir,' he replied.

'Is that how many suspects you have?' Swift asked, apparently taking this seriously, although I knew he loved these sorts of processes.

'It is, sir. Sir Richard Fitzroy has 12 stars and is my number one suspect. He alone knew Mr Brodie was coming.' He duly placed the card at the top of the rows.

'We can't be sure he was the only one,' I warned.

'Indeed, sir.' I could tell he wasn't listening. 'Then Lady Peggie, Mr Craggie, Mrs Craggie, Professor Coltrane, Miss Belinda, Mr Malone, Mr Daniel Addison, Mr Lars, Miss Molly and then Miss Susannah – who I do not consider a suspect at all, sir. Oh! And the Railwayman, McDuff, whom I have only just added.' As he hadn't seen McDuff, this picture was very simply of a round face and cap. Needless to say, it looked nothing like the wizened old man.

'Lady Peggie and the Craggies were together when Malone was attacked,' Swift pointed out.

'Ah, indeed, sir.' Greggs reached for their cards.

'Or so they say,' I said.

His hand hesitated. 'Should I leave them in place.'

'Yes,' Swift said.

'You need to move Addison further up the line,' I told him. 'He's a dark horse in all this.'

'Very well, sir.' He took Daniel's card and added more stars then placed him next in line after Lady Peggie. 'What of Professor Coltrane, sir?'

'Innocent,' I said. 'The American police would have investigated his colleague's death thoroughly.'

'But the professor may have pushed him from the window, sir, and unless there was a witness, he could very easily have got away with it.'

'No,' Swift countered. 'It is possible to set someone up to fall, but the man came into the room of his own accord and was presumably already very agitated. If he were in a fight, or attacked by Coltrane, there would be evidence. Ripped clothes, blood spattered inside the room or on the assailant's clothing. It would all indicate murder.'

'Unless he used subterfuge.' Greggs turned to me. 'As you have yourself encountered, sir,' he reminded me.

'Well, not directly,' I said, thinking back to a murder I'd been accused of, and hadn't done, obviously. 'But Brodie was murdered with a knife. Stabbing someone in the back is very different from shoving someone out of a window.'

Greggs frowned at the professor's card, but returned it to its place in the line-up. 'Could it simply have been an opportunist murder, sir?'

'No,' Swift replied. 'The knife had been stolen from the kitchen.'

'But Mrs Craggie denied this, sir.'

'She either didn't know or was covering up,' I said.

'Perhaps the killer simply intended to murder *someone*, sir? Without any particular care who it would be.' He wasn't giving up.

Swift considered that. 'You mean a random murder? If that were the case, the culprit would want to create enough fear to drive the heirs from the castle. They'd have made sure the murder was obvious. But that does not fit either Brodie's or Sullivan's murders.'

'Exactly,' I said. 'Sullivan's murder was designed to look like an accident.'

'But Mr Malone's was not, sir,' he said.

'Yes,' I said. 'I think at first the killer wanted to remove the competition without arousing suspicion. But having failed to do so, changed their mind and is now trying to frighten them away.'

'I agree,' Swift said.

I dug in my pocket to draw out the gold dowry coins and put them on the tabletop. 'I think the incident this morning was part of trying to frighten people.'

'Sir!' Greggs stared at them, wide-eyed. 'I thought the coins had been locked away.'

'So did we,' Swift said, then told him what happened.

'But that is appalling, sir.' Greggs was understandably upset. 'The poor lady.'

'You've put her as suspect number two,' I said.

'Well, yes, sir, but that was before I realised she had suffered this cruel atrocity.'

'She could have fabricated it all,' Swift said, then thought about it. 'Actually, no, I retract that. She couldn't have known we'd find her.'

'Would she have to have witnesses?' I countered. 'She could have run back to the castle and showed Fitzroy the coins.'

'Hm…' Swift raised his hand to his chin. 'It's too obvious, she had easy access to the coins.'

'As did Sir Richard Fitzroy,' Greggs said, pointing to the card of his suspect number one.

'Let's bring him in here,' Swift said.

'Wait a minute,' I countered. 'What motive would he have?'

'Perhaps he has had a secret longing to take the castle for himself,' Greggs offered.

'Why?' I said.

'I cannot know the desires of men,' he replied, rather pompously.

I refrained from rolling my eyes.

'I'll go and find him,' I decided.

'And I must telephone Billings,' Swift stated. 'He might have news from Stirling, or the old ladies at The Collegium of British Genealogists.'

'Really?' I grinned.

'No stone unturned, Lennox,' he replied. 'However unlikely.'

CHAPTER 21

I didn't get very far. As far as the top of the stairs to the landing, actually.

'Murder! Murder!' Craggie was calling out, his voice hoarse. 'Come, sir, come,' he called when he spotted me.

'What?'

'Murder, sir. Another one dead.' He looked dishevelled, his hair on end, butlering togs more crumpled than ever, his eyes rounded with shock. He didn't even have his umbrella with him.

'Where? Who?' I demanded.

'Come. Come,' he stuttered then lowered his voice to almost a whisper. 'Murder.' He turned and tottered ahead of me, along the landing, then stopped to pull at a panel set in the wall below the arch leading to the men's quarters. It revealed a set of simple stone steps leading upwards, and was obviously another servants' passage. I cursed myself for not having explored the place more thoroughly, even though we hadn't been here two full days yet.

'Who is it?' I demanded again.

I don't think he heard, or was in too much of a state to

listen. He climbed ahead of me, breathing heavily. The stairs were steep, the treads too shallow, as was often the case with servants' stairs. I guessed we were going to the old part of the castle, and was proved right when he pushed the rickety door open at the top.

'Blasphemy,' he muttered, then shambled quickly across the dusty floorboards towards the next set of steps and up again, heading to the room housing the wedding party.

He stopped on the threshold, then stepped aside, an arm raised, his shaking finger pointing at the figures arranged in the far corner. 'Murder.'

My eyes fell first on the 'bride'. A large knife had been driven through the veil resting on top of the neck of the dummy and into the canvas body. There was something horrifying about it, as was the blood spattered on the knife and the faded white fabric of the gown and veil.

The blood came from the body lying on the floor in front of the wedding party. I strode quickly over to kneel next to him. The knife had been used on him first. He'd been stabbed in the back, blood already congealing on his jacket and the slashed fabric around the wound site. The killer must have waited for him to die – I doubt it took very long judging by the amount of blood – then removed the knife and stabbed it into the bride's neck.

I knew who he was. I was tempted to turn him over, but decided against. I felt his neck, just in case there was any chance he might somehow not be dead. He was already cold. Death must have come early this morning. Dawn or shortly afterwards.

'Go and find Inspector Swift,' I told Craggie. 'Tell him to come immediately.'

'An abomination, an abomination,' Craggie muttered over and over. He was nodding, half bent over, his hands clasped together.

'Go, now,' I ordered him loudly.

It seemed to snap him out of the shock and he looked up at me with fearful eyes. 'Yes, the inspector, yes.' He shuffled off, heading back to the stairs.

I stood in silence for moments, feeling the sense of outrage, and loss, for the taking of an innocent life. Then I sent a prayer to the man upstairs, and hoped that the poor soul would rest in peace.

Then I decided to search for clues, although I thought the chance of finding anything was slim to none. *Damn it, why?* I thought as I stalked around the echoing room gazing at the floor. There was nothing, of course. I returned to the wedding party and the desecrated bride. It was a blacksmith-made knife, very probably from the kitchen, as I was sure the one that had killed Brodie was. Apart from the knife and blood there was nothing obvious to be seen. I sighed. The killer may not be very proficient; that had been obvious from the mistakes made in the murders of Sullivan and Brodie, but whoever it was, was utterly ruthless. And cruel. And clever. They must realise that this murder would be enough to release the heirs to scatter back to wherever they'd come from.

'Lennox?' Swift called out.

'In here,' I shouted and heard the sound of running feet.

'Craggie said murder,' Swift had called out then stopped when he saw me, then the body at my feet. 'Who is it?'

'Professor Coltrane,' I said gazing down at his mortal remains.

'Hell and damnation.' Swift stalked over and immediately knelt by the body. He too felt for a pulse in the neck, discovered there was none, then he examined the torn fabric in the jacket. He was diligent and systematic as always; he examined the professor's head, just in case he'd been hit first. He hadn't. Then he ran hands over his clothes, finding a pen, a handkerchief and not much else. 'He's already cold. He must have been killed around breakfast time, or shortly afterwards,' he said.

'Yes,' I agreed, having thought the same.

'Help me turn him over,' Swift said.

'Right.' I knelt down and we gently lifted him between us and placed him on his back.

His glasses were broken, his bow tie crushed and askew. Dust and grime were smeared on his shirt and waistcoat, the skin on his face showing light impressions of the floorboards he'd lain on. The small indignities of a life taken.

'His notebook,' I said as I plucked it from where it must have fallen beneath him.

'Looks like he was holding it when he was stabbed,' Swift said.

'Yes,' I agreed and began leafing through it as Swift examined the body for anything useful. 'He was making notes on everything, including the murders.'

'Was he now?' Swift looked up. 'Did he come to any conclusions?'

I carried on flicking through the pages. The pages were creased, but free of blood, which I was thankful for. 'There's an entry for last night…' I read down the page, the writing small and cramped but legible. 'He thought Fitzroy was behind it.'

'Really? I'm not so sure…' he said then sighed. 'Damn it, I liked Coltrane.'

'So did I.'

He was still kneeling beside the dead man and carefully lifted Coltrane's hands and crossed them over his chest. 'Poor chap. Susannah will be upset.'

'Something of an understatement, Swift.'

'I know,' he said then swore. 'We're not letting them get away with this, Lennox. Do you have any idea at all?'

I looked down at the crumpled face of Professor Coltrane. There was an indignity, a violation of a decent man, that made my blood boil. And the senseless attack on the 'bride', done for no reason other than pure spite. 'I think I do, Swift, but we need to gather them all together and hear what they have to say for themselves.'

'In the drawing room?'

'No, here, initially. I want them to see the evil in their midst. If anyone is hiding anything I want it brought into the open.'

'I wouldn't usually put innocent people through this,' he said. 'Susannah shouldn't witness it. Nor Lady Peggie.'

'Fine,' I said. 'But let's have the men. And Fitzroy can explain how the hell the coins were so easily accessed.'

'Do you want to stay here while I go and find them?'

'No, but I will,' I replied.

He went, striding across the floorboards, his feet pounding on the wood in echoing footsteps.

There was nowhere to sit down, so I stood with the dead man for a while longer, then went for a wander about. I found a narrow door in the next room and practically pulled it off its hinges to open it. I knew it was the round tower that I'd seen from outside, and it inevitably housed a winding staircase. Except it didn't wind, it went down a few steps and then plummeted into the dark. Something must have collapsed somewhere below, and without support the stairs had gone with it. I closed the door then had to bang it with my shoulder to push it back into place.

Who wanted this castle so badly? That was the question, and I was beginning to formulate an answer. There were gaps, and I might even be entirely wrong. I paced back to the desecrated wedding party, and Professor Coltrane. He wasn't stiff yet and his head had flopped to one side. We probably shouldn't let the others see him. I knew they'd never be able to wipe the memory from their minds for as long as they lived. Only the guilty deserved to witness this.

His arms suddenly flopped to his side with a bang as they hit the floor. I almost jumped out of my skin. I stared, aghast for a moment wondering if we'd missed some signs of life. I checked the carotid artery again for a pulse. He was stone cold, there was nothing, he simply wasn't stiff enough yet for them to hold in place. I debated what to do then gingerly crossed his arms back over his chest. Then stepped away from him.

Voices rose from the next room, reverberating up the stairs Craggie had brought me up, and Swift, obviously. I went to intercept them, my initial fury at the murder and desecration fading into sympathy and cold hard determination.

'Stay where you are,' I called out.

'Lennox?' Swift shouted a reply. 'I've brought the men.'

'Right,' I replied, then nodded. 'Fine.' I walked back to the corpse and the dummies, and waited to face them.

Their reactions were predictable. Swift was at the rear, herding them forward. Fitzroy led the way. He stopped the instant he saw the bloodied knife sticking out the top of the bride's neck, his hand flying to his mouth.

Lars was the first to spot the body. 'Min Gud!'

'Oh, noooo,' Malone almost wailed. 'Not the prof. He was a real gent. What the hell is this?'

'Is he really dead?' Daniel asked. None of them had advanced any further, until Fitzroy came tentatively closer. His eyes flicked between the body of Coltrane and the bloodied bride. 'Was he stabbed?'

'Yes, in the back,' I replied. 'The act of a coward.'

'This is a monstrosity,' he uttered, then glanced at me. 'Don't allow Lady Peggie to witness this.'

'We won't,' I replied.

'Why?' Lars asked, anger in his voice. 'Why do this?'

'I want you all to gather around me,' I told them.

'Major Lennox, for God's sake,' Daniel said. 'Is this necessary?'

'One of you did this,' I replied.

'Move,' Swift ordered.

Lars moved, so did Fitzroy. The other two shuffled behind. Malone had left the plaster off his scalp today, but still wore the kilt and his stolen highland finery. Lars was back in cream sweater and light pants. Fitzroy looked as though he was ready for a day at the office, bow tie perfectly positioned, although his silver hair was a little dishevelled. Daniel wore the same tailored grey suit as usual.

'When was this obscenity enacted?' Fitzroy demanded.

'Early this morning,' Swift replied, coming around them to stand by the other side of the corpse. 'What time did you all go to breakfast?'

'Eight,' Lars said. 'I was warm in bed and did not wish to stir.'

'We had breakfast together,' Fitzroy said. 'You weren't there and neither was...' His voice tailed off, and he nodded at Professor Coltrane, whose colour was already becoming mottled even in this short time.

'It was the dancing last night,' Malone said. 'We thought he was tired out. He was enjoying himself. We all were.'

'Did anyone ask after him?' I said.

'Yes, everyone, but we didn't want to disturb him,' Daniel replied. 'Susannah joked about him being worn out by the jitterbugging.'

'Did he have his notebook with him?' Fitzroy asked suddenly.

'No,' I lied. 'Why?'

'He spent a lot of time writing in it,' he replied. 'I thought it might be the cause of...' He took a breath. 'His death.'

'It wasn't.' Swift backed my lie.

'Who wants to leave the castle now?' I asked.

'I do,' Fitzroy was the first to respond.

'I do not,' Lars said. 'I want to stay until this is done.'

'And I,' Daniel echoed.

'I'm not going anywhere,' Malone said. 'The prof deserves justice.' He glared suddenly at us and demanded, 'You're not giving up, are you?'

'No,' Swift and I replied at the same time.

'D'you think he suffered?' Malone asked.

Swift glanced at Coltrane's corpse. 'I doubt it. Or not for long anyway.'

That didn't really make anyone feel any better. I took the dowry coins out of my pocket and spread them in my hand. 'We found these this morning.'

'What, where?' Fitzroy demanded. 'How could they have been taken from the safe?'

'That's a question you need to answer,' Swift replied coldly.

Fitzroy stared. 'Look, I don't know what you're hoping to achieve by this, Inspector, but it sounds as if you are trying to implicate me.'

We ignored that.

'Did anyone go outside before breakfast?' I asked.

They all said no, of course. I was outside myself early this morning, but I was equally aware we hadn't found all the doors leading in and out of the place. Then I thought of Coltrane's notebook. He'd been mapping the place, he could easily have shared his information with someone, not that we'd ever know now. I thought it curious the killer had left the notebook with the corpse; if it were me, I'd have burned it.

'Should we say a prayer?' Daniel offered. 'I'd like to, with permission.'

'Yes, of course,' Swift agreed.

Daniel began to recite an old prayer I hadn't heard in a long time. *'Almighty and merciful God, we commend into Thy hands Thy servant who has departed this life. Grant unto him rest eternal and let light perpetual shine upon them. May he go forth in peace, and may Thy holy angels lead him to his rest. Comfort those who mourn, and strengthen our hearts with the hope of resurrection, through Jesus Christ our Lord. Amen.'*

We all muttered *Amen* together, then Coltrane's hands slid from their clasp across his chest again, his arms once more falling to the floorboards with a bang.

'Argh!' They all jumped backwards, including Swift.

'It's nothing to be alarmed about.' I tried to sound reassuring. 'Rigor Mortis hasn't set in yet.'

'Check him for life, check him for life,' Fitzroy yelled, horror on his face, all semblance of assured self-control entirely gone.

'I'll do it.' Daniel leapt forward and knelt over him. We waited as he listened carefully for breathing and felt for a pulse. 'I think he's dead. I mean he is, I'm sure of it.'

'I help.' Lars also moved to lean over the body. 'I have medical knowledge.' He was a little longer in checking for signs of life, then shook his head. 'Nay, he is dead.'

'I'm sorry.' Swift was shaken. 'I crossed his hands over. It was a mark of respect. I should have left him as he was.'

I didn't say anything, but thought Professor Coltrane would have been rather amused by the incident. I let a moment pass before turning to Fitzroy.

'Sir Richard, come with us, we need to interview you.'

'But you must call an ambulance, and the police,' he said, unable to drag his eyes from the body.

'Later,' Swift said. 'Please proceed ahead of us. The rest of you must go to your rooms and remain there until instructed otherwise.'

'You're not going to leave him here on his own, are you?' Malone said.

'Yes,' I replied. 'Now do as you're told.'

CHAPTER 22

They trudged out and down the stairs, Swift and I bringing up the rear. We went with Fitzroy to the library and he led us straight across to the small safe. It rested on a shelf, fixed to the back of the bookcase, 'hidden' behind a small pile of books. A child of moderate intelligence would have found it within five minutes.

'It's locked, look.' Fitzroy demonstrated by tugging at the brass dial in the centre of the squat iron box. 'And I have the combination in my wallet.' He reached to draw it from the inner pocket of his superbly tailored jacket. 'Here, you can see it. Lady Peggie opened the safe for me, told me the combination, and I wrote it down.' He fumbled with the wallet, his hands trembling slightly; it was obvious the morning's events had disturbed him. 'This is it.' He removed a folded piece of cheap grey-white paper, put the wallet on the bookshelf next to the safe, and handed it to Swift.

He read it carefully. 'Did you tell anyone the combination?'

'No of course not,' Fitzroy spluttered.

I'd noticed a pad of the same paper on the desk near the fireplace and went over to pick it up. 'You used this pad to write on?' I held it up.

He glared at it. 'Yes, what of it?'

I tilted the pad in the sunlight coming through the windows. 'You left an imprint on the page below,' I said, and showed him the indent. It was quite clear, and an exact copy of what he'd written on his own sheet of paper before he tore it from the pad.

He gave a faint groan then lifted his hand to his forehead. 'Oh, God. This is appalling. What sort of fiend is among us?' He dropped his hand, weariness and worry in his handsome face. 'Where did you find the coins?'

Swift told him, succinctly and calmly, how we found Lady Peggie in the graveyard this morning. It horrified the lawyer. 'That was cruel, why poor Lady Peggie? Why attack her? And the wedding clothes... If she discovers what happened she will be distraught.'

'I think the killer has decided to frighten everyone out of the castle,' Swift said.

'They said they wouldn't leave, you heard them,' Fitzroy retorted.

'But you could order them out,' I said.

'Yes, and I will,' he replied. 'This cannot continue.'

'What happens if the clan do not agree on a new Laird, or Lady?' I asked.

'Then Lady Peggie will remain in place until such a time as a Chief can be chosen.' He sighed. 'I think that could be quite a long way off, given the circumstances.'

'What about you?' I asked. 'What will you do?'

He gazed at me. 'What do you mean? I will carry on as before.'

'Who will administer the estate?' I persisted. 'You or Lady Peggie?'

'Me, as you are very likely aware, Major Lennox,' he said, anger in his voice. 'It is standard practice until all the legalities are processed.'

'And how long will that take?' Swift said.

'Until a new clan chief is decided upon,' Fitzroy replied heavily. 'As I thought I'd made clear.' He took a breath. 'Have you informed all the heirs of Professor Coltrane's death?'

'Not yet,' Swift replied.

'We will gather everyone in the drawing room in one hour,' I decided.

'To announce his death?' Fitzroy demanded.

'Yes, and to expose the murderer,' I replied.

Swift looked sideways at me but didn't react.

'What?' Fitzroy's silver grey brows rose then drew together. 'You know who it is? Tell me.'

'No,' I replied. 'Inform the household they must all go to the drawing room one hour from now,' I instructed him, then turned and walked out.

Swift caught me up. 'That was a good observation on the notepad, Lennox.'

'It wasn't difficult to put two and two together once I saw the paper he'd written the code on.'

'Hm…' He considered that. 'Do you really know who's behind this?'

'Yes,' I said, then admitted, 'I'm pretty sure of it, anyway.'

He glanced at me. 'Do you need anything?'

'No…I still have the coins.' My head was spinning with trying to think of everything. 'Perhaps some vinegar.'

'Vinegar?'

We were crossing the hall; Lars and Malone suddenly appeared on the landing.

'Detectives, wait,' Lars called down.

They came down the stairs quickly, Malone's overlong kilt dragging behind him on the treads.

'We gotta tell Susannah,' Malone said when they came to us. 'We need your permission to move around.'

'I want to ask Molly to come,' Lars offered. 'We can go to see her first.'

'Right,' Swift said. 'I agree, we can't spring this news on Susannah as part of an announcement, nor the rest of the household.'

'*Gut*. Come Malone, we go, quickly now.' Lars was already heading back to the stairs.

'But don't say anything about the bride,' I called after them.

'We will not,' Lars called back.

Malone had to pluck up the kilt to run up the steps. They made a strange sight between them: the tall and muscular Dane, the short, stumpy American in his unlikely get-up.

'Did you call Billings again?' I asked Swift as we watched them rush across the landing towards the ladies' quarters.

'Yes.' He shoved his hands in his pockets. 'I meant to tell you, but with everything that's been going on… A sergeant went over to talk to the old ladies who run the Collegium of British Genealogists. He couldn't get much sense out of them, they're both very old, but they allowed him to go through their files and he found correspondence from when Fitzroy first contacted all the potential heirs. He confirmed that Brodie had been in touch and appeared to have the best claim. His letters to the old ladies implied he'd been contacted by some of the other claimants, but didn't state who.'

'Presumably the old dears were working for Brodie?'

'No, he'd told them he'd carry out his own research. He sounded very sure of himself, judging by the tone of his letters.'

'Was he a wealthy man?'

'Not by the sounds of it. The Stirling police searched his flat; they weren't impressed. He was a bachelor and careful with what money he had. He kept himself to himself. The neighbours saw him leave on April the second, but he didn't tell them where he was going. The police didn't find any papers either, presumably he brought them all here with him.'

Mrs Craggie came bustling into the hall, a basket full of peat turfs on her hip. 'Is this all ye're doin' when there's good folk dead and the girl's grave's been dug over?' She glared at us.

Swift frowned but didn't respond. 'Come on, Lennox.'

'I'll catch you up,' I replied. 'I'm going to call Persi.'

'Right,' he said. 'I'll see you in the incident room as soon as you've finished.' He pulled back his cuff to check his watch. 'We have forty minutes.'

'Fine,' I said and strode towards the room housing the telephone.

'Lennox? Oh, how lovely to hear from you,' Persi said once I finally got through to her.

I'd managed to shut the door by lifting the chair onto the desk, shoving the door closed then putting the chair down with its back resting against the damn door. I thought it might be the only way I could talk to her without being overheard. I kept my voice low anyway. 'How are you?'

'Perfectly fine,' she said, laughter in her voice. 'Being pregnant isn't an illness, you know.'

'I know but you haven't done it before.'

'There's a first time for everything, and I'm perfectly fit and well. Now tell me what you and Jonathan have found out.'

That took quite some time, and she sounded upset at the violation of Fiona's grave and the murder of the professor. 'Why leave the coins there? Was it to imply the girl was too poor to have a dowry?'

'I think so, and was forced to sew her own clothes, although it sounds to me she'd have done it anyway.'

'How could anyone know Lady Peggie would go there?'

'I don't know, and we don't know when the coins went missing from the safe either,' I replied.

'Strange they should add the missing ones,' she mused.

'Brodie's and the one stolen when Malone was attacked? Yes,' I agreed. 'It's almost as though they're taunting us.'

'Who do you think did it?' she asked.

I told her, almost whispering it, just in case.

'Really? Gosh, that's a surprise,' she replied. 'Do you have enough evidence to make an arrest?'

'No.'

'It's not going to be easy, Heathcliff.'

'I know,' I said and sighed. Then turned the subject before we both grew downcast. 'What did you find at the cairn?'

'Oh it's fascinating, and huge. Its origins date back to prehistoric times. They started with two huge walls built in concentric stone circles, rather like the outline of a dough-nut, but with a passageway cut into it so that the centre can be reached. And then they started placing loose stones between the walls in memory of those who died, and then they just carried on. It's extraordinary that they have kept up the continuity for thousands of years.'

'And an indication of how isolated the clan is,' I replied then told her about the tower I'd visited on the hill.

'It sounds similar in principle with a slightly different structure,' she remarked then asked, 'Would the local clan really accept an outsider as Laird? Blood runs deep in these places.'

'I know, but sometimes they need new blood. Look at what Swift has achieved at Braeburn with the whisky.'

She murmured agreement, then asked what I was going to do. We discussed various ideas, but it really would be dic-tated by the reactions of those present, and the murderer, of course. Then we switched to talk of home and babies and the practicalities of what we'd need, such as prams and layettes and whatnots that were a total mystery to me. I just agreed to everything.

A banging on the door gave me pause. 'Costin' more than pennies this time.' Craggie's voice was muffled but loud enough to hear.

'I have to go, old stick,' I said. 'We will be home later today.'

'Really?' She sounded pleased. 'Do let us know what time and we'll meet you on the mainland.'

'Fine,' I said, then said my goodbyes, and my love, and finally put the receiver back on its hook when Craggie banged on the door again.

I handed him a shilling after I'd rearranged the chair to get out of the room. 'Fifteen minutes,' I told him. 'You and Mrs Craggie in the drawing room. And Lady Peggie.'

'I've been told,' he rasped back. 'We all got to be there. You're goin' to get the monster killin' folk.'

'Probably,' I said and made a rapid escape towards the gunroom.

'Sir.' Greggs was sitting at the worktable with Swift. 'This is a tragic state of affairs. Poor Professor Coltrane. I was most distressed to hear the news.'

'Yes, I know,' I replied tersely.

They were drinking coffee and eating flapjacks.

'May I pour a cup, sir?' Greggs stood up and offered.

'Yes, please.'

He duly did so and I reached for a flapjack and sat down.

'We've been going over Greggs' notes, and Coltrane's,' Swift said. He had both notebooks open on the table in front of him. 'Coltrane had made a good job of mapping a plan of the castle. There are doors in panels, and servants' stairs all over the place. Some had crosses over them. I think that meant they were inaccessible.'

I thought of the winding stairs in the round tower. 'Were there many doors leading outside?'

'Yes, a surprising number,' Swift said. 'Given that this was once a fortress, but I expect they were built in more peaceful times.'

'I have collected together the statements, fingerprints, and evidence, sir,' Greggs said. 'There is only the glove, the shillelagh, and the dowry coins, sir.'

'We haven't removed the knife from the dummy yet,' Swift said. 'But the doctor is on his way. Craggie had called him, though he won't be here for a time because he has to go to another glen to patch up an injured farmer.'

'Right…did you fingerprint the knife used to kill Coltrane?' I asked.

'Yes.' Swift nodded. 'There was nothing, the killer had almost certainly worn gloves.'

'There is very little to show for our detecting, sir,' Greggs said.

'As I am aware,' I replied.

'I hope you're sure about this, Lennox,' Swift said.

'It will be fine,' I decided. Regardless of my assurances, we spent the next few minutes arguing over details and what I would say and how likely it was that I'd force a confession, or an admission, anyway. I emptied my coffee cup and finished off the flapjacks when Greggs announced we had to leave.

'You have the coins?' Swift fussed.

'Yes.'

'I have brought the notepad from the library and–'

'We don't need it,' I cut in.

'You can't be sure.'

'Yes I can. Come on Swift.'

With that, we left to make our way up to the drawing room, and the gathering of what was left of the Clan McFee.

CHAPTER 23

I ran my gaze over them all as they stared back at me.

'Why did William Sullivan have to die?' I began.

Malone put his hand up.

'It's rhetorical,' I said.

'What?' he replied.

'Please remain silent, Mr Malone,' Fitzroy told him. 'Unless the major asks you a question.'

'He just did.'

'No, he didn't,' Fitzroy said.

'Quiet your mouth now, Malone,' Lars told him.

They had arranged themselves in the drawing room on their usual places on the sofas and armchairs nearest to the fire. The sun had slipped away behind billowing clouds and allowed the cold to creep back in. Lady Peggie was there, her face weary and taut. Susannah's eyes were red-rimmed, she held a handkerchief in her hand, looking as though she'd aged ten years in a day. Molly sat next to her, holding her hand. Lars was on the adjacent chair. Most were pale, the tension clear in their faces. Daniel was almost ashen, his brow creased, his face drawn. Even Belinda looked abashed, her usual hectoring bravado subdued, her eyes, lightly made up, were round with worry. The Craggies sat at the rear, uncomfortable and red-faced, veering between defensiveness in protection of Lady Peggie and fear of what more revelations might bring. Greggs sat to one side, glasses perched on his nose, rather in the way of a court recorder who had seen it all but rose above it regardless. He had brought his notebook, pen, and the cards he'd carefully prepared. I couldn't think of a use for them but I'd assured him I'd try.

'Sullivan's death was supposed to appear an accident.' I tried a different tack. 'The killer botched whatever plan they had—'

'Why have you got my vinegar?' Mrs Craggie shouted out.

I held my hand up to stop her. 'I will come to that.' I stood quietly for a moment, then continued. 'The killer also botched the next murder. That of Douglas Brodie. His body was supposed to wash away in the waters of the river, but somehow he was held up, probably by the stank stones damming the blackwater. I believe the killer hoped his body would never be observed, his arrival here unattested apart from the station master, Jock McDuff. Would he have raised an alarm at the disappearance of a stranger? I'm not sure he'd have even noticed.'

'He wouldnae have done,' Mrs Craggie called out. 'He had no time for ootlanders, they were all the same to him.'

'And yet the killer couldn't know that when devising their plan.' I ignored the interruption. 'One thing they did know was that Brodie had the best claim, and all he had to do was present his official papers to Sir Richard Fitzroy and he would become the new Laird of Clan McFee. Isn't that right, Sir Richard?' I addressed him.

'If he indeed had the requisite papers then it was quite possible,' he replied evenly; he seemed to have recovered his usual composure.

'Weren't you surprised when he didn't turn up?' I asked.

'Yes and no.' He gave the classic lawyerly response. 'He may have merely been bragging in his letters to me, or had simply discovered in his research that his claim wasn't as strong as he'd assumed.'

'Why would he write to you that he was coming then?' Molly asked.

'In my extensive experience at the bar,' Fitzroy replied, 'it is not uncommon for individuals to engage in behaviour that may appear anomalous or inexplicable.'

'You mean people are weird,' Malone called out.

'One could say so, yes,' Fitzroy replied.

'Jock McDuff attested to Brodie's arrival on April the second. That was the day after everyone else had arrived,' I continued. 'We know he had a dowry coin because he'd held it in his glove.' This was the cue for Greggs to pick up the now dried out glove and hold it up. A few mutterings of distaste resulted, for which I couldn't blame them because the glove looked more like a shrivelled hand than ever. 'Thank you Greggs,' I said. He sat down, smiling to himself at his role played in the proceedings. 'We found an imprint of a coin inside the glove, and we have interviewed a witness who saw the glove in the river on April the second.' I might have slightly exaggerated the role of the chap who'd handed it to me.

'So the glove was taken from the hand of a dead man?' Lars said.

'Yes,' I replied. 'In order to remove the dowry coin.'

'What happened to the papers he'd brought with him?' Daniel asked, raising his hand at the same time.

'We believe they're in the depths of the blackwater,' Swift replied for me.

'Surely someone could prove the validity of Brodie's claim though?' Daniel continued.

'To what end?' Fitzroy answered. 'The man is dead, he cannot inherit, and he doesn't have any family to step forward and make the claim.'

'Would he have had enough money to renovate the castle?' Belinda asked.

'I think that's unlikely,' I said. 'He was said to live by modest means, and he had not chosen to use the Collegium of British Genealogists to carry out research for him. That may be because he was careful with money, or he couldn't afford it.'

'Maybe that's why he was killed, because he'd have run the place further into the ground,' Belinda said tactlessly.

'This estate is not run into the ground.' Lady Peggie leaned forward to give a sharp reply.

'Are you saying he was killed because he wasn't wealthy enough to save the place?' Molly asked Belinda. 'Because that implies it was done by someone who really wanted it saved – like Lady Peggie.'

'Don't put words into my mouth like that,' Belinda retorted, colour rising in her cheeks.

It seems our talk to her about not making enemies of the clan members hadn't had much impact.

'Enough,' I snapped. 'What you're talking about is motive. Why were Sullivan and Brodie killed?'

Malone raised his hand again.

'Stop now,' Lars hissed at him.

I carried on regardless. 'Sullivan was possibly wealthy enough to pay for the renovations needed to the castle. He had his own construction company, and he was so keen to become Laird he even had his own highland outfit made in the McFee tartan.' I aimed a look at Malone as I said this. 'I don't think either man was killed because of money. I think it was simply because they both had the best claim to the castle.'

'Which is why I got bonked on the head,' Malone called out.

'You have not proved this,' Fitzroy reminded him.

'I'll do it. I'll get them Genie 'ologists to do it for me.' Malone twisted round in his chair to reply to the lawyer.

'Do you have any illegitimate births in your line?' Fitzroy demanded.

'How would I know?' Malone replied.

'Have you ever been to jail?' Fitzroy continued. 'Because I can assure you, I will find out.'

Malone turned back in his armchair and looked down at his hands. 'I was too young to know what I was doing.'

'What was it, Malone?' I asked out of curiosity.

'Selling steak out of the butcher's store I worked in,' Malone muttered without looking up.

'You must explain more,' Lars said. 'This is not clear.'

'I stole some of the best cuts and sold them to people I knew in the neighbourhood,' Malone said. 'I got eighteen months when the boss found out.'

'You were not too young to know that was wrong,' Lars told him.

'Well, maybe,' Malone grumbled. 'But I've kept my nose clean ever since.'

'The motive for your attack,' I said, 'could have been a panicked reaction by the killer. Swift and I had arrived to investigate, we didn't believe the death of Sullivan was an accident, and we'd just witnessed Brodie's body floating away down the river with a knife in his back. The killer now wanted to scare everyone enough so that they would demand to be allowed to leave.'

Greggs waved the shillelagh in the air at this point, but nobody noticed.

'And is that why poor Robert Coltrane was murdered this morning?' Susannah called out, her voice cracking with emotion.

I glanced over at Swift, who nodded.

'Yes, we think that was the reason,' I replied.

'For nothing,' Susannah carried on, tears now running down her face. 'His life was taken for nothing.' She broke on a sob and raised the handkerchief to cover her eyes.

Mutterings of sympathy were made by everyone in the room.

'And was it the reason for the dowry coins buried in my daughter's grave this morning?' Lady Peggie demanded, her voice high and taut.

'Probably,' I replied then explained what we'd found in short and precise words. I took the six coins from my pocket and laid them on my palm so they could see them all together.

'How could someone break into the safe?' Daniel asked. 'Sir Richard said he had locked them away.'

'Swift?' I said.

He stood up, picking up the cheap notepad we'd found in the library and went on in pedantic detail about how it had been done. I left the coins on a low table and went to pick up a glass of water Greggs had left for me on the long sideboard. Despite having been in there numerous times, I hadn't had much of a chance to look around. The picture on the wall next to me was of an austere-looking man in full highland regalia. The frame was gilded and quite fresh; it made the dark red painted wall behind it look dull and tired. *Laird Neville Ramsey Duncan McFee*, was inscribed below the portrait. The Laird himself. He was frowning at me from under bristling grey brows. A hard man judging by his cold eyes, clenched jaw and combative expression.

'Lennox?' Swift called to me.

'Right.' I put the glass of water down, wishing I'd told Greggs to find a decent claret instead, and went back to tormenting the murderer as I closed in slowly but surely.

'The killer knew such a desecration would be deeply hurtful, and that Sir Richard would be furious. It would be logical he'd call a halt to the gathering after such an escalation of terror.' None of us had said a word to Lady Peggie about the knife stabbed into the bride's wedding dress. Fitzroy told us he would ask Mrs Craggie if repairs could be made to cover up the atrocity, but we weren't particularly confident of it. 'Burying the coins was a mistake, because the murderer made another blunder, this time leaving fingerprints on one of the coins.' That was a lie but it made them all sit up.

Greggs raised his hand. '*Ahem*, sir.'

'Not now, old chap,' I told him firmly. I knew he was about to remind me that we hadn't had time to brush the coins for prints. 'It was left on the coin that had belonged to Brodie, and that stupid error will cause them to hang.'

'Who?' a few of them called out. 'Who was it?'

Fitzroy raised his voice. 'Major Lennox, I was under the impression that you and the inspector believed it may be two people working together?'

'We considered the possibility but realised it was the work of a single individual,' I replied.

'Tell us who it was?' voices called out again.

'The person who had the most to gain and the least to lose by coming to live in this remote castle, far from the prying eyes of the authorities and the whispers of murder.'

'Who are you talking about?' Daniel shouted.

I ignored him. 'There was candle wax in Sullivan's hair. It was caused by hot wax being spilled from the guttering candles in the chandelier hanging in the hall. Which of you would not realise the wax would spill when they dropped the iron chandelier onto Sullivan's head?' In my mind's eye I could see the three younger members gazing up at the candles burning in the chandelier above them the evening we arrived. 'Most of us have lived with candles at some stage in our lives. Gas lighting and electricity have been slow to arrive in remoter parts of the world. But those fortunate to have been raised in modern houses, with modern comforts, would never have used candles. They wouldn't have realised the consequence of dropping the chandelier onto Sullivan's head.' I now had the killer firmly in my sights. 'The plan was poorly thought out and poorly executed. Sullivan was too drunk to push down the stairs, and I suspect he was sick from all the liquor he'd had. Which was why the circular rug in the hall smelled of vinegar, didn't it Mrs Craggie?'

'Aye, I could smell sick on it as well as the blood, that's why I used the vinegar,' she replied.

'The killer made use of the opportunity and killed Sullivan when he'd lurched over to the bannister rail and leaned over it. Once he was dead, his body was dragged to the stairs and rolled down it.' I eyed the culprit, who was beginning to squirm. 'You were quite clever in telling me you suspected murder when we spoke at dinner the night we arrived,' I directed the words at him. 'You had realised by then the mistakes you'd made – such as the blood on the second step down. You knew that couldn't have happened had Sullivan fallen of his own accord. You wanted to know what we knew, or had discovered–'

'You mean Daniel did it?' Belinda called out, leaping up from her seat and pointing. 'He murdered three men?

Just for this decrepit old castle? My God I thought you were just a stupid sap, but now I see what a stinking little coward you are.'

'Be quiet and sit down,' Swift ordered her.

'Sure,' she retorted and plonked down, staring daggers at Daniel. 'But I hope you're going to hang him, and I hope it hurts like hell.'

'So do I,' Molly said, fury in her voice. 'Poor Professor Coltrane, he should be sitting here with us right now.'

'Enough,' Swift snapped.

'Mistake after mistake,' I said to Daniel, who was trying to crawl back in his chair. 'One botched attempt after another.' I raised my head to look over at Mrs Craggie. 'Why didn't you admit the knife that killed Brodie was missing from your kitchen, Mrs Craggie?'

The look she aimed at her husband was enough to tell us the answer to that question.

'I didnae do a thing, though I were sore tempted,' Craggie rumbled at her.

'After your failures to cover up the murders, you panicked, didn't you?' I continued to berate Daniel, who'd become red-faced and furious, his shoulders hunched, his lips curling; he was beginning to look like a cornered rat. 'You wanted to frighten everyone into leaving and tried to kill Malone. You even botched that, so you decided to ratchet it up. You knew the tale of Lady Peggie's daughter; I imagine you'd seen her at some time in the graveyard and decided to play a nasty trick on her, and kill Professor Coltrane to create even more terror. You made mistake after mistake,' I said evenly. 'Despite having carefully planned everything–'

'How?' Lars spoke up. 'How was it possible to plan this?'

'Daniel's father, who I've no doubt died at his hands, had been writing to the ladies at The Collegium of British Genealogists,' I replied to Lars then turned back to Daniel. 'I assume you returned to England with suspicion hanging over your head and any chance of a career completely destroyed. You knew about this castle from your father and decided it would become your refuge. You lived in London, you could easily have travelled to Stirling to discuss matters with Brodie. You certainly wrote to him. You inherited your father's wealth so you could afford to bribe him and Sullivan, though I doubt Sullivan would have taken you up on it. But Brodie might have agreed to it, or at least to sell you his dowry coin. Did you arrange to meet Brodie here so you could pay him first? I imagine you must have done, because he had no sooner taken his glove off to hand over the coin than he was stabbed in the back. You pushed him and his glove into the river immediately afterwards thinking both would be washed away forever.'

'I think you've said enough, Major,' Daniel snarled from his chair, all eyes fixed with varying degrees of horror upon him. 'You have no proof. You have nothing on me, this is just a nasty bullying tactic to get me to confess. You want to tell your chief at Scotland Yard how clever you've been and you're making me a scapegoat because you have no idea who really did it.' He was practically spitting out every word.

I picked the coins back up from the table I'd put them on. 'These tell a different story,' I said in cool tones. 'There's no doubting your prints are on them. Can you explain how they got there? You didn't have a coin of your own, did you?'

'My prints aren't on there, they can't be,' he yelled. 'They can't be.'

'Why can't they be?' I shouted at him. 'You got careless, you botched this like you botched everything else.'

'I didn't, I didn't. Leave me alone. Leave me alone. I didn't do anything,' he yelled.

'Yes, you did.' I took a step closer to him.

He stared in fear at me, his tie askew, his legs beginning to rise up as he pushed back in his seat.

'You tell the major,' Lars bellowed, suddenly losing his temper. He got up, grabbed Daniel by his shoulder and hauled him to his feet. 'You tell him what you did.' He shook him like a rag.

'I wasn't…I didn't…' Daniel was almost gibbering. 'He's lying. I didn't touch the coins.' He burst into loud sobs of fear and self-pity. 'I didn't, I didn't,' his voice rose in a shriek, then he struck out at Lars, fists flailing. Lars merely held him at arm's length.

'What did you do? Tell me, what did you do?' Lars growled at him.

'I didn't do anything, there's no proof…' Daniel twisted around to shake him off, almost writhing out of his jacket as he did.

I stepped forward. 'Tell us or you'll hang.'

He slumped, buckling at the knee and still Lars held him. 'I'm sorry, I'm sorry, I'm sorry.' He began crying again and shouting, almost incoherently, 'They made me do it. They deserved it, they should have gone away. It's mine, it's mine.'

Lars let him go and he fell back into his seat and curled up into a ball, sobbing and raging like a child in a tantrum.

Swift moved forward with handcuffs at the ready. Greggs came behind; I've no idea what he thought he would do. But he always was a game old soldier.

CHAPTER 24

There was nothing dignified about it. Daniel fought and screamed as Swift applied the handcuffs; Lars and I held his arms behind his back. Then we marched him down to the dining room and tied him to the old Laird's chair, it being more than strong enough to hold him without suffering damage.

Swift went to call Billings to inform him of the arrest, and ask him to send a contingent of the local police to haul him away. Lars and I stood guard while this took place, as did Malone, although I thought his brawling days were probably done.

Greggs and the Craggies went to make tea and scones along with a few shots of whisky in an attempt to calm the nerves of the remainder of the traumatised clan. The doctor and ambulance arrived at the same time as the police. We went up with them to gather poor Professor Coltrane, and we recovered the knife at the same time. Perhaps Mrs Craggie would be able to mend the damage done to the 'bride', and maybe some of the clan ladies would help her.

Eventually both victim and cruel perpetrator were taken

away, along with all the evidence we could provide – apart from the dowry coins, because we preferred to keep them safely at the castle. Daniel continued to shout and scream his innocence; the coppers threatened him with a straight-jacket if he carried on.

We returned to the drawing room afterwards and tried to answer their questions as best we could. The tray of tea and goodies was largely ignored, but a few took a tot of whisky, including me. Lady Peggie and Susannah were still tearful. Fitzroy was badly shaken. Belinda helped Molly to try and soothe them with kindness, which Belinda actually managed quite well. Malone added his own version of compassion; although it was rather rough and ready. Lars was mostly silent, no doubt reflecting on what he'd seen and heard, and like the rest of us, probably wondering if there was anything he could have done to stop Daniel from killing Professor Coltrane.

The morning wore through with more questions, more tears and what few answers we could provide. Nobody felt up to lunch and Greggs brought in a tray with soft buttered rolls stuffed with sausages and bacon, followed by a cake dish piled high with every sort of cake and biscuit Mrs Craggie could think of.

We made our recommendations and told them we would keep in touch, and then made our escape as the clock struck two.

I cranked up the Bentley's engine, wound up the revs and raced her across the bridge and along the old track, causing the car and occupants to bounce. They didn't complain, we were all glad to be on the road and heading back to the relative comforts of Braeburn, to sit before the fire with our loved ones and to take a good dose of Braeburn malt.

EPILOGUE

April 14th Braeburn Castle

'Have Scotland Yard discovered anything more about Daniel Addison?' Persi asked me as I came back into the cosy parlour she and Florence retreated to when the rain swept in.

'Swift's still talking to Billings,' I replied, 'and Fitzroy has sent a letter.' I waved it, then moved Tubbs from my favourite spot on the sofa next to Persi and sat down. 'Greggs had it from McDonald and I prised it out of his hands before he had a chance to steam it open. He's bringing tea and whatnots up shortly.'

'We could sneak a look.' Florence looked up from her sewing. She was making a tiny lace bonnet that looked as though it would barely fit the cat.

'Florence Braeburn, I am shocked at such a suggestion!' Persi raised her brows in mock horror.

Florence laughed. 'Well, Jonathan shouldn't be allowed to have all the fun.'

'Actually I've already slit the flap of the envelope open,' I said as I moved to slide the contents out.

'Ah, miladies, and sir.' Greggs arrived with a clinking tray. 'Cook has baked raspberry jam tarts topped with cream,' he announced, and placed the tray on the pretty side dresser. He had seen the envelope and was regarding me with a gimlet eye.

'We're waiting for Swift,' I said.

'Indeed sir,' he intoned and picked the lid from the teapot to give it a stir with a silver teaspoon.

Fogg and Nicky's ears pricked up from where they were lying flat out on the hearthrug. Then they both yawned and came over to see what was being served.

'He's confessed. He thinks it might save his neck, though I doubt it.' Swift came in, looking serious but satisfied, his lean face hawkish. He'd got his man, or we had, anyway. And now the culprit was in the custody of Scotland Yard.

'There's a letter from Fitzroy,' I said. I reached out to my lovely wife and laid an arm across her shoulders. She snuggled in closer, and smiled at me.

'What does it say?' Swift asked.

'Tell us what Billings reported first,' I replied.

He had sat next to Florence who put aside her sewing. Persi had given up on knitting and was now sewing small squares of fabric together to make a patchwork quilt. It was slow work by the looks of it.

'He said Daniel had tried to pretend he was insane, though no-one believed it. They brought in a psychiatrist to interview him. The man said he was as sane as most, but narcissistic and self-absorbed. He had no concept of empathy, and all that mattered was that he got his own way.'

'Even to the point of murder?' I asked as Greggs handed out the teacups.

'Absolutely,' Swift said.

'Had he murdered his father?' Persi asked. We'd told them both the whole tale when we'd arrived back at the castle.

'The foreign office thought it probable, but it was impossible to prove,' Swift said. 'The head of security had fled with his daughter who may well have been attacked by Daniel's father. George Addison was every bit as bad as Daniel made out, but like father like son. They were both without either morals or conscience.'

'But why did the head of security run away if he was innocent?' Florence asked.

'I suspect it would have been to protect his daughter,' Persi provided a possible answer. 'If she had been violated in any way, her reputation would be ruined. She may never find a husband and might even be ostracised for bringing shame on her family.'

'That's appalling,' Florence said.

'It's just different cultures, I'm afraid,' Persi replied.

'And one or both of the Addisons were the cause of it.' Swift spoke sternly. 'Daniel's father died of his wound before the doctor arrived. No-one in the embassy would admit to seeing or hearing anything. The Foreign Office held an inquiry, which was inconclusive, though they thought it very likely Daniel had shot his father. They sent him back to London afterwards and made it clear he would always have the accusation hanging over his head.'

I knew how the establishment worked, by word of mouth and private enquiry. Daniel would never hear the whispers, but they would be there and they'd follow him for the rest of his life. And he saw Castle McFee as his private retreat, where he could afford to run a fiefdom, away from prying eyes. Or at least that's what I suspect he'd told himself.

'Had he been in contact with Brodie?' I asked.

'Yes,' Swift replied. 'He'd told Brodie he accepted his greater claim and would support him financially, providing he made the castle over to him. It seemed Brodie was mostly interested in making some money from it. Daniel insisted he bring the dowry coin and all his documents to the castle to prove his claim, and that they must meet privately before presenting the arrangement to Fitzroy. Daniel waited in the front doorway and once he saw Brodie arrive, ran out to meet him. It was lucky for him that it was raining and no-one was around to see him, but I suspect he had another plan up his sleeve if the first attempt to kill Brodie failed.'

'Did he plan any more murders?' I asked.

'Yes, he wanted to kill Lars. He was quite vitriolic whenever his name came up. He was frightened of him and hadn't decided how to tackle him, but he was determined that he would kill him somehow. He hit Malone over the head as an experiment to see if such a means of killing would work. It didn't, as you know, and he reverted to using a knife on Professor Coltrane. Lars would have been next.'

We drank tea and ate the delicious tarts as we contemplated this.

'It seems quite deranged to me,' Persi said after a while.

'But he worked out what he was going to do,' I said. 'He had planned it, and I'm not sure deranged people are really capable of that.'

'Well, I'm very glad you both caught him,' she replied.

'So am I,' Florence added.

'What's in your letter?' Persi smiled at me, switching away from the darkness brought by Daniel's appalling crimes.

'Ah, well, we are about to find out,' I replied and opened it up:

Castle Mcfee April 12th 1924.

Dear Major Lennox and Inspector Swift, I must thank you for your diligence and determination in uncovering the foul deeds of Daniel Addison. I will forever regret the circumstances of his presence at the castle. The taking of three lives by this felon is beyond forgiveness and I will be plain in saying that I hope he will hang.

In more positive news the remaining members of the clan have unanimously decided upon Lars Olafson as the new Laird. I doubt this will come as a surprise to you. He and Molly are close and Lady Peggie and I believe it possible they may make a match of it.

Belinda Guthrie has returned to her home in California. She was somewhat contrite in her behaviour towards other clan members but I think it unlikely she will visit the castle again. Unless perhaps her family wish to do so.

Malone is remaining at the castle. He is quite a capable cook, and the Craggies are keen to retire to the cottage designated for them in the village.

Miss Susannah has also opted to stay for the spring and summer months. She has invited her son to join her, although she has had no news of this yet. Nevertheless her spirits have improved and she is working alongside Malone in the kitchen. They appear to be quite firm friends now. Malone has adopted three kittens from a local clansman and they are caring for them together.

Lady Peggie also remains as the castle chatelaine for the instant, and I have agreed to stay to aid her. We have become somewhat closer in the time we have spent together, and I may make a home in the district if our companionship should warm further.

Lars has already begun to make changes. He is very capable and appears to be quite wealthy. He aims to invest in more cattle and is actively seeking stockmen to care for them. His preference is for the men of the village, although most are too old for such work. Some of the younger generations have written to their parents to state that they are willing to return to the glen if work can be provided. Lars has given his word that it will be.

I am encouraged to believe more families will return. A list of outstanding work is already being compiled, and a schedule for such is underway. Lars has begun clearing the pastures behind the stables and stock shed with the help of a small team of villagers. He has even agreed to wear the tartan, and the kilt, although I am not aware that he has made any order for the cloth.

This is very much the resolution I had hoped for, although the means by which it was arrived at have been marred by tragedy. Nevertheless I am optimistic for the future.

As no family have come forward to claim Professor Coltrane's body, the decision has been made to bury him in the kirk grounds. His funeral will be held on April 17th and you would all be very welcome should you wish to join us at the castle.

I remain at your service and keenly await the trial of Daniel Addison, where I will stand as a witness for the prosecution.

Yours faithfully,

Sir Richard Fitzroy KC

'That sounds as if it turned out as well as one could hope for,' Persi said.

'*Ahem*, indeed, milady,' Greggs said quite loudly.

'And your help must have been invaluable, Greggs,' Persi told him.

'I always thought you would make a fine deputy detective,' Florence added.

He simpered with a smile, then looked meaningfully at me.

'Yes, it was well done, Greggs, but I think it's above and beyond your butlering duties.'

'I can assure you, sir, that I am quite capable of fulfilling both roles,' he replied loftily.

'But we will need much more help around the house after baby is born,' Persi reminded him. 'And Miss Fairchild has offered to stay at Ashton Steeple for a while to support us.'

Greggs and Miss Fairchild had been quite close for a while, and he'd even gone so far as to offer her his hand in marriage after one heady evening of champagne and whirling around the dance floor.

'Ah, yes, well I am still willing to offer detecting services in addition to aiding Miss Fairchild, should I be needed,' he added hastily.

'Excellent,' I said, as Persi smiled at me. Although I wasn't at all in favour of Miss Fairchild taking up residence, however temporary. I'd already decided I'd have to come up with a diversionary tactic of some sort.

'I think the outcome for the McFee clan is very encouraging too now,' Florence said. 'They will be able to turn their fortunes around, just as we have ours.' She squeezed Swift's hand as she said this.

'I'd love to go and visit the glen.' Persi looked at me. 'And the least we can do is attend the professor's funeral.'

'Swift?' I asked him.

'Yes, I think we should,' he replied in a serious tone. 'I'd like to pay my respects, and give my condolences.'

I nodded. I knew what he was thinking. The question of whether we might have saved the professor by letting the heirs leave would forever haunt us.

'And I'd love to see the mummified head behind the dining room fireplace,' Persi said.

'Persi, will you please stop searching for long-dead bodies,' I told her.

She laughed. 'Why on earth should I? I don't object to you going off hunting down murderers.'

'Fine,' I said, and sighed, because she was right – as always.

I do hope you have enjoyed this book and if you'd like to leave a review, I will be eternally grateful!

Would you like to take a look at the Readers Club website? As a member of the Readers Club, you'll receive the FREE audio short story, including the ebook; 'Heathcliff Lennox – France 1918'. You will also have access to the 'World of Lennox' page, where you can view portraits of Lennox, Swift, Greggs, Persi and Tommy Jenkins. There are also 'inspirations' for the books, plus occasional newsletters with updates and free giveaways.

You can find the Readers Club, and more, at karenmenuhin.com

You can also follow me on Amazon for immediate updates on new releases, plus special deals, sales and free giveaways.

* * *

Here's the full **Heathcliff Lennox series** list to date. All the ebooks are on Amazon. Print books can be found on Amazon and online through your favourite book stores.

Book 1: Murder at Melrose Court
Book 2: The Black Cat Murder
Book 3: The Curse of Braeburn Castle
Book 4: Death in Damascus
Book 5: The Monks Hood Murders
Book 6: The Tomb of the Chatelaine

Book 7: The Mystery of Montague Morgan
Book 8: The Birdcage Murders
Book 9: A Wreath of Red Roses
Book 10: Murder at Ashton Steeple
Book 11: The Belvedere Murders
Book 12: The Twelve Saints of Christmas
Book 13: Valentine's Day Murder
Book 14: The Gathering of Clan McFee
Book 15: The Murder of Viscount Montcrief – ready for pre-order now

Here's the list of the **Miss Busby series** to date.

Book 1: Murder at Little Minton
Book 2: Death of a Penniless Poet
Book 3: The Lord of Cold Compton
Book 4: A Very Elegant Murder
Book 5: The Mystery of the Midnight Swan – ready for pre-order now.

There are Audio versions of the Heathcliff Lennox series read by Sam Dewhurst-Phillips, who is superb. He 'acts' all the voices – it's just as if listening to a radio play.

The audio versions of Miss Busby Investigates are narrated by the amazing Corrie James and extremely popular. These can be found on Amazon, Audible and Apple Books.

A little about Karen Baugh Menuhin

1920s, Cozy crime, Traditional Detectives, Downton Abbey – I love them! Along with my family, my dog and my cat.

At 60 I decided to write, I don't know why but suddenly the stories came pouring out, along with the characters. Eccentric Uncles, stalwart butlers, idiosyncratic servants, machinating Countesses, and the hapless Major Heathcliff Lennox. A whole world built itself upon the page and I just followed along.

Now, some years later I have reached number 1 in USA and sold over a million books. It's been a huge surprise, and goes to show that it's never too late to try something new.

I grew up in the military, often on RAF bases but preferring to be in the countryside when we could. I adore whodunnits, art and history of any description.

I have two amazing sons – Jonathan and Sam Baugh, and his wife, Wendy, and five grandchildren, Charlie, Joshua, Isabella-Rose, Scarlett and Hugo.

My wonderful husband is Krov Menuhin, a retired film maker, US special forces veteran and eldest son of the violinist, Yehudi Menuhin.

We live in the Cotswolds.

For more information you can contact me via my email address, karenmenuhinauthor@littledogpublishing.com

Karen Baugh Menuhin is a member of The Crime Writers Association, The Author's Guild, The Alliance of Independent Authors and The Society of Authors.

Printed in Dunstable, United Kingdom